TWO WOMEN ARE OPPOSITE SEX

MARCUS WESTFALL

© 2010, 2013, 2024 Marcus Westfall. All rights reserved.

All rights reserved. No part of this book may be reproduced, stored, or transmitted by any means—whether auditory, graphic, mechanical, or electronic—without written permission of both publisher and author, except in the case of brief excerpts used in critical articles and reviews. Unauthorized reproduction of any part of this work is illegal and is punishable by law.

ISBN: 979-8-89419-155-3 (sc)
ISBN: 979-8-89419-156-0 (hc)
ISBN: 979-8-89419-157-7 (e)

Because of the dynamic nature of the Internet, any web addresses or links contained in this book may have changed since publication and may no longer be valid. The views expressed in this work are solely those of the author and do not necessarily reflect the views of the publisher, and the publisher hereby disclaims any responsibility for them.

Website: https://www.marcuswestfall.com/

One Galleria Blvd., Suite 1900, Metairie, LA 70001
(504) 702-6708

Because of so many ways of talking and physical touching between 2 women and not 2 men. It is all viewed as feminine and not masculine.

That is why we see so much discrimination toward straight men and gay men.

There is no law against these things about women or about men. It is just society. Society allows women to do these things with other women. But not men with other men.

Straight men and especially gay men face a lot of discrimination. On the job people can see religious discrimination. And nationalistic discrimination. And race discrimination. And age discrimination. And even discrimination against women. But they cannot see discrimination against straight men and gay men.

This book does NOT say nor ask if a man is straight or gay. Nor does it say if it is right or wrong to be gay. What this fiction story does. It teaches all the cultural things that discriminate against straight men and gay men everywhere they go. But especially on the job.

The family is at home and the father and mother Ben and Mary are in the living room watching television while their little kids are up stairs in Katrisha's bed room playing with the girl and boy dolls. The children are putting the doll clothes and doing their hair. Since the kids are so quiet the father Ben decides to go upstairs and check on the kids to make sure they are ok. When Ben opens the bed room door Katrisha has a girl and boy doll in her hands and walks over to Ben. Katrisha first shows Ben the girl doll.

Katrisha says daddy look at my doll.

Ben says honny she is pretty.

Then Katrisha shows Ben the boy doll and says look at my other doll.

Ben says honny he is pretty too.

Tommy has a girl and boy doll in his hands and walks over to Ben and first shows Ben the boy doll. Tommy says daddy look at my doll.

Ben says he looks nice.

Now Tommy shows Ben the girl doll and says look at my other doll.

Ben puts a mad look on his face and says in a mad voice. What are you doing playing with girl dolls? Boys don't play with girl dolls. Boys only play with boy dolls. Give the girl doll back to your sister. Tommy puts a sad look on his face then gives the girl doll back to Katrisha.

Ben says don't ever let me see you playing with girl dolls again.

Ben goes back down stairs to the living room and sits down and looks at Mary and says the kids were up stairs in Katrisha's room playing with the dolls. But Tommy was also playing with the girl dolls.

Mary put a confused look on her face and says what is wrong with a boy playing with a girl doll?

Ben says that is not a masculine thing for a boy to play with girl dolls.

Mary says well what is the purpose of a girl playing with a girl doll? It is to pretend to be a mother to her daughter. If she plays with a boy doll it is to pretend to be a mother to her son. Because when a mother gives birth she gives birth to sons as well as daughters. So they need to know how to be a mother to sons as well as daughters. Men are the same way. When men produce they produce daughters as well as sons. So men need to know how to be a father to their daughters as well as to their sons. Little girls are taught from child hood on up how to feed and bathe and change diapers and put on pretty clothes and do their hair. They are learning how to take care of a child. Little boys need to learn the same thing how to feed and bathe and change and put on pretty clothes. That is 1 problem with society toward most men. Most men are only being taught to have sex but they are not being taught take care of your responsibility. So there is nothing wrong with a boy playing with a girl doll pretending to be a father to his daughter.

Now Ben goes back to Katrisha's room and opens the door and looks at Tommy and in a kind voice says come here Tommy.

Tommy walks over to Ben.

Ben gets on his kneese and puts his hands on Tommy's shoulders and looks Tommy in the eyes and in a kind voice Ben says your mother corrected me. I was wrong. There is nothing wrong with a boy playing with a girl doll pretending to be a father to his daughter.

Ben looks at Katrisha and says let me see the same girl doll Tommy was playing with.

Katrisha gives the girl doll to Ben.

Ben looks Tommy in the eyes again and says here honny you can take the doll.

Tommy takes the doll and smiles.

Ben gives Tommy a hug with both arms and says I love you.

8 YEARS LATER

Tommy and Mike and Katrisha had become teenagers. Ben and Tommy and Mike are at home in the basement and Ben is trying to teach the boys how to wrestle and box. Both boys try to refuse.

Tommy says I don't like violence.

Mike says I don't like violence either. I don't want people hitting on me and I don't want to hit others.

Now Mary and Katrisha are both carrying a basket of laundry in their hands and walk into the basement. Mary looks at Ben.

Mary says what is going on?

Ben says I am trying to teach the boys how to wrestle and box so they can defend themselves like a man should. What if they get married someday? Then they will need to know how to defend their wife and kids.

Mary says 1st of all there is a difference between defending your self and being violent. This is not defending your self this is violence. Second of all you think because a man is suppose to be masculine and defend his self and his family that he is suppose to fight. Well fighting is not being masculine it is just being violent. That is why so many men in the world today are so violent. Because society makes a man harsh. Men have been taught that a man is suppose to be physically strong and rough and know how to fight and give a punch and take a punch. All this violence only leads to an early death. Pluss you don't have to fight to survive in life. You just have to watch the people you hang around. If you hang around people who like to fight then you will find yourself fighting to survive. If you hang around people who like to be friendly and peaceful then you do not to fight at all. Instead of teaching them how to fight you need to teach them how to show love to one another.

Mike looks at Katrisha and says Katrisha you are fortunate you are a girl. Because people do not expect a woman to fight AS MUCH as they expect a man to fight. Most of the time a woman is taught to get her boyfriend or husband. People would think a man was crazy if a man says I am going to get my girlfriend or wife.

Katrisha says that is true, but there are times when a woman is taught to fight.

Mike says that is true too but most of the time a woman is taught to get her boyfriend or husband.

Katrisha says yes that is true.

It is now the next day and the kids are at school in Tommy's class and Tommy looks at the clock and the clock says 11:55am.

Angela raises her hand.

Mrs. Smith says yes Angela.

Angela says my other teachers gave us home work this weekend. Are you going to give us home work this weekend?

Mrs. Smith says yes I will give you home work this weekend.

Angela puts a disappointed look on her face and in a sad voice says maaan I was invited to a party with my girlfriends.

Tommy says I was invited to shoot pool with my boyfriends.

For 3 seconds the whole class laughs.

Mrs. Smith puts a shocked look on her face and says your what?

Tommy says my boyfriends.

In a shocked voice Mrs. Smith says ok.

Dale looks at Tommy and asks are you gay?

Tommy says no way my sexual preference is women I like a vagina. I noticed nobody laughed when Angela said my girlfriend. For my opinion since a woman can call her women friends her girlfriend then a man can call his men friends his boyfriend. I know society disagrees with me on that. But I disagree with society.

Then the bell rings and all the students are leaving but Tommy is the slowest. Tommy is slow putting his books in his back pack. Then after all the students have gone then Tommy starts walking toward the door.

Mrs. Smith says Tommy come here I need to talk to you.

Tommy stands next to the desk.

Mrs. Smith says I purposely waited until the class left because I did not want to embarrass you. Are you gay?

Tommy says no I am straight. My sexual preference is women.

Mrs. Smith says then why did you call other men you boyfriend?

Tommy says I will tell you just like I told Dale. For my opinion since a woman can say my girlfriend, then a man can say my boyfriend.

I know society disagrees with me but I disagree with society. A woman can say my girlfriend but a man cannot say my boyfriend. I disagree with that. Do you sometimes call your female friends your girlfriends?

Mrs. Smith says yes I do but that is viewed as a girly thing.

Tommy says well for my opinion since a woman saying my girlfriend is a girly thing then I feel it's a guy thing for a man to say my boyfriend.

Mrs. Smith says well Tommy I don't want people to think as a teacher of this class I am encouraging my students to be gay. Because I am not that kind of teacher.

Tommy says well do they think that way when your girl students say my girlfriend?

Mrs. Smith says no they don't.

Tommy says well they shouldn't think that way when a boy student says my boyfriend.

Mrs. Smith says Tommy I am not going to argue with you. Take this as a verbal warning. I do not want you to call men your boyfriend in my class again.

It is still lunch time and all the students are on the playground and Tommy and Mrs. Smith are standing a few feet away from Angela and watching her. Angela is sitting on another girls lap talking to her.

Mrs. Smith says Tommy congratulations you are graduating this year. I am very proud of you.

Tommy says thanks Mrs. Smith.

Mrs. Smith asks do you know what you want to become some day?

Tommy says I want to become a computer engineer. I want to do technical things on computers.

Mrs. Smith says with the way technology is today computers is the thing to get into.

Mrs. Smith and Tommy walk up to Angela.

Mrs. Smith says Angela you are graduating too this year congratulations. I am very proud of you.

Angela says thank you.

Mrs. Smith says what do you want to become some day?

Angela says I want to become a lawyer. Both of my parents are lawyers and they have given me lots of encouragement.

Mrs. Smith says there is good money in that.

Mrs. Smith walks away to supervise other students but stays on the same side of the building where she can see Tommy from behind him.

Dale comes over to Tommy and puts 1 arm around him and puts a romantic look in his face and in a romantic voice says Tommy how is your boyfriend? And blew a kiss to him.

Mrs. Smith looks up and sees Tommy immediately knock Dale's arm off his shoulder and push Dale real hard onto the ground onto his back. Then Tommy sits on Dale's chest locking Dale in between Tommy's legs. Then grabs a hold of Dale's neck and in a mad voice Tommy says I told you I am not gay.

Mrs. Smith runs over to Tommy and Dale and in a mad voice says Tommy get off of him.

Tommy gets off of Dale.

Mrs. Smith says both of you lets go to the office right now.

When they get into the office Mrs. Smith talks to the principle and says Mrs. Day I am very sorry I had to bring these 2 young men in here but my eyes seen Tommy push Dale onto the ground and then chocking him.

Mrs. Day says thank you Mrs. Smith I will take care of them.

Mrs. Smith leaves the office.

Mrs. Day says ok gentlemen tell me what happened.

In a mad voice Tommy says Dale came up to me and put his arms around me and talking in a romantic tone of voice and asked me how is my boyfriend and blew a kiss to me. I got so angry before I know it I knocked Dale's arm off me and pushed him onto the ground and chocked him. How would you feel if another woman put her arms around you and asked you in a romantic voice how is your girlfriend and blew a kiss to you?

In a firm voice Mrs. Day says Tommy calm down. I am going to get this solved.

Mrs. Day looks at Dale and says Is that true Dale? Did you approach Tommy in that way?

Dale says yes but the only reason why I did it is because Tommy gave me the impression that he is gay because of calling his male friends his boyfriends.

Mrs. Day says well first of all I know Tommy is not gay. He is straight. Second of all even if he was his sexual preference would be his business. There is nothing we can do about a person's sexual preference. And rather you are some one's same sex or opposite sex that does not give you the right to just go up to them and put your arms around them. Even the girls can not just go up to Tommy and put their arm around him without Tommy first giving them his permission. That can be viewed as sexual harassment. Also people have a right not to be touched at all by anybody. So Dale you were wrong to just touch him without his permission first.

Mrs. Day looks at Tommy and says Tommy in your case after knocking Dale's arm off your shoulder you should have just reported it to a teacher or principle. You don't knock some one onto the ground and then chocking them. That is literal violence. Doing bodily harm.

Now because of you both conducting your self this way. Dale I am giving you a detention. When you get home today let your parents know that tomorrow you have to stay after school for a detention. Tommy in your case I am going to have to suspend you for 1 day. This means you can not come to school tomorrow.

Mrs. Day takes a piece of note pad paper and grabs a pen and walks over to her student file cabinet and looks up Tommy's home phone number and writes it down. Then goes back to her seat and picks up the phone and dials Tommy's phone number.

The phone rings and Tommy's mother Mary Cloud picks up the phone and says hello.

Mrs. Day says hello this is Mrs. Day from Wise High School. May I please speak to Mrs. Cloud?

Mary says this is Mrs. Cloud.

Mrs. Day says Mrs. Cloud I am very sorry to bother you but your son Tommy was involved in a fight today and so unfortunately I had to suspend him for 1 day. So I need you to come and pick him up from school early today. He will be waiting in my office.

Mrs. Cloud says ok I am on my way. I will see you in a few minutes.

Mrs. Day says ok bye.

Mrs. Cloud says bye.

Then they both hang up the phone.

Mary gets in her car and drives to Wise High School. When she gets to the school she goes to Mrs. Day's office and first looks at Mrs. Day.

Mary asks what happened?

Mrs. Day says well Dale put his arm around Tommy and blew a kiss to him and them Tommy knocked Dale real hard onto the ground and chocked him. So unfortunately I had to give Dale a detention and suspend Tommy for 1 day.

Mary looks at Tommy and asks is that true Tommy?

Tommy says yes.

Mary looks at Mrs. Day and says I am very sorry about this.

Then Mary looks at Tommy and says lets go Tommy.

Mary and Tommy went to the car and drove home.

It is now 4 hours later at 5 pm Ben comes home from work and Mary and Tommy are sitting in the living room. Then Ben goes to the living room where they are and Mary informs Ben about what happened at school.

Mary says Tommy was involved in a fight today at school so unfortunately he was suspended for 1 day. The principle Mrs. Day told me that Dale came up to Tommy and put his arms around him and then blew a kiss to him. Then Tommy knocked Dale's arms off of him then pushed Dale real hard onto the ground and chocked him. And so Mrs. Day gave Dale a detention and suspended Tommy for 1 day.

Ben says I am real sorry about that Tommy.

Mary says honny this is partly your fault. You are the 1 that taught the boys that every problem they have with some one they should fight about it because this is being manly. So when this happened Tommy took it too far and got violent. He was not being manly he was being violent.

Ben says honny you are right and I am very sorry about this.

Then Ben says Tommy I know you were wrong for getting violent. But it is my fault for teaching you boys how to box and wrestle. Mary is right it is not being manly it is just being violent. And violence does not solve anything it only makes matters worse. We don't want to make matters worse we want to solve them.

TWO DAYS LATER

Mary dropped Tommy off in the front of the school yard and Tommy's friend Wendle is sitting in the front of the school on the steps with Wendle's other friends. When Tommy turns around and starts walking toward the school. Then Wendle sees Tommy and yells his name.

Wendle says hey Tommy come over here and sit with us.

Tommy walks over to the steps where Wendle is sitting. When Tommy gets to the front of the steps he does not turn his whole body just his head. Looking around the crowded steps, Tommy notices other than one single aisle for walking up and down the steps, there is no other place to sit.

Wendle says Tommy sit on my lap.

Then Tommy sits on Wendle's lap.

Wendle says it is good to see you again.

Tommy says it is good to see you again too.

And they both start talking to each other in general.

Then Mrs. Smith parks her car in front of the school and gets out and walks toward the front of the school and up the stairs where Tommy and Wendle are sitting and every one sees her and says hi Mrs. Smith.

Mrs. Smith says hi every one.

Then Mrs. Smith looks at Tommy and gives Tommy a nice warm smile.

Mrs. Smith says welcome back Tommy.

Tommy says thanks Mrs. Smith.

Now the bell rings and all the students go to their class room.

It is now 3 hours later in Mrs. Smith's class. After taking attendance Mrs. Smith says Wendle and Tommy may I please see both of you in the hall way?

When they get in the hall way Mrs. Smith says I am talking to you out here because I do not want to embarrass you.

Mrs. Smith 1st looks at Tommy and says this morning out side on the front steps Tommy you were sitting on Wendle's lap. You know men do not sit on other men's lap because that is not a masculine thing.

Tommy says well when I got to the steps I noticed there was no place to sit. So Wendle let me sit on his lap.

Mrs. Smith says Tommy you know how this makes a man look. It looks like he is gay.

Tommy says I disagree with that. When a woman sits on another woman's lap it doesn't look like a woman is gay. Since a woman can sit on another woman's lap then a man can sit on another man's lap.

Now Mrs. Smith looks at Wendle and says Wendle you know it is not proper for a man. I am from the old school. Men don't let other men sit on their lap. I am surprised at you. You were letting him do it.

Wendle says well it did not bother me because I see nothing feminine about Tommy plus I know Tommy is straight. I seen there was no place for Tommy to sit and I did not want to keep him standing so I told him to sit on my lap. I was trying to be considerate.

Mrs. Smith says Wendle since this is my first time saying anything to you about doing things not proper for a man then I am just going to give you a verbal warning. Consider this as your verbal warning. In a mad voice Wendle says WHAT DO YOU MEAN A VERBAL WARNING!

Mrs. Smith says I am not going to take action against you by disciplining you. I am just giving you a verbal warning. Now go back to class.

Mrs. Smith says Tommy this is my 2nd time I have had to say some thing to you about doing things not proper for a man. The last time I just gave you a verbal warning. This time you have to write sentences. I expect you to write 100 times I will not sit on men's lap. Your sentences will be due tomorrow.

In a frustrated voice Tommy says MRS. SMITH THAT IS NOT FAIR! IF IT WAS A GIRL SITTING ON ANOTHER GIRL'S LAP YOU WOULD NOT GIVE A GIRL SENTENCES TO WRITE! Just 2 days ago during lunch out side on the play ground you were talking to me and Angela both about careers. Me and you both seen Angela sitting on another girl's lap and you did not give Angela sentences to write nor did you say any thing to her. What is the difference?

Mrs. Smith says it makes a man look gay.

Tommy says I disagree. If it does not make a woman look gay then it does not make a man look gay.

Mrs. Smith says Tommy what would you think if your father sat on anther man's lap?

Tommy says I would not think he was gay, because if my mother sat on another woman's lap I would not think she was gay. For my opinion since a woman can sit on another woman's lap then a man can sit on another man's lap.

Mrs. Smith says Tommy I am not going to argue with you. Wait right here.

Mrs. Smith walks to her desk and pulls open the drawer and pulls out her carbon pad slip for writing sentences and fill it out and walks back into the hallway.

Mrs. Smith says here this is to remind you that you have to write sentences and they are tomorrow.

With a ticked off look on his face Tommy takes the slip.

Mrs. Smith says you may go back to class now.

When Tommy gets back to his seat he puts the carbon slip in his note book. Wendle is sitting next to him.

Wendle says she was not fair to me she gave me a verbal warning.

Tommy says she was not fair to me either. She told me I have to write sentences.

Wendle says what do you have to write?

Tommy says I have to write 100 times I will not sit on men's lap.

Later that night at the Cloud's house the family is in bed and Mary wakes up and looks at the clock. The clock is saying 12:15am and Mary rubs her nose and decides to go to the bath room to blow her nostrils. On the way to the bath room Mary notices that the bedroom light to Katrisha's room and Mike's room is off and she opens the door just to make sure they are still sleep and ok. But Mary also notices that Tommy's bed room light is the only light still on so Mary opens the door.

Mary says Tommy what are you doing still up? Do you realize it is 12:15 in the morning?

Tommy says I am trying to finish my home work. I am all most done.

Mary says ok hurry up you have to get some sleep for school in the morning.

Tommy says ok.

Mary closes his bed room door. Then she goes to the bath room and blows her nose. Then Mary goes back to her bed room and goes back to bed.

THE NEXT DAY

It is career day at Wise High School and the teachers and principles are trying to encourage the students and especially the seniors to think about what kind of careers they would like to get into after graduation. They are in Mrs. Smith's class and Mrs. Smith explains to the class who
She invited to her class and why.

Mrs. Smith says for a parttime job I do cosmetology. And the reason why I invited 2 cosmetology staff is because some people think since cosmetology is doing hair and make up and nails. They think the services are only given by women and only on women but they fail to realize that you also have some men that give and receive cosmetology services.

Mrs. Smith points to her guess speakers and says this is Alisha and KC now I will let them talk to you.

Alisha says there are many things a person can do in cosmetology to make money. Not the only but 1 of your biggest money makers is hair coloring. Lots of people love to get their hair colored. A simple rule in coloring. If you have light colored hair and you want it darker you just apply the darker color. If you have dark hair and you want a light color then before putting on the lighter color you have to first bleach out the darker color then put in the lighter color. If you want to stay the same color but just your regrowth done then you have to use 1 shade lighter on your regrowth. Then when it finishes processing then you put the rest of the color on the rest of the hair. If the customer wants to get a hair cut and a curl then you first do the hair cut so all hair strands are the same length. Another big money maker in cosmetology is doing perms. Just make sure you know what you are doing when you apply chemicals to a person's hair because if you apply the wrong chemical and burn a person's hair out then you can be sued.

Now you won't make as much money doing nails but doing nails is not as risky. Doing nails is a chemical service but if you use the wrong chemical you can easily wipe it off and you do not have to worry about burning off their nail. Doing make up is the same way. You make money with it but not as much because it does not take as long pluss the risk is not as high. Now I will let you hear a little bit from KC.

KC says as Mrs. Smith mentioned earlier. Men do give and receive cosmetology services. Men do not receive the services to the same extent as women but they do receive the services. Men can get a hair cut. Men with curly hair may also want a perm. Men also have their nails done. But when men get their nails polished they do not use colored polish they only use clear polish. If they get make up then it is strictly the color of their skin tone.

Alisha says also when you are choosing a make up color and nail color make sure all your colors and designs in your clothes match. See my hair is blonde and my top is a cream color and my skirt is a gold color and my lipstick and eye shadow and even my shoes all match.

Angela says the way you have every thing blending you look real cute.

Alisha says thank you.

KC says now seeing that I have red hair I had to dress with a little bit different colors than Alisha. I have on a turqois colored shirt and black pants and brown shoes.

Tommy says you look cute. I like how every thing goes together.

KC says thank you.

At the same time for 4 seconds Mrs. Smith gives Tommy a mad look on her face.

Alisha says this is a field of work where you have to build clientele. When you first set started you will be paid a minimum wage hourly rate. But when your customers build up high enough to the point where you make a lot more on commission than you do hourly.

Then the company takes you off hourly pay and puts you on strictly commission pay.

KC says there's lots of money to be made in this field of work if you are willing to do the work.

Wendle says how long have you been doing this work?

KC says for 9 years.

Wendle says I suspected you had lots of experience with your color coordinating. You look cute.

KC says thank you.

At the same time for 4 seconds Mrs. Smith gives Wendle a mad look on her face.

Alisha asks are there any questions?

Wendle asks what are the educational requirements for being a cosmetologist?

Alisha says the requirements is just a high school diploma and so many hours of training in an accredited school. Then when you finish your training then you have to take a state board test. After you pass your state board test then you pay a fee to get your license.

Angela says while you are building a clientele what is the least amount hourly you will be paid?

KC says the least amount you will be paid is the federal minimum wage.

Alisha says are there any more questions?

Nobody raises their hand.

KC says are there any more comments?

Again nobody raises their hand.

Alisha says well if nobody has anymore questions or comments then we will be leaving at this time because we both have to be at our salon in 1 hour.

Mrs. Smith says thank you both for coming.

All the students at the same time say thank you.

Mrs. Smith leads the class into applauding the guess speakers.

Now Alisha and KC leave for work. At the same time the bell rings for the students to go to lunch and Tommy and Wendle are the last 2 students preparing to leave the room.

Two Women Are Opposite Sex

Mrs. Smith says Tommy and Wendle before you 2 leave I want to talk to you.

Tommy and Wendle says what do you want now? Did I do some thing wrong again?

Mrs. Smith says you 2 highly embarrassed me today. You told the man speaker he was cute. I do not want my guess to think I am teaching the boys in my class to be gay.

Wendle says what is wrong with a man telling another man he is cute.

Mrs. Smith says it is not a manly thing. Wendle this is my 2nd time I have had to say some thing to you about doing things that is not right for a man. So this time Wendle I expect you to write 100 sentences. I will not say men are cute.

Mrs. Smith looks at Tommy and says Tommy this is my 3rd time saying something to you. This time you have a detention. You have to serve your detention tomorrow after school.

Tommy and Wendle put a firm look on their face.

In a firm voice Tommy says Mrs. Smith that is not right. Angela said Alisha is cute and you did not give Angela a detention.

In a mad voice Wendle says NOR DID YOU MAKE ANGELA WRITE SENTENCES. AND ANGELA WAS TALKING ABOUT THE SAME SEX JUST LIKE WE WERE. THAT IS NOT FAIR.

Mrs. Smith says gentlemen if I allow you to talk this way then it makes me look bad.

Wendle says did it make you look bad when Angela said another woman is cute?

Mrs. Smith says no it did not.

Wendle says then it does not make you look bad when we say a man is cute.

Mrs. Smith says you know me I do not argue.

Then Mrs. Smith opens her desk drawer and pulled out 2 different carbon pad slips 1 for Wendle's sentences and the other for Tommy's detention and fills them out. Then Mrs. Smith hands Wendle his slip.

Mrs. Smith says Wendle your sentences are due tomorrow.

Then she hands Tommy his slip.

Mrs. Smith says your detention is due tomorrow.

Both boys put a ticked off look on their face and put the slip in their note book.

Wendle says Mrs. Smith what time do you have your prep period?

Mrs. Smith says at 2:15pm. You boys may leave now.

When Tommy and Wendle leave the class room Mrs. Smith gets on her desk phone and calls Tommy's mother.

At the Clouds house Mrs. Cloud is late trying to finish cooking dinner. While Mrs. Cloud is taking dinner out of the oven and turning off the stove then the phone rings. She picks up the receiver.

Mrs. Cloud says hello.

Mrs. Smith says hello this is Mrs. Smith from Wise High School. May I please talk to Mrs. Cloud?

Mrs. Cloud says this is Mrs. Cloud speaking.

Mrs. Smith says Mrs. Cloud may I please make arrangements with you to speak with you at school tomorrow at 2:15pm that is when I have my prep period. I would like to talk to you about your son Tommy. It is some things he is saying in class and some things I have seen him do. I hate to tell you this but I believe your son Tommy is gay.

In a surprised voice Mrs. Cloud says oh my god!

Mrs. Smith says since I don't have students at 2:15 can I talk to you at that time tomorrow?

Mrs. Cloud says yes I will be there at 2:15 tomorrow.

Mrs. Smith says thank you.

Mrs. Cloud says you are welcome.

Mrs. Smith says bye.

Mrs. Cloud says bye.

Then they both hang up the phone.

Now it is 3:30 pm in the afternoon and Mary and Tommy and Katrisha and Mike are in the living room watching television until Ben comes home.

Mary says Tommy I got a phone call from Mrs. Smith today. She wants me to come to the school tomorrow to talk to her about you because of some comments she said you are making. And some things she seen you do. She told me you might be gay.

In a mad voice Tommy says she told you I am gay? All because I will say another man is cute. And I call my male friends my boyfriends.

Mom I will tell you just like I told Mrs. Smith I disagree with society a woman can call her female friends my girlfriend but a man cannot call his male friends my boyfriend. A woman can say another woman is cute but a man cannot say another man is cute. I disagree with that. And that is why she told you I am gay. But I am not. My sexual preference is women. Mrs. Smith accused me of being gay but she did not tell you she gave me a detention for telling a man cosmetologist speaker he is cute. She said that Wendle and I embarrassed her. She does not want people to think that she is teaching the boys to be gay. At the same time Angela told the lady cosmetologist speaker she is cute and Mrs. Smith did not say anything to her. Angela did not get a detention but I did.

In a mad voice Mary says Mrs. Smith gave you a detention for that?

Tommy says yes. I have to stay after school tomorrow to serve my detention. Pluss the other night around midnight when you woke up and came into my bed room and asked me what am I doing up so late?

It is 12:15am. I told you I am doing homework. Mrs. Smith had me writing 100 sentences saying I will not sit on men's lap.

In a mad voice Mary says Mrs. Smith had you writing sentences because you sat on another man's lap?

Tommy says yes. We were outside sitting on the front steps and there was no where else for me to sit. So Wendle told me to sit on his lap. And she had me writing sentences for that. I will get the slips and show them to you.

Tommy goes up stairs to his bedroom and opens his note book and pull out both slips. Then takes both slips down stairs and shows both slips to Mary.

Tommy says here mom these are the slips she wrote for my sentences and detention.

Mary takes the slips and reads them and says when she had you writing sentences why didn't you tell me?

Tommy says I thought I had to take the discipline.

In a firm voice Mary says oooh no you don't. I wish you had've told me this earlier when she had you writing sentences, but still I am glad you are telling me now before serving your detention. When I go to the school tomorrow I am going to talk to her about this. So now I am glad she wants me to come to the school tomorrow. I got some thing to tell her. Pluss tomorrow do not serve your detention.

Mary hands the slips back to Tommy and says ok put these back.

It is now later in the evening and Ben is home and the family sits down to eat dinner. Mary tells Ben about what happened to Tommy and Wendle at school from Mrs. Smith.

Mary says honny I got another call from the school today. Mrs. Smith called me and asked me to come to the school tomorrow. She is accusing our son of being gay.

In a firm voice Ben says what in the world is she accusing him of that for?

Mary says because he will call his male friends his boyfriend. Pluss he will say another man is cute. Pluss he sat on wendle's lap. She even had Tommy writing sentences and late gave Tommy a detention for saying a male speaker is cute.

Ben says well after hearing this I am glad you are going to the school tomorrow to talk to the teacher. Something is wrong with that teacher.

Now at the Velet's house Wendle and his mother Rose are sitting and eating dinner. Wendle is telling his mother about Mrs. Smith.

Wendle says mom at school today we had 2 cosmetology speakers. One was a man and the other was a woman. The man speaker was talking about the way his clothes matched with his hair color. He had every thing blending in so good. I told him he looked real cute. And he told me thank you for the complement. After the speakers had left Mrs. Smith told me and Tommy that we embarrassed her. And so she told me I have to write 100 sentences saying I will not say men are cute.

In a mad voice Rose says she is making you write sentences all because you said another man is cute?

Wendle says yes. I will go get my slip and show it to you.

Wendle goes up stairs and opens his note book and pulls out his slip for writing sentences, then goes back down stairs and shows the slip to Rose.

Wendle says here mom this is the slip Mrs. Smith gave me to remind me about my sentences.

Rose takes the slip and reads it.

Tommy says Angela said the lady speaker is cute but Mrs. Smith did not give her any sentences to write.

Rose says what is wrong with Mrs. Smith would she rather you say another man is ugly. It sounds like a complement to me.

Wendle says do you want me to put that back into my note book?

Rose says no I want to keep this. I will call the school tomorrow and see what time is her prep period so I can talk to her.

Wendle says she told me her prep period stars at 2:15.

Rose says ok then I will go to the school tomorrow at 2:15 and talk to her about this.

THE NEXT DAY

Mary and Rose both are at Wise High School and they both walk into the front office at the same time and then introduce them selves to the secretary.

Mary says hello my name is Mrs. Cloud. I am Tommy Cloud's mother I need to get a visitor's pass to see Mrs. Smith.

Rose says I need to see Mrs. Smith too. I am Mrs. Velet. Wendle Velet's mother. I need to get a visitor's pass too.

Mrs. Afflian says my name is Mrs. Afflian I am 1 of the secretaries. I will get your passes.

Mrs. Afflian goes to her desk and pulls out the visitor passes and fills them both out and gives them to Mary and Rose.

Mrs. Afflian says here you go.

Mary and Rose both say thank you and walk to Mrs. Smith's room. They both arrive at the same time.

Mrs. Cloud sees Mrs. Smith and says hello I am Mrs. Cloud. Tommy Cloud's mother. You asked me to be here at 2:15 to talk to you about Tommy.

Rose says I am Mrs. Velet. Wendle Velet's mother. When you are done with Mrs. Cloud I need to talk to you about Wendle.

Mrs. Smith says ok I will be glad to talk to you immediately after.

Mrs. Velet says ok.

Mrs. Smith says while you wait would you like to have a seat and look through Wendle's folder to see how he is doing and his grades?

Mrs. Velet says yes thank you.

Mrs. Velet takes a seat and Mrs. Smith pulls out Wendle's work folder and gives it to Mrs. Velet.

While Mrs. Velet is looking at Wendle's folder she is also listening to what Mrs. Cloud and Mrs. Smith are saying.

Mrs. Smith says Mrs. Cloud I hate to tell you this but there are times in class when Tommy calls his male friends his boyfriends.

Mrs. Cloud says what is wrong with Tommy calling his male friends his boyfriend?

Mrs. Smith says it is not a manly thing.

Mrs. Cloud says what is so unmanly about it?

Mrs. Smith says it Makes it look like he is gay.

Mrs. Cloud says let Me ask you this. Do the girls in your class call their female friends their girlfriend?

Mrs. Smith says yes.

Mrs. Cloud says then do you think the girls look like lesbians.

Mrs. Smith says no.

Mrs. Velet looks at Mrs. Smith with a ticked off look on her face and in her Mind she says what is the difference?

Mrs. Smith say just yesterday I had a Man cosmetologist in class Tommy told the Man he is cute.

Mrs. Cloud says what is wrong with a Man saying another Man is cute?

Mrs. Smith says I told you it Makes him look gay.

Mrs. Cloud says do the girls in your class say other women are cute?

Mrs. Smith says yes.

Mrs. Cloud says do they look like lesbians?

Mrs. Smith says no.

Mrs. Velet looks at Mrs. Smith again with another ticked off look on her face and in her Mind she says there is no difference.

Mrs. Smith says well what about More physical things. I seen it with My own eyes. Just 2 days ago out side the front of the school Tommy was sitting on Wendle's lap. How do you explain that?

Mrs. Cloud says well do the girls in your class sit on other women's lap?

Mrs. Smith says yes.

Mrs. Cloud says there is no difference. If the women do not look gay then neither do the Men.

Mrs. Smith says I can't believe this after hearing that he is calling other Men his boyfriend and sitting on other Men's lap you don't think he is gay. For My opinion Tommy needs to see a child psychiatrist. Because he is gay.

Mrs. Cloud puts a ticked off look on her face and in a Mad voice she says hooold it now. You go to a psychiatrist when some one has a Mental problem. You don't go to a psychiatrist when you thing some one has a hormone problem and My son Tommy does not have a hormone problem. Because My son Tommy is straight. You are judging My son the wrong way. Pluss I've noticed you've been telling Me what you think he did wrong but you have not told Me you had him writing sentences for sitting on Wendle's lap. Pluss he told Me you gave him a detention for saying the Male cosmetologist is cute. What you did is wrong.

Mrs. Smith says but that was very inappropriate.

Mrs. Cloud says was it inappropriate when Angela said the lady cosmetologist is cute?

Mrs. Smith says no but when Tommy said that about the Man I was very embarrassed.

Mrs. Cloud says you weren't embarrassed when Angela said the woman is cute. I will tell you right now Tommy does not have to serve that detention.

Mrs. Cloud leaves the room and goes back to the front office and sees the secretary Mrs. Afflian.

Mrs. Cloud says May I please speak to Tommy's principle?

Mrs. Afflian says let Me see is she busy right now.

Mrs. Afflian goes to Mrs. Day's office and sticks her head inside and sees there's nobody in the office with Mrs. Day. Mrs. Afflian gets Mrs. Day's attention.

Mrs. Afflian says are you busy right now?

Mrs. Day says no I am not. Do you need some thing?

Mrs. Afflian says Tommy's Mother Mrs. Cloud would like to speak to you.

Mrs. Day says tell her to come on in.

Mrs. Afflian looks at a Mrs. Cloud and says Mrs. Cloud you May come on in.

Mrs. Cloud goes into the principle's office and looks at Mrs. Day and says hello.

Mrs. Day says hello.

Mrs. Cloud says how are you doing?

Mrs. Day says I am fine how are you?

Mrs. Cloud says well I received a phone call from Mrs. Smith yesterday and she asked Me to come in today and talk to her about My son Tommy Cloud. So when I got here she told Me she is concerned about Tommy because of some comments she heard Tommy Make in class. Pluss she said there is some thing she seen him do. Mrs. Smith said that Tommy calls his Men friends his boyfriends. Pluss she had a Male speaker in her class and Tommy embarrassed her and told the Male speaker he is cute. She also said the physical thing that Tommy did. She seen Tommy sitting on Wendle Velet's lap. She told Me because of these things she is convinced that Tommy is gay and needs to see a child psychiatrist.

Mrs. Day puts a firm look on her face and in a firm voice she says you are Tommy's Mother and she told you that?

Mrs. Cloud says yes. I told her I disagree with her. My son is straight.

Mrs. Day says yes he is very straight.

Mrs. Cloud says then I asked her do the girls in her class call their female friends their girlfriends and she told Me yes. I said do they sit on other womens' lap. She said yes. I said do you think they are gay. She said no. I said there is no difference. Pluss she did not tell Me but Tommy told Me Mrs. Smith gave him sentences to write when he sat on Wendle's lap. And when he said the Male speaker is cute she gave Tommy a detention.

Mrs. Day is interrupted with a phone call from her boss.

Now in Mrs. Smith's room Mrs. Smith patiently waited for Mrs.
Velet to finish looking through Wendle's folder.

Mrs. Smith says I think Wendle does excellent work in school.

Mrs. Velet says yes he does. But I did not come to the school because of his work. I came because he told Me you gave him sentences to write all because he said another Man is cute.

Mrs. Smith says I am sorry Mrs. Velet but I am not going to go through this again. I am not going to argue with you.

In a Mad voice Mrs. Velet says exscuse Me. I am not going to argue with you either. But I disagree with you. You are wrong. The girls can do these things with other girls but the boys can't do them with other boys. I am going to the principle's office.

Mrs. Smith says that won't do any good because the principle will agree with Me.

Mrs. Velet leaves Mrs. Smith's room and goes back to the front office. When she gets to the front office she sees Mrs. Afflian .

Mrs. Velet says May I please speak to Mrs. Day It is very important.

Mrs. Afflian says let Me see is she still speaking with some one else. Mrs. Afflian gets on her speaker phone and pushes Mrs. Day extension number.

Mrs. Afflian says Mrs. Day are you still speaking with some one?

Mrs. Day says yes.

Mrs. Afflian says ok.

Then she looks at Mrs. Velet and says I am sorry but Mrs. Day is still talking to some one. Would you like to have a seat until she is done?

Mrs. Velet says yes. Thank you.

Then Mrs. Velet sits down.

Now in Mrs. Day's office Mrs. Day is about to end her conversation with her boss.

Mrs. Day says ok I will be here. Bye.

Mrs. Day hangs up the phone and says I am sorry about the interruption Mrs. Cloud that was my boss.

Mrs. Cloud says I understand so that is ok.

Mrs. Day puts a firm look on her face again and in a firm voice says you are Tommy's mother and she said that to you?

Mrs. Cloud says yes.

Mrs. Day asks did you also say Mrs. Smith gave Tommy a detention for saying a male speaker is cute?

Mrs.Cloud says yes she did.

Mrs. Day gets on her speaker phone and dials Mrs. Afflian's extention.

Mrs. Day says Mrs. Afflian would you please look up Tommy Cloud's schedule and see who is his 6th hour teacher and tell the teacher to send him to my office with his books. His mother is here so I am letting him out of class early today.

Mrs. Afflian says I sure will.

Then she looks in her desk drawer and pulls out a pen and piece of note pad paper and walks over to the file cabinet with student schedules and looks up Tommy Cloud's 6th hour teacher then writes down the name then walks over to the class room intercom and pushes the button to speak to Tommy's teacher.

Mrs. Afflian says Mrs. Great.

Mrs. Great says yes.

Mrs. Afflian says would you please send Tommy Cloud to Mrs. Day's office? Tell him to bring his books because his mother is here , he might be going home early.

Mrs. Great says ok. I sure will.

Mrs. Afflian says thank you.

Mrs. Great says you are welcome.

Mrs. Great says Tommy did you hear that?

Tommy says yes.

Tommy puts all his books in his back pack and puts his back pack on his back.

Tommy says have a good evening Mrs. Great.

Mrs. Great says you too Tommy.

Then Tommy leaves the room and walks to the front office.

When Tommy gets to the front office he first sees Mrs. Afflian.

Tommy says you paged for me?

Mrs. Afflian says yes. Mrs. Day wants to see you she is in her office.

Tommy walks into Mrs. Day's office and says hi Mrs. Day.

Mrs. Day says hi Tommy.

Then Tommy sees Mrs. Cloud and says hi mom.

Mrs. Cloud says hi Tommy.

Tommy says I hope I am not suspended again.

Mrs. Day says no. You are not suspended again.

Tommy says good. I want to graduate this year.

Mrs. Day says Tommy I pulled you out of class early because I wanted to tell you before the school day ended to don't serve your detention. I heard from your mother what Mrs. Smith had you doing with the sentences and detention. May I have your reminder copies for your sentences and detention?

Tommy looks in his back pack and pulls out his books and opens it and pulls out the slips and hands them to Mrs. Day. Then puts the book back into his back pack.

Mrs. Day puts both slips in her desk drawer and looks at Tommy.

Mrs. Day says I disagree with her on the disciplining.

Tommy says wow! Thanks Mrs. Day. Did you need me for any thing else?

Mrs. Day says no that's all. You may leave with your mother.

Mrs. Cloud says thank you so much Mrs. Day.

Mrs. Day says you are welcome too Mrs. Cloud.

Then Mrs. Day looks at the clock and says it is 2:50 did you want me to page Katrisha and Mike so they can leave with you?

Mrs. Cloud says well since we only have around 16 minutes left then Tommy and I will just wait in the car. But thank you any way.

Mrs. Day says ok I won't page them. You all have a good day.

Mrs. Cloud and Tommy says thank you. And leave the office and go sit in the car.

In the mean time while Mrs. Day has nobody in her office she walks to her office door and sees Mrs. Velet.

Mrs. Day says are you waiting to talk to me?

Mrs. Velet says yes.

Mrs. Day says come on in.

When Mrs. Velet gets into Mrs. Day's office she takes a seat.

Mrs. Day says how are you doing?

Mrs. Velet says I'm fine but. Yesterday my son Wendle Velet came home from school and told me that Mrs. Smith had a man and woman speaker in her class and they were talking about the way they were groomed. Then a student named Angela told the lady speaker she is cute. Then later Wendle told the man speaker he is cute. When both speakers left then Mrs. Smith gave Wendle sentences to write. But did not give Angela any discipline at all. That is not right. Angela doesn't get disciplined but Wendle does.

Mrs. Day says I agree with you. It is not right the girls can say that but the boys can't.

Mrs. Velet says I have heard other parents complaining about this same thing. When I complained to her she told me she is not going to go through this again, and she is not going to argue with me. Wendle gave me the slip she gave him for writing sentences.

Mrs. Day says do you still have the slip he gave you?

Mrs. Velet says yes.

Mrs. Velet opened her purse and pulled out the slip and hands it to Mrs. Day.

Mrs. Day says when were the sentences due?

Mrs. Velet says the sentences were due today.

Mrs. Day says well by this time of day he's already did the sentences. So what I will do is have a talk with Mrs. Smith. And since I can't undo him writing the sentences. I am going to compensate Wendle by giving Wendle a coupon for a free meal at his favorite smorgasboard for 1 whole day.

Mrs. Velet says ok thank you Mrs. Day.

Mrs. Day says you are welcome.

Mrs. Velet says I am sure Wendle will appreciate this.

Mrs. Day says do you need any thing else?

Mrs. Velet says no thank you. I hope you have a good day. Bye.

Mrs. Day says you have a good day too.

Mrs. Velet leaves the room and goes to her car and waits for Wendle.

In the mean time Mrs. Day gets on her desk and dials Mrs. Smith's extension to her classroom.

Mrs. Smith picks up her phone and says Mrs. Smith speaking may I help you?

Mrs. Day says this is Mrs. Day may I please speak to you in my office.

Mrs. Smith says yes I will be there in a few minutes.

Two Women Are Opposite Sex

Mrs. Day says ok bye.

Mrs. Smith says bye.

Then they both hang up the phone.

Mrs. Smith shuts off her lights and closes her door and locks it and walks to the office.

When she gets inside of Mrs. Day's office.

Mrs. Day says Mrs. Smith I hate to tell you this but I have had parents comming to me and complaining that you are not treating all your students the same.

Mrs. Smith says well I don't care what my student's religion or nationality or race is. It makes no difference to me. I don't even see them in that way.

Mrs. Day says that's not what I am talking about. When the girls call their female friends their girlfriends or when the girls sit on another girls lap or when the girls say another women is cute. Then you think nothing of it. You take no action against it. But on the other hand when the boys call their male friend. Then you punish the boys for it. What you are doing is wrong.

Mrs. Smith says how could it be wrong when these things between girls is viewed as a feminine thing.

Mrs. Day says ell if you are going to view this conduct between 2 women as feminine then you have to view the same conduct between 2 men as masculine. If you don't then you are showing favoritism. You have to treat every body the same regardless.

Mrs. Smith says I am from the old school.

Mrs. Day says I understand what school you are from. But you still have to treat every body the same regardless.

Mrs. Day opens the drawer and pulls out the slips for Tommy's sentences and detention and Wendle's sentences and shows them to Mrs. Smith.

Mrs. Day says I am sorry Mrs. Smith but you can't do this. It is not right. I hate to tell you this. But you are fired. For showing favoritism. Take your things out of your desk and leave.

2 WEEKS LATER

It is now 2 weeks later at Wise High School and Mrs. Day has hired a new teacher to work in Mrs. Smith's place. The new teacher's name is Mrs. Gold. Mrs. Gold is in her class room talking to her class. She first introduces herself.

Mrs. Gold says first of all good morning. My name is Mrs. Gold. Now I can't say any thing in detail. But I can say this. Mrs. Smith is no longer working for the school district. So in this class I will be your teacher for the rest of the year.

It is now the last 30 minutes before lunch.

Mrs. Gold says may I have your attention please. Before lunch today the principle's want the teachers to choose a class president for each hour. So what we'll do first. If you want to be class president. Write on a piece of paper why you should be class president. I will give you 10 minutes.

Now the 10 minutes is up.

Mrs. Gold says I want each candidate to stand up.

All the candidates stand up.

Mrs. Gold says now we'll go vertically down each aisle and each candidate will read what they wrote on their paper.

Now all the candidates have spoken.

Mrs. Gold says now I will give each person 1 piece of note pad paper and on the paper you will write the name of the person you are voting for. I will give you 1 minute to decide.

Now 1 minute is up and Mrs. Gold collects all the votes then goes to her desk and puts all the same names together, then counts all the same names and writes down the count.

Now Mrs. Gold is finished counting.

Mrs. Gold says congratulations Doug. You are now our class president.

Doug says thank you.

Now the bell rings and the class ends. Most of the students leave the class room but Chase and Doug and a few other students stay in the room with Mrs. Gold to eat their lunch. Mrs. Gold looks up and sees Chase walk over to Doug.

Chase says Doug congratulations. I am very proud of you.

Doug says thank you.

Then Chase and Doug give each other a hug with both arms each. And Chase kisses Doug on the cheeks 1 time.

Mrs. Gold says Chase don't ever let me see that again.

Chase says what did I do wrong?

Mrs. Gold says you kissed Doug on his cheeks.

Chase says well I know 2 men are not supposed to kiss on the lips. No waaay. But I didn't see any thing wrong with a kiss on the cheeks.

Mrs. Gold says 2 men are not supposed to kiss each other at all. Straight men don't do that.

Chase says well I am straight.

In a kind voice Mrs. Gold says that's good. Take this as a verbal warning.

Mrs. Gold looks at Doug.

Mrs. Gold says Doug you just got appointed as class president. So I hate to tell you this but don't let other guys kiss on you. Even on the cheeks. Any kind of wrong conduct can cause you to loose your position. Because you are expected to set an example. I hate to say it but this is a verbal warning for you too. It will hurt me to have to take your position away. So please watch your conduct. Now do you know what all is involved in being class president?

Doug says I do know I have to assist the teacher.

Mrs. Gold says you also have to keep your grades up and watch your conduct. Now seeing what a smart and intelligent young man you are. Pluss you are a very nice young man. I know you can do it. And you are going to do an excellent job.

Doug says thanks Mrs. Gold.

Later that evening in the home of the Styles family the father Jeff is in the kitchen looking in the refrigerator and notices there's very little food left in the refrigerator. Jeff closes the refrigerator door and walks to the living room and looks at his wife Grace.

Jeff says honny we need to go to the grocery store because we are too low on food.

Grace says ok honny.

Then Grace looks at the rest of the family Derek and Doug and Tina and says are you all ready?

Doug and Tina says yes.

Derek says I really don't feel like grocery shopping right now.

Grace says do you feel ok?

Derek says yes. But I just don't feel like grocery shopping. You know me I feel grocery shopping is boring. Do I have to go?

Grace says no honny you don't have to go. Just don't get mad if we don't come back with things you like to eat. Because you weren't there to pick out what you like. Ok.

Derek says ok.

Then the rest of the family goes to the car and drives to the grocery store.

In the meantime at home, in his mind Derek is saying I don't feel like grocery shopping, but I do feel like clothes shopping.

Now from his mouth Derek says I better hurry up before they get back home.

Derek sneaks to a near by all women's clothing store and looks around at the skirts. Derek also looks at the staff and notices the way the staff is looking at him. Like he's got a serious problem. Then Derek picks out a skirt of his size and walks over to the hills and picks out a pair of heel his size and then walks over to the tops and picks out a top his size. Then Derek walks toward the dressing room to see if he can fit the clothes comfortably. When Derek gets to the dressing room, right before he goes in, then the cashier Jean gets Derek's attention.

Jean says sir.

Derek says yes.

Jean says you might want to go into the bath room just in case some ladies come. They won't feel comfortable with a man in the women's dressing rom.

Jean points to where the bath room is and says the bath room is right over there.

When Derek gets inside the bath room he takes off all his men's clothes and puts on the women's clothes. Then Derek looks at himself in the mirror in side the bath room and sees that the clothes look good and feel good on him. Then Derek takes off all the women's clothes and puts his man's clothes back on and then Derek takes the clothes to the cashier. When Derek gets to the cashier.

Jean says hi, how are you doing?

Derek says oh I am fine. I am paying with cash.

Jean says that is fine. The company won't get any interest with cash but it is still fine.

Jean finishes ringing all 3 items and tells Derek the total.

Derek hands Jean the cash.

Jean hands Derek his change and receipt. Then she puts the clothes and shoes in a bag.

Jean says have a nice day

Derek says thank you .You too.

Derek walks back home real fast.

Derek says I hope I get home before the family does.

When Derek gets back home, he notices the family car is not home yet.

Derek says good I made it back home before the family got back.

Now Derek goes into the house then goes to his bed room and keeps his clothes in the plastic bag but he takes the heels out of the shoe box an puts the heels in the plastic bag with the clothes, then Derek closes the plastic bag and hides it in his back pack. Then Derek closes the back pack and sits it next to his bed. Then Derek takes the shoe box and puts it in the trash can out side. Then Derek goes back to the living room and sits down where he was at first.

It is now 15 minutes later and the family comes home from the grocery store.

Doug and Tina goes to sit in the living room until Jeff and Grace finish putting the groceries away and have dinner ready.

When dinner is on the table Grace goes to the living room.

Grace says it is time to eat.

While the family is eating Grace looks at Derek.

Grace says Derek when we left you was watching an interesting movie on television what happened on the show?

Derek says well I don't know to my shock I actually dozed off to sleep.

THE NEXT DAY

It is now the next day at school and the students are passing from the 2nd hour class to the 3rd hour class, while Derek is in the hall way he goes to the bath room with his back pack and then goes to the camode area and closes the door and locks it. Derek takes off his men's clothes and puts on his women's clothes. When he finishes getting dressed then the bell rings to start 3rd hour. Derek walks to Mrs. Gold's class. When he walks through the door way Mrs. Gold sees him come in and he sees her starring at him as he walks to his seat. When he sits down Mrs. Gold walks up to Derek's seat.

Mrs. Gold says what is wrong? First you come in late, then you are wearing women's clothes.

Derek says Mrs. Gold I was late because I was in the bath room. Pluss I feel that a woman's clothes is more comfortable.

Mrs. Gold says I don't allow people to cross dress in my class.

Derek says If it were a girl would you let a girl cross dress in your class?

Mrs. Gold says I am not going to argue about it. I do not want you in my class dressed like that. Would you please step in the hall way?

Derek goes to the hall way.

Mrs. Gold goes to her desk and pulls out a detention slip and fills it out. Then Mrs. Gold pulls out a referal form and fills it out. Then she takes both forms to the hall way where Derek is.

Mrs. Gold says I am giving you a detention for being late AND a referral for coming to class crossed dressed. Now go to the principle's office.

While Derek is gone, before he gets to Mrs. Reasha's office , Mrs. Gold gets on the office pager and pulls the button for Mrs. Reasha.

Mrs. Gold says Mrs. Reasha.

Mrs. Reasha says yes.

Mrs. Gold says I am sending Derek Styles down to your office with a referral. I am telling you just so you will know he is coming.

Mrs. Reasha says ok thank you.

Mrs. Gold says bye.

Mrs. Reasha says bye.

Derek walks into the front office.

Mrs. Sealer sees him wearing the women's clothes and puts a surprised look on her face.

Mrs. Sealer says may I help you?

Derek says I have to see Mrs. Reasha.

Mrs. Sealer says let me see is she busy.

Mrs. Sealer dials Mrs. Reasha's extention and says Mrs. Reasha this is Mrs. Sealer, are you busy.

Mrs. Reasha says no I am not. Can I help you?

Mrs. Sealer says Derek Styles is here to see you.

Mrs. Reasha says ok send him on in.

Mrs. Sealer says you may go in now.

Derek walks into Mrs. Reasha'a office.

Mrs. Reasha notices that Derek is wearing women's clothes.

Derek takes a seat.

Mrs. Reasha says I see why Mrs. Gold sent you tome.

Derek lays his detention slip and referral form on Mrs. Reasha's desk.

Mrs. Reasha reads the referral form and hands the detention slip back to Derek.

Derek says I'll tell you the same thing I told Mrs. Gold. I feel that women's clothes are more comfortable.

Mrs. Reasha says I am sending you home. I will not allow you to give this school a bad reputation because of wearing women's clothes. You have to change your clothes.

Mrs. Reasha grabs a pen and piece of note pad paper and looked in her student file for Derek's number. When she finds it she writes it down. Then she goes back to her seat and gets on her phone and calls Derek's house.

At the Styles house the phone rings and Mrs. Styles picks it up.

Mrs. Styles says hello.

Mrs. Reasha says this is Mrs. Reasha from Wise High School may I please speak to Derek Style's mother?

Mrs. Styles says this is Mrs. Styles.

Mrs. Reasha says Mrs. Styles I don't know how to tell you this but your son Derek is in my office. Derek went into his 3rd hour class wearing a women's skirt and a women's top and heels. I am sorry but I can't let him stay in school dressed this way. I need you to come to the school and pick him up so he can change his clothes.

Mrs. Styles says I can't believe what I am hearing. Ok I will pick him up. I will be there in a few minutes.

Mrs. Reasha says ok bye.

Mrs. Styles says bye.

Then they both hang up the phone.

Grace grabs her keys and gets in her car and drives to the school. When she gets to the school she goes to the front office. First Mrs. Style's sees Mrs. Sealer.

Mrs. Styles says may I please see Mrs. Reasha?

Mrs. Sealer says let me see is she still busy.

Mrs. Sealer gets on her speaker phone and dials Mrs. Reasha's extension.

Mrs. Sealer says Mrs. Reasha are you still busy? There is some one here to see you.

Mrs. Reasha says is it Mrs. Styles?

Mrs. Sealer looks at Mrs. Styles and says are you Mrs. Styles?

Mrs. Styles says yes I am.

Mrs. Sealer says It's Mrs. Styles.

Mrs. Reasha says tell her to come on in.

Mrs. Styles says thank you and walks into Mrs. Reasha's office.

When Mrs. Styles gets into the office she has a mad look on her face and she 1st looks at Derek and then she looks at Mrs. Reasha.

Mrs. Styles says Mrs. Reasha I am very sorry about this.

Mrs. Reasha says it is not your fault. I am very sorry I had to bother you. But I can't let Derek stay in school wearing women's clothes.

Mrs. Styles looks at Derek and says this evening when your father gets home. Your father and I are going to have a talk with you. I dare you to embarrass me like this. Right now you are going home and changing your clothes and coming right back to school. You are not getting the rest of the day out of school. Now go get in the car.

Mrs. Styles looks at Mrs. Reasha and says you have a good day.

Mrs. Reasha says thank you. You too.

Then Grace goes to the car with Derek and she drives home.

When Grace and Derek get home.

Grace says now the only thing I want you to do right now is go upstairs and change those clothes.

Grace waits at the bottom of the steps.

Derek goes to his bed room and changes his clothes. When he has his men clothes back on Derek comes back down stairs.

Grace says now get back in the car.

They both get in the car and Grace drives back to the school.

When they get back to the school they both get out of the car and walk to Mrs. Sealer's office.

Grace says I brought Derek to your office so you could see that his mother just brought him and he could get a pass to class.

Mrs. Sealer says ok and gets out her hall passes and fill one out then hands it to Derek.

Derek says thank you.

Mrs. Styles looks at Derek and says now you go to class.

Derek goes to class.

Mrs. Styles says thank you Mrs. Sealer.

Mrs. Sealer says you are welcome have a good day.

Mrs. Styles says you too.

Now Grace leaves the school and drives back home.

LATER THAT EVENING

Later that evening at the Styles home Jeff and Grace are in the living room watching the news as it is going off. The kids are up stairs doing their home work.

Grace says Jeff honny there is something I need to tell you. Pluss you need to call Derek down here. I want Derek to hear this.

Jeff says ok.

Jeff goes up stairs and knocks on Derek's door.

Derek says yes.

Jeff says Derek come down stairs. Your mother needs to tell you and I something.

Derek says ok. Here I come.

Jeff and Derek walk down stairs into the living room and have a seat.

Grace says honny I got a phone call from the school today. Derek's principle called me today. She said Derek came to 3rd hour wearing a women's skirt and a woman's top and a woman's heels. She told me she had to call because she couldn't let Derek stay in school wearing women's clothes. He got sent home long enough to change his clothes and then I drove him back to school.

Jeff says Derek why in the world would you put on women's clothes?

Derek says dad I don't mean to be rude but for my opinion I feel that women's clothes are more comfortable. If it were a girl crossed dressed would you complain about it?

Jeff says son your mother and I don't accept people cross dressing in our home. Every body in our home is expected to wear clothes for their sex only. Pluss since you have caused your mother the embarrassment. We are going to put you on a punishment. This mean for the rest of the night you have to stay in your bed room. Except for going to school or the bath room.

In a sad voice Derek says what about eating dinner?

Jeff says you have to eat dinner in your bed room. So now up stairs you go.

Derek goes up stairs to his bed room.

THE NEXT DAY

It is now the next day of school and it is senior recognition day and all the principles and teachers and students are in the gym. The teachers and freshman and sophomores and juniors and principles are sitting on the bleachers. The seniors are sitting on chairs in the middle of the floor. The head principle's name is Mrs. Heather. She is sitting on a chair in front of the seniors, facing them. Mrs. Gold is sitting on the bottom row of the bleachers and on the end seat where she can see the front row of the seniors. Angela Wing and Tina Styles are 2 seniors sitting in the front row next to each other. Now as Mrs. Heather calls individual senior names, the senior will go up and stand next to Mrs. Heather. And Mrs. Heather will tell every school organization the senior was involved in and all the good things the senior did for the school and then hand them their reward for their hard work. Then the senior goes back to their seat.

Now Mrs. Heather gets down to the last 3 names and says Angela Wing.

Angela walks up and stands next to Mrs. Heather.

Mrs. Heather tells all the school organizations that Angela was involved in and all the good deeds that she did for the school. Then Mrs. Heather hands Angela her rewards.

Angela walks back to her seat. When Angela gets to her seat then Angela and Tina Styles gives each other a hug and Mrs. Gold sees Tina kiss Angela on the cheeks.

Mrs. Heather says Tommy Cloud.

Tommy Cloud walks up and stands next to Mrs. Heather.

Mrs. Heather tells all the organizations Tommy was a part of and all the good deeds Tommy did for the school. Then she hands Tommy his rewards.

Tommy walks back to his seat and sits down.

Mrs. Heather says Wendle Velet.

Wendle walks up and stands next to Mrs. Heather.

Mrs. Heather tells all the organizations Wendle worked in and all the good deeds Wendle did for the school.

Mrs. Heather gives Wendle his rewards.

Wendle walks back to his seat and sits down.

Mrs. Heather says I am very proud of all our seniors. They all have worked very hard for their reward. Every one lets give the seniors an applause for their hard work.

Every one claps. When the clapping is over.

Mrs. Heather says now that all the seniors have their rewards it is lunch time and we all are hungry. So at this time I am going to let the teachers dismiss the students but we are going to start with the seniors. Let the seniors go first. And since Mrs. Gold is standing so close I am going to ask Mrs. Gold to lead the seniors out.

Mrs. Gold says ok I want 2 lines. One from each side and then 1 row at a time.

Mrs. Gold starts walking across the gym floor and she walks into the hall way and she stops and tells the crowd to keep going. Then when Tina and Angela come out she gets their attention and stops them.

Mrs. Gold says Tina and Angela I need to talk to you.

Mrs. Gold first looks at Tina and says Tina I seen it when you kissed Angela on her cheeks. That was very inappropriate. Take this as a verbal warning. Don't ever let me see that again.

Mrs. Gold now looks at Angela and says Angela you let her kiss you on your cheeks. You were just as wrong.

Angela says what is wrong with a girl kissing another girl on her cheeks?

Mrs. Gold says you don't kiss the same sex even on the cheeks. You both are going to graduate this year and you are very close to that day so don't let your conduct get you in trouble. Now go to lunch.

While Tina and Angela are eating lunch they start talking about Mrs. Gold.

Tina says I couldn't believe Mrs. Gold she gave us a verbal warning just because I kissed you on the cheeks.

Angela says don't she realize that's what girls do when they are friends and they are proud of each other.

Tina says she probably was never a girl. She might be a man with women's clothes on. I know what I am going to do.

Angela says what?

Tina says I am going to complain to the senior principle. This is not right. You don't give 2 girls a verbal warning because they kissed each other on the cheeks. We were just showing that we are proud of each other.

Later that day after school Angela meets Tina In the hall way and says do you want to come with me to talk to Mrs. Day about Mrs. Gold?

Tina say yes.

Then both girls walk to the office.

When they get into the office, they see Mrs. Afflian.

Tina says I have a complaint about a teacher. May I please see Mrs. Day?

Mrs. Afflian says Mrs. Day had an important meeting out side the school building she had to go to. So you will have to talk to the head principle Mrs. Heather.

Tina says that is fine.

Mrs. Afflian says let me see is she busy.

Mrs. Afflian dials Mrs. Heather's extension and says Heather this is Mrs. Afflian there are 2 students out here to see you. They said they have a complaint about a teacher.

Mrs. Heather says send them on in.

Mrs. Afflian says you girls may go in now.

Both girls go into the office and have a seat.

Mrs. Heather says hello ladies. How may I help you?

Tina says 1st thanks for being willing to listen to us.

Mrs. Heather says sure. I will make time to listen to all my staff and students and visitors. Now what can I help you ladies with?

Tina says we were just doing feminine things that girls do together and Mrs. Gold gave us a verbal warning for that.

Mrs. Heather says that's all you did just feminine things and Mrs. Gold gave you a verbal warning for it?

Angela says that's right.

Mrs. Heather says ok I will take care of this. Let me call Mrs. Gold to my office.

Mrs. Heather gets on her phone and dials Mrs. Gold's extension number and the phone rings and Mrs. Gold picks up the phone.

Mrs. Gold says this is Mrs. Gold.

Mrs. Heather says this is Mrs. Heather. Mrs. Gold some thing very serious about you has come to me. Would you please come to my office right away.

Mrs. Gold says yes I will be there right away.

Mrs. Gold drops what she is doing and walks to the hall way and locks her door and walks to Mrs. Heather's office.

When Mrs. Gold gets to Mrs. Heather's office she is surprised to see Tina and Angela sitting in the office.

Mrs. Gold says what is going on?

Mrs. Heather says ladies please tell Mrs. Gold what you just told me.

Tina says I just told Mrs. Heather we were just doing feminine things that girls do together and you gave us a verbal warning for that.

Mrs. Gold says I know what you are talking about. During the senior recognition program after Angela got her reward then took her seat and you 2 hugged each other and then Tina I seen you kiss Angela on her cheeks. Then after the program I pulled you 2 to the side and told you it is not appropriate to kiss the same sex even on the cheeks. One of the boys in my class did that and I gave the boys a verbal warning for it. And I did the same thing with you girls. Because I treat every body the same.

Mrs. Heather says well ladies if she gave the boys a verbal warning for it then she did right to give you girls a verbal warning.

Mrs. Heather says Mrs. Gold I am very sorry I had to bother you.

Thank you for coming. You may go back to your class room now Mrs. Gold leaves the office.

Mrs. Heather says ladies I am very sorry this did not turn out good for you. But if you ever need to talk to me again feel free to come to my office. That is what I am here for. Now did you ladies need any thing else.

Angela says no.

Mrs. Heather says ok you are dismissed.

Angela and Tina leave the office. While they are in the hall way

Angela says Tina how would you like it if I ask my mother can you come over and spend the night tonight?

Tina says that sounds fine. But I will have to ask my mother too if I can come.

Late that evening at the home of the Wing Family. Angela's mother Dolly Wing is sitting in the kitchen playing solitaire and Angela comes from her bed room to the kitchen.

Angela says mom since I have finished my home work can Tina spend the night tonight and go to the movies with me and then tomorrow she will ride to school with us.

Dolly says if her mother says she can come, then yes she can spend the night with you. Just make sure she has money for the movies.

Angela gets on the phone and dials Tina's number.

Then at Grace Style's house the phone rings and Grace picks it up. Grace says hello.

Angela says this is Angela may I please speak to Mrs. Styles? Grace says this is Mrs. Styles speaking.

Angela says is it ok with you if Tina goes to the movies with me tonight and spends the night at my house? She can ride to school with me tomorrow.

Mrs. Styles says if she wants to she can. Let me see if she wants to go.

Mrs. Styles looks at Tina and says Tina this is Angela she wants to know if you want to go to the movies and spend the night at her house.

Tina says yes. Thanks mom.

Grace says you are welcome honny.

Grace speaks into the phone and says Angela she wants to come.

Angela says ok thanks. I will come and pick her up.

Grace says ok bye.

Angela says bye.

Grace says Tina you better get ready Angela says she will pick you up. I don't know exactly what time she will be here.

Now Tina goes to her bed room and pack her bag with her pajamas and her school clothes for the next day.

At the same time at the Wing's house Angela gets in her car and drives to Tina's house. When she gets to Tina's house she goes to the door and knocks, then Grace opens the door.

Grace says hi Angela come on in.

Angela comes in.

Tina comes down stairs and says mom I will see after school tomorrow.

Grace says ok honny.

Both girls get in the car.

Angela says Tina do you have plenty of money for the movies?

Tina says yes.

Angela says just to add a little more fun to it. Since we have permission to go to the movies do you also have money for shopping?

Tina says yes.

Angela says ok lets go shopping as well. Now if we go to the movies first. When the movie is over, then the stores will be closed. So let's go shopping first. Then go to the movies.

Tina says ok.

Now Angela drives to the mall. When they get there they go to a store with women's and men's clothes. First they go look for tops, then pick out the top they like. Then they go look for skirts then pick out the skirt they like. They go look for heels then pick out the heels they like. Now they both go to the dressing room and try the clothes on. When they see the clothes fit comfortably then they take off the store's clothes and put their clothes back on. Then they both come out of the dressing room.

Angela says are you ready to go to the cashier?

Tina says yes.

They both go to the cashier and pay for their clothes.

Angela says well I guess we can go to the car now.

They both walk to the car and when they get there Tina opens the door to the back seat and puts her bags on the seat.

Tina says I am sorry Angela there is some thing I forgot I forgot I want to get. Do I have time to go get it?

Angela says yes. We still have an hour and a half before the movie starts.

Tina rushes back into the store to look for some more clothes. This time Tina goes to the men's clothes. First Tina looks at men's pants then picks out the kind she likes. Then Tina looks at men's shirts then picks out the shirt she likes. Then Tina looks at men's shoes then pick out the shoes she likes. Then Tina looks at the men's ties then picks out the tie she likes.

At the same time a male staff named Jerry is in the dressing room making sure there are no clothes left in the empty rooms. While Jerry is checking the dressing rooms Tina walks toward the rooms and when she gets to the door way Jerry sees her.

Jerry says sorry mam. You can't come in here. This is a men's dressing room. You will have to go to a women's dressing room.

Tina says but I have men's clothes to try on.

With a firm look in his face and a firm voice Jerry says I see that and that does not look good either. You have to go to a women's dressing room.

Tina turns around and walks to a women's dressing room. When she gets to the dressing room she tries on the men's clothes. When she sees the clothes fit comfortably then she takes off the men's clothes and puts her women's clothes back on. Tina comes out of the dressing room and goes to the cashier to pay for her clothes. While Tina is paying for her clothes. Out side Angela is sitting in the car and looking at her watch.

Angela says what is taking so long?

Now Tina is finished paying for her clothes and comes out to the car.

Tina says Angela I am sorry it took so long.

Real happily Angela says what did you get?

Tina says I don't want to say. I bought some more dress up clothes. Your eyes will be amazed when you see how nice I dress up.

Angela says ok then we better get these clothes to my house before the movie starts.

Then Angela drives to the Wings house. When she gets to the house both girls take the shopping bags out of the car and into the house and into then into Angela's bed room. Then both girls get back into the car.

Angela says now let's go to the movies so we won't be late.

THE NEXT DAY

It is now the next day and Angela and Tina are just finishing breakfast and going to the car with their bags to go to school. Angela parks her car at the school.

Tina says Angela thanks for inviting me over to spend the night.
Angela says you are welcome.
Tina says I have to run to the girl's bath room. I will see you in 3rd hour.
Angela says ok.

3 HOURS LATER

The students are passing from 2nd hour class to 3rd hour class and Tina is in the girl's bath room inside the camode area changing from her girl clothes to her men's clothes. When she finish changing she goes to Mrs. Gold's class room. Mrs. Gold is not in her room yet. Tina sits in her seat. The students notice how she is dressed and stares at her. Around 1 minute after Tina sits down the bell rings and at the same time Mrs. Gold enters the room.

Mrs. Gold first takes attendance.

Then Mrs. Gold says today your assignment is not in your textbook. Your assignment is on a worksheet. I am going to pass out the assignment and then explain it on the board.

Mrs. Gold starts passing out the assignment. She goes down each row, handing out the assignment to each student. When she gets to Tina Mrs. Gold puts a surprised look on her face.

Mrs. Gold says what is this?

Tina takes the assignment and says well you haven't explained it on the board yet.

Mrs. Gold says I am not talking about the assignment. I am talking about the clothes you are wearing.

Tina says what is wrong with the clothes I am wearing?

Mrs. Gold says Tina you are wearing men's pants and men's shirt and men's men's shoes and a man's tie.

Tina says but Mrs. Gold women do that. They cross dress and wear men's clothes.

Mrs. Gold says not in my class you don't. Just like I don't allow the boys to cross dress I don't allow the girls to cross dress either. Tina go in the hall way.

Tina walks to the hall way.

Mrs. Gold walks to the teacher's desk and pulls out a referral form to send Tina to the office. When she finish filling out the slip she goes to the hall way and hands Tina the slip.

Mrs. Gold says you are a woman you should be wearing women's clothes and not men's. Now go to the office.

Tina takes the slip to the office. When she gets there she sees Mrs. Afflian.

Mrs. Afflian puts a surprised look on her face and says may I help you?

Tina says I got a referral to see Mrs. Day.

Mrs. Afflian says Mrs. Day is not in her office today. You will have to see Mrs. Heather. Let me see is she available.

Mrs. Afflian pushes the button on her speaker phone and says Mrs. Day there is a student here that needs to see you.

Mrs. Day says tell them to come on in.

Mrs. Afflian says go on in.

Tina walks into Mrs. Day's office.

Mrs. Day notices how Tina is dressed and puts a shocked look on her face.

Tina hands the referral form to Mrs. Day.

Mrs. Day reads the form.

Then Mrs. Day says I understand why Mrs. Gold sent you to me. I don't understand why some women want to wear men's clothes. I am sorry Tina but this can not be accepted at school. Cross dressing. Wearing clothes for the opposite sex. I am going to have to call your mother and send you home to change your clothes.

Mrs. Heather grabs a pen and piece of note pad paper and walks over to her file with student home phone numbers and looks up Tina's number and writes it down. Then she goes back to her seat and gets on her phone and dials Tina's number.

At the Styles house the phone rings and Grace pick up the phone.

Grace says hello.

Mrs. Heather says this is Mrs. Heather from Wise High School may I please speak to Mrs. Styles?

Mrs. Styles says this is Mrs. Styles.

Mrs. Heather says Mrs. Styles I am sorry to bother you but I have your daughter Tina Styles in my office unfortunately Tina was given a referral for coming to class crossed dressed. She is wearing men's pants and a man's shirt and a man's tie and men's shoes. We need you to come and pick her up and take her home because we can't allow kids to cross dress in school.

Mrs. Styles says oh my god I can't believe what I am hearing. Ok I will be there. Give me a few minutes.

Grace gets in her car and drives to Wise High School. When she gets to the school she goes to the office. She first sees Mrs. Afflian.

Grace says I am Tina Styles mother. Mrs. Day just called me and she is expecting to see me.

Mrs. Afflian says go on in.

Grace walks into Mrs. Day's office.

Mrs. Day says I am very sorry I had to bother you Mrs. Styles.

Mrs. Styles says that's ok I understand.

Mrs. Styles looks at Tina and in a mad voice says what is your problem? Why in the world would you want to dress like a boy?

Tina says mom other girls dress like boys.

Grace says that's other girls you are not other girls you are mine. And your father and I are highly against wearing clothes for the opposite sex.

Mrs. Styles says Mrs. Day I am very sorry about this.

Mrs. Day says it is not your fault.

Mrs. Styles says Tina go get in the car now.

Tina leaves the office and gets in the car.

Mrs. Styles says Mrs. Heather you have a good day.

Mrs. Heather says you too.

Now Mrs. Styles gets in her car and drives home.

While they are riding home Tina says mom what is wrong with a woman wearing men's pants and men's shirts because after all women do wear pants and shirts too.

Grace says that's true women do wear pants and shirts but they should wear a women's pants and a women's shirt. NOT MEN'S. They should wear women's shoes not men's. And a tie is a men's garment not a women's.

Now Grace and Tina get home.

Grace says I don't want you to do anything else but go up stair to your bed room and change those clothes. Put on women's clothes. And then get right back down here.

Now Tina goes up stairs to her bed room and takes off all the men's clothes and puts on her women's clothes. When Tina gets finished dressing, then she comes back down stairs.

Grace says you are not getting the rest of the day out of school. You get back in the car and I am taking you back to school.

Tina and Grace go back to the school, when they get there Grace takes Tina to the office. At the office they see Mrs. Afflian.

Grace says I came in with her so you could see that her mother just got her back. Can she get a pass to class?

Mrs. Afflian says yes, then grabs her hall passes and fills it out and hands it to Tina.

Tina says thank you.

Mrs. Styles says now you go to class.

Tina leaves the office and goes to class.

Grace says Mrs. Afflian thank you. You have a good day. Bye.

Mrs. Afflian says bye.

Grace leaves the office.

LATER THAT EVENING

Later that evening at the Styles home Jeff and Grace are sitting in their bed room.

Grace says honny wait right here I am going to get Tina. There's some thing I need to tell you with her present.

Jeff says ok I will be right here.

Grace goes to Tina's bed room and knocks on the door.

Tina says yes.

Grace says Tina come to me and your dad's bed room. There's some thing we need to talk about.

Tina says ok I'm coming.

Grace and Tina walk to Grace and Jeff's bed room and sit down.

Grace says honny I got another call from the school today. We had the same problem with Tina that we had with Derek. Tina was crossed dressed in school today. Wearing every thing of a man's.

Jeff says Tina why would you wear men's clothes?

Tina says dad that's what some women do, they cross dress.

Jeff says sorry honny that is some thing your mother and I don't accept is wearing clothes for the opposite sex. I will tell you just like I told your brother. Since you did this and caused your mother embarrassment you will be on a punishment. For the rest of today and tomorrow you will have to stay in your bed room except for school time and going to the bath room. You have to eat dinner in your bed room. Now go to your bed room.

Tina goes to her bed room.

THE NEXT DAY

It is now the next day and graduation day at Wise High School. All the seniors and their family and close friends are at the graduation to watch the seniors receive their high school diploma. They are in the gym room. The seniors are sitting on chairs in the middle of the gym. The teachers and principles and family members and their friends are sitting on the bleachers. The head principle Mrs. Heather is sitting in front of the seniors facing them in the middle, with the podium next to her.

Mrs. Heather walks up to the podium and speaks through the microphone.

Mrs. Heather says first of all it is an honor to be here and represent all of my seniors. They all have worked very hard to get here. After 12 long years they deserve. I am very proud of all of them and I am going to miss them. I wish them the very best if they choose to go to college or chose a trade school or choose employment that just requires only a high school diploma. And for the ladies even if you choose to be a house wife. I wish you the best huspand who can afford to keep you at home and treat you good. Pluss I hope you all come back and see me.

Now as I call your name will you please come up and receive your diploma. After you receive your diploma please go back to your seat until all seniors have their diploma.

Mrs. Heather gets down to her last 4 seniors and says Tommy Cloud.

Tommy Cloud walks up and receives his diploma.

Every body claps.

Tommy goes back to his seat.

Mrs. Heather says Wendle Velet.

Wendle Velet walks up and receives his diploma.

Every body claps.

Wendle goes back to his seat.

Mrs. Heather says Angela Wing.

Angela Wing walks up and receives her diploma.

Every body claps.

Then Angela goes back to her seat.

Mrs. Heather says Dale Trade.

Dale walks up and receives his diploma.

Every body claps.

Dale goes back to his seat.

Mrs. Heather says now since all of our seniors have finally graduated how about a nice applause for all of the seniors?

Every body claps for all of the seniors.

The clapping is done.

Mrs. Heather says now the seniors have graduated so I thank all of you for coming. Every body is dismissed.

The family members and friends and teachers and principles leave the bleachers and give the seniors a graduation hug.

Katrisha walks up to Angela and says Angela since you are leaving high school I want to be able to keep in touch with you.

Angela says sure I like keeping in touch with friends. Then Angela reaches into her purse and pulls out a pen and piece of paper and writes down her name and number and gives it to Katrisha.

Angela says write down your name and number for me.

Katrisha says do you have an extra piece of paper?

Angela says yes. Here you go.

Katrisha writes her name and number and gives it to Angela.

Angela says now you better keep in touch.

Katrisha says I will I promise.

Derek walks up to Angela and says I am so proud of you. May I please give you a hug?

Angela says of course.

They both embrace each other with a hug.

Derek says would It be ok if I keep in touch with you?

Angela says yes. Do you want to exchange phone numbers?

Derek says yes.

Angela reaches into her purse again and pulls out a piece of note pad paper and pen and writes down her name and number and gives it to Derek.

Angel gives Derek a blank piece of paper and pen and Derek writes down his name and number and gives it to Angela.

Wendle walks up to Tommy.

Wendle says hey boyfriend I am going to miss you.

Tommy says boyfriend I am going to miss you too.

Wendle says lets keep in touch. Even though we won't be at the same school any more, that does not mean we can't stay in touch. Lets exchange numbers.

Tommy says ok, then looks at Mary and says mom do you have a pen and piece of paper in your purse so I can write down my number for Wendle?

Mary says yes, then reaches into her purse and pulls out a pen and paper and hands it to Tommy.

Tommy writes his name and number on the paper, then hands it to Wendle.

Wendle says Mrs. Cloud may I have a piece of paper.

Mrs. Cloud says yes. Then hands Wendle a piece of paper and pen.

Wendle writes his name and number and gives it to Tommy.
Wendle says keep in touch.
Tommy says I will.
Mrs. Gold walks up to Tommy and says congratulations Tommy I am very proud of you.
Tommy says thank you Mrs. Gold.
After they all finish the hugs and exchange numbers, then they all leave.

12 YEARS LATER

ALL THE SCHOOL ARE ADULTS NOW AND HAVE THEIR OWN HOME.

Ben Cloud is at work at a bank, Ben is a teller. A female teller is Amy. The Teller manager is Joe. Ben and Joe both are watching Amy talk to a female customer named Mrs. Quote.
Amy says hi Mrs. Quote. Come on up.
Mrs. Quote walks up to Amy's window.
Amy says how may I help you?
Mrs. Quote says I just need to cash this check.
Mrs. Quote hands the check to Amy.
Amy starts the transaction. At the same time, she says this is the first time I have ever seen you dressed up. What is the occasion?
Mrs. Quote says I am on my way to a revival at my church. Most places I go to I usually do not dress up. I wear a pair of jeans. But to me church is a special occasion so I dress up for church.
Amy says between the way you did your hair and your lovely dress. You look real cute.
Mrs. Quote says thank you.
Amy finishes the transaction.
Mrs. Quote leaves the teller window.

2 HOURS LATER

It is now Two hours later Joe is watching Ben talk to a male staff named Bill.

Ben says Bill usually you just wear a button up shirt and slacks. But today you've got on a 3 piece suit. What is the occasion?

Bill says next week is my parent's wedding anniversary. So as soon as I get off work all of their kids are getting together to have a portrait picture taken for them as a surprise.

Ben says you look real cute.

Bill says thank you Ben. I appreciate the complement.

It is now 15 minutes later Joe walks up to Ben.

Joe says when you take your break I want to talk to you in my office.

Ben says ok.

Later when Ben takes his break he goes to Joe's office.

When he gets to the office Joe says you want to close the door?

Ben closes the door.

Joe says earlier you were talking to Bill and you made a comment to him. You told Bill he is cute. I am sorry Ben but it is not proper for a man to say another man is cute.

Ben says what is wrong with a man saying another man is cute? To me it is a very nice complement. Earlier Amy said a woman customer is cute. But Amy did not get in trouble. Amy was talking about the same sex just like I was.

Joe says I am sorry Ben but that is just the way it is. I need you to read this slip and sign it.

Ben says Bill even told me he appreciates the complement.

Joes says Ben read the slip and sign it.

Ben reads the slip. Then Ben notices the slip is a write up form.

Ben says I am not signing this. This is not right.

Joe says ok if you refuse to sign it. Then I will get back with you later. You may leave my office.

Ben goes back to his teller window.

Ben says Bill I have a question for you. Earlier when I told you that because of the way you are dressed, that you look cute. Did I offend you or make you feel uncomfortable?

Bill says no. I appreciate the complement.

Ben says our manager just pulled me into the office, and tried to write me up because I was talking to someone of the same sex.

Bill says it doesn't bother me for another man to tell me I am cute. Now if he touches me in a sexual way then that would bother me. Because I am all the way straight.

Now in the mean time Joe goes to the administrator's office and knocks on the door.

The administrator Kevin says come on in.

Joe says I am sorry to bother you Kevin. But I am having a problem with 1 of my employees. I hate to tell you this but Ben Cloud made a wrong comment to his coworker Bill. Ben told Bill he is cute. I told Ben it is not right for a man to say another man is cute. Plus he said it in the lobby where customers could hear it. So I prepared a write up form for Ben and pulled him into my office to sign the form and he refused to sing it. So I decided to come to you.

Kevin says ok I will take care of this.

Now in the lobby it is a slow period and Ben hears his name paged over the intercom. Kevin is paging Ben.

Kevin says Ben Cloud please come to the Kevin Firm's office.

Since Ben has no customers at the present time he leaves his chair and walks to the Kevin's office. When Ben gets to Kevin's office he sees Joe.

Kevin says Ben will you please close the door?

Ben closes the door.

Kevin says Ben I am sorry I had to pull you in here. But Joe tells me you are not cooperating with him. You are telling other men that they are cute. Plus you said it in the lobby where customers can hear you. This makes the bank look bad.

Ben says I told Joe I noticed when Amy said a female customer is cute Amy did not get in any trouble. This is not right. I am not signing this.

Kevin says Ben if you refuse to sign the write up form, then I will have no other choice but to suspend you without pay for a week for refusing to respond to discipline by a department manager and an administrator.

Ben puts a ticked off look on his face and signs the form.

Joe says thank you Ben. You may go back to your teller window now.

When Ben gets back to his teller window he still has a ticked off look on his face.

Bill says you look like some thing is bothering you. What is wrong?

Ben says Joe wrote me up for telling you that you are cute. I tried to refuse to sign. But then Joe went and told Kevin what I told you, he also told Kevin I was refusing to cooperate by signing the slip. Then Kevin said if I refuse to sign the slip he would suspend me for a week without pay. I can't afford to loose pay so I signed it.

Bill says Kevin and Joe did you wrong. I feel for you.

LATER THAT EVENING

Later that evening Tina Styles is at her home. She lives by her self. She is wearing men's clothes. As an adult Tina always wears men's clothes every where she goes 24 hours a day 7 days a week. Tina gets on the phone and calls her brother Derek. Derek is at his home and watching television and the phone rings. Derek picks up the phone and says hello.

Tina says hi brother this is your sister Tina.

Derek says hi Tina good to talk to you.

Tina says same here. I was wondering do you remember years ago when I graduated from Wise High School?

Derek says yes.

Tina says do you remember a girl graduating with me named Angela Wing?

Derek says yes we keep in touch. She is a friendly lady.

Two Women Are Opposite Sex

Tina says please get in touch with her and ask her can your sister Tina have her phone number.

Derek says I sure will.

Tina says will you call her as soon as we finish talking?

Derek says I sure will.

Tina says ok thanks Derek.

Derek says you are welcome. Bye.

Tina says bye.

Derek keeps holding the receiver in his hands and pushes down on the button to hang up the phone then Derek releases the button and dials Angela's number.

Now at Angela's home Angela lives by her self. She is sitting on a chair with a soda and a phone on a table next to her and reading a book and the phone rings.

Angela picks up her phone and says hello.

Derek says hello Angela this is your friend Derek.

Angela says hi Derek.

Derek says do you remember years ago graduating from Wise High School?

Angela says yes.

Derek says do you remember my sister Tina?

Angela says of course I remember Tina we went to the movies together.

Derek says Tina just called me and she told me to ask you if I can give her your phone number. She wants to call you.

Angela says sure. She is your sister. She can have my phone number.

Derek says are you going to be home in a few minutes? Because as soon as I finish talking to you. I will immediately call Tina and give her your number. Tina might call you immediately.

Angela says ok. I will be right here reading my book.

Derek says ok bye.

Angela says bye.

Then they both hang up their phone.

Now Derek picks up the phone again and dials Tina's number.

Tina's phone rings and she picks it up.

Tina says hello.

Derek says hello Tina this is Derek again.

Tina says ok.

Derek says I called Angela and she said it is ok for you to have her phone number. Do you have some thing to write it down?

Tina says yes.

Derek says it is 4871046.

Tina says thank you Derek.

Derek says you are welcome.

Tina says I am going to call her right now.

Derek says ok bye.

Tina says bye.

Then they both hang up their phone.

Now Tina picks up her receiver again and dials Angela's number.

The phone rings at Angela's house and Angela picks it up.

Angela says hello.

Tina says this is Tina Styles. May I please speak to Angela Wing?

Angela says this is Angela, how are you doing Tina?

Tina says I am fine.

Angela says it is good to talk to you again. How many years has it been?

Tina says at least 12. I did not think you would remember me.

Angela says of course I do. We used to go shopping and to the movies together. I call those the good old days.

Tina says I am now buying a house, would you like to come and look at my house?

Angela says yes. Where do you live?

Tina says 802 w. cook.

Angela says I know where that is. I will be there in 30 minutes.

It is now 30 minutes later and Angela arrives at Tina's house and walks to the door and knocks.

Tina opens the door and says come on in.

Angela steps into the living room.

Angela says boy this living room sure does look nice.

Tina says let me show you the rest of the house.

Tina takes Angela around the whole house and then brings her back into the living room and they both sit on the couch.

Angela says are you dating any one?

Tina says no. Are you dating any one?

Angela says no. I have a problem with that.

Tina says what is the problem with dating?

Angela says Tina I hope I don't offend you. I am sexually attracted to women. All my life I have felt a sexual pull toward masculine women. So I am a lesbian.

Tina puts a shocked look on her face.

Angela says I hope I am not offending you.

Tina says are you gay.

Angela says yes.

Tina says after all these years I never suspected it. Because you are so feminine. Like people expect a woman to be. To be honest with you I am gay too. After all these years I never told you because I did not want to offend you. Because I thought you were straight.

Angela says years ago when we were in high school and you came to Mrs. Gold's class crossed dressed. I knew you were. Because the way I see it what other reason would a woman wear men's clothes. Because she is gay. Plus I knew I liked you. But I did not know if you liked me.

Tina says let me ask you this what kind of women do you like?

Angela says I like masculine women. I see women as cute and gorgeous. I do not see men as cute and gorgeous. I want the woman's role. What kind of women do you like?

Tina says I like feminine women. I see women as cute and gorgeous too. Not men. I want the man's role.

Angela says are you attracted to me?

Tina says yes. Are you attracted to me?

Angela says yes. How would you feel about a relationship between you and me?

Tina says that is fine. My firm law is no cheating. We will treat the relationship like a straight married couple.

Angela says I agree. Let me slide over next to you, then put your arms around me.

ONE WEEK LATER

It is now 1 week later at Mike Cloud's house in the basement and Mike is having a party. All his immediate family and close friends are there. The tables are set up with most of the food on them. Except they realize there is no where for Katrisha and Doug and Chase to put the food that's in their hands. So Mike realizes he's going to have to get some more tables for the rest of the food to sit on.

Chase says Mike do you have an extra table?

Mike says yes I do.

Derek has no food in his hands.

Mike says Derek the extra table is pretty heavy. And it is in the yard shed. Will you come with me to get it?

Derek says yes.

Mike and Derek walk through the back yard to get to the yard shed.

While they are in the shed Mike stands next to Derek.

Mike says Derek are you married?

Derek says no.

Mike says do you have a romantic girlfriend?

Derek says no.

Mike says how old are you?

Derek says 33.

Mike says I like how feminine you are. I've always been attracted to feminine men.

Derek says thank you. Are you gay?

Mike says yes. Are you gay?

Derek says yes.

Mike says are you looking for a relationship?

Derek says yes. Are you looking for a relationship?

Mike says yes. How would you feel about a relationship between you and me?

Derek says I like masculine men. But if I get into a relationship. I have a very strict rule. No cheating from either partner. The first time I catch you cheating on me we will be done.

Mike says I am a firm believer in being faithful.

Derek says well then a relationship between us is fine with me.

Mike puts his arms around Derek and Derek puts his arms around Mike.

Mike says good. Are you ready to lift this table?

Derek says yes.

They both lifted the table and took it to the basement. Then they wiped the plastic table with a damped cloth and then covered the table with a white table cloth then put food on it.

Around 4 hours later after every one finished eating and played some games then they all sat down and socialized.

Katrisha says you guys we all need to do this more often. Plus not only this but go some where for entertainment. Like go to the movies together or to a night club. So we can all have fun together.

Now at the bank in the lobby Joe is in the hall way and sees the lead teller Jennifer walking toward the men's bath room.

Joe sees Jennifer and says where are you going?

Jennifer says I am looking for Bill. He went on his break and is supposed to be back now. I checked in the break room and he is not there. So I am now going inside the men's bath room to look for him. Because I hear some talking in there.

Joe says ok.

Jennifer opens the door and walks over to where she can see the whole sink area.

The men stare at Jennifer.

When she sees other men standing there and not Bill then Jennifer looks at the door to the toilet area.

Jennifer says Bill are you in there? Your break is over.

Bill notices Jennifer's voice and says I am coming back. On my last 4 minutes that bath room feeling hit me. That's why I am late.

Jennifer says ok and walks out of the bath room. Then goes back to her teller window.

When she gets back to her window Joe is standing behind the teller counter.

Joe says did you find Bill?

Jennifer says yes. When I went into the men's bath room I found him there.

Ben says you actually went into the men's bath room?

Jennifer says yes. When I am looking for a male staff if they are not in the break room then I will go in the men's bath room looking for them.

Joe says ok I will leave it alone I am going back to my office.

Now in the lobby a customer named Mrs. Jet went to high school with Amy and Mrs. Jet went to Amy's window.

Amy says hi. Good to see you Mrs. Jet.

Mrs. Jet says good to see you too. I remember you from high school.

Amy starts the transaction and says I remember you too.

Mrs. Jet says I was going to school to get my real-estate license. And look here.

Mrs. Jet pulls out her license and says look here. I finally got it.

Amy says I am so proud of you.

Joe Is watching as Amy raises her arms to give Mrs. Jet a hug and then Mrs. Jet hugs Amy in return. And Amy kisses Mrs. Jet on the cheeks.

Amy says you have worked so hard for this. I am so proud of you.

Then Amy finishes the transaction.

Mrs. Jet leaves the bank.

Now Clay Dot who's Ben's close friend comes up to Ben's window.

Clay says hi Ben it's been quite a while since we seen each other.

Ben says yes it has. Good to see you.

Clay says good to see you again too.

Ben starts the transaction.

Clay says since I didn't know where you lived and I am just now seeing you. I want to give you a last minute invitation to my wedding.

Ben says are you getting married?

Clay says yes I am tomorrow.

Ben says congratulations. I am so happy for you.

Then Joe looks up and sees Ben and Clay raise their arms and give each other a hug. And Ben even kisses Clay on his cheeks.

Clay says thank you I needed that.

Two Women Are Opposite Sex

Clay reaches into his pocket and pulls out an invitations card and gives it to Ben.
Ben says thank you I will be there.
Ben finishes the transaction.
Clay says I will see you tomorrow at the wedding.
Ben says I will be there.
Now in Joe's office Joe dials the administrator's extension number.
Kevin's phone rings and he picks it up.
Kevin says Kevin speaking how may I help you?
Joe says Kevin this is Joe. I need you to be my eye witness. Could you please come to my office and back me up?
Kevin says sure I will be right there.
Joe says ok bye.
Kevin says bye.
Then they both hang up their phone.
Kevin walks to Joe's office.
When he's in the office Kevin says I will be right beside you.
Now in the front lobby there's no customers. Ben gets a phone call from Joe.
Ben says hello.
Joe says Ben this is Joe.
Ben says ok.
Joe says will you please come to my office?
Ben says ok.
Joe says bye.
Ben says bye.
Then they both hang up their phones.
Ben locks his drawer and walks to Joe's office.
When Ben gets to Joe's office he notices Kevin in the office too.
Ben says what's wrong?
Joe says will you close the door?
Ben closes the door.
Joe says earlier I seen you hug a male customer. On the job any kind of hugging is viewed as not proper. You even kissed the male customer on the cheeks. The kiss is viewed as sexual harassment or sexual abuse. In the past when you spoke to a male staff in the wrong

way you just received a write up. Ben I am sorry but this time I am going to have to suspend you for a week without pay.

Ben says the last time you told me the only way you would suspend me is if I refuse to sign the write up form.

Joe says I did say that but I have to look at both issues. What you did and are you accepting the discipline. In this case you may accept the discipline. At the same time look at what you did. So this time if you refuse to sign the suspension form I will have no other choice but to fire you.

Ben puts a ticked off look on his face and picks up the pen and signs the suspension form.

Joe says I need you to get your cash drawer and all your financial statements and bring it all to my office and we will balance your drawer together.

Ben says ok.

Then Ben leaves the office.

Joe says Kevin thank you for being my eye witness.

Kevin says you are welcome.

Kevin goes back to his office.

Now it is 35 minutes later and Ben gets home early.

Mary says honny it is past your lunch time. And I am happy to see you. But what are you doing home early? This is not like you to come home early.

Ben says I am ticked off at my boss.

Mary says hold it. First you come home early. Then you say you are ticked off at your boss. You did not quit your job did you?

Ben says no.

Mary says what happened?

Ben says do you remember my friend Clay Dot?

Mary says yes I remember Clay Dot.

Ben says he came in the bank today and came to my window and told me he was getting married. So I told him congratulations. Then we both gave each other a hug and I kissed him on his cheeks.

My boss seen me kiss Clay on his cheeks and told me it is not right to kiss the same sex. Even on the cheeks. So he suspended me for a week with out pay. The part that ticked me off the most is that Amy kissed the same sex on the cheeks and she did not get suspended.

ONE WEEK LATER

It is now a week later at the bank and in the lobby and Ben is almost finished cashing a check, he is counting money and giving it to a customer. When he finished the customer leaves the bank.

Ben says Jennifer I have to go to the bath room real bad! I can't hold it.

Jennifer says ok.

Ben walks to the men's bath room, when he gets there he opens the door and walks around to the sink area and notices how crowded it is. Men are waiting in line to use the urinals and toilets. Since he has to go so bad, he even goes to check the men's bath room in the basement of the bank. When he gets there he notices the same thing. Men are standing in line waiting to use the urinals and toilets. So Ben decides to go to the hall way when he gets out there a lady staff named Orletta comes out of the women's bath room.

Ben says excuse me Orletta.

Orletta says yes.

Ben says the men's bath rooms up stairs and down stairs are all filled up. Men are standing in line to use the toilet. I am about to use the toil in my pants. Could you please check the ladies bathroom to make sure there are no ladies in there?

Orletta says sure I will check.

Orletta goes in to check. When she comes out she says there are no ladies in there. Go ahead I will watch the door for you.

Ben goes into the women's bath room.

As soon as he goes in Joe comes walking toward the bath rooms and sees Orletta standing next the bath room door.

Joe says are you ok?

Orletta says yes. I am standing here to warn the ladies that a man is in the women's bath room. Because both men's bath room is filled up. Men are standing in line to use the urinals and toilets. A male staff was about to go in his pants. So I made sure the women's bath room was clear and told him to go in. And I would watch the door for him.

Ben finished and washed his hands and came out.

Ben says thanks Orletta I highly appreciate it. I just barely made it. Oh what a relief it is.

Joe says Ben do you feel better?

Ben says oh yes.

Ben goes back to his window.

Joe goes back to his office then sits down and dials the extension to Ben's window.

Ben's phone rings and he picks it up and says this is Ben speaking.

Joe says Ben this is Joe please come to my office.

Ben says ok.

Then they both hang up their phone.

Ben locks up his drawer again and walks to Joe's office.

Joe says Ben earlier you went into the women's bath room. If a woman had to go in there that would have made the bank look real bad.

Ben says the only reason why I did it is because I had to go real bad and the men's bath room up stairs and down stairs were filled up. And I was about to move bowels in my pants. Orletta 1st made sure the women's bath room was clear.

Joe says that's not the point. You should've have done just like the other men and continued waiting in the men's bath room. It is very inappropriate for a man to go into a women's bath room.

Ben says well a week ago Jennifer went into the men's bath room and you did not say a word to her.

Joe says that is more acceptable by people for a woman to go into a man's bath room but not for a man to go into a woman's bath room. Ben first of all you tell a male staff he is cute. Then you hug a male customer and kiss him on his cheeks. Now you go into the women's bath room. Ben I am sorry to tell you this but you are fired.

Ben says Amy and Jennifer did the same thing and they did not get fired. That is discriminating.

Joe says it is not discriminating. It is just not acceptable. Ben go get your time sheet and sign out and bring your time sheet to me and I will balance your cash drawer for you.

Ben comes to his window and Bill and Amy sees every thing Ben is doing.

Ben grabs his time sheet and signs the time he is leaving and also pulls out his cash drawer.

Bill says why are you signing out early and pulling your drawer out?

Ben says I just got fired.

Bill and Amy both put a shocked look on their face.

Ben takes the time sheet to Joe. Then he walks to Kevin's office. When Ben gets to Kevin's door he knocks.

Kevin says come on in Ben.

Ben says I have a complaint about Joe.

Kevin says ok go ahead.

Ben says Joe just fired me for an unfair reason. The men's bath room up stairs and down stairs was filled up. Men were waiting in line to use the toilet. I had to go so bad I was about to move bowels in my pants. Orletta made sure the women's bath room was clear. So I went to use the women's bath room I just barely made it. I sat down just in the nick of time. Joe seen me come out and later called me into his office. He told me it was very inappropriate. I told him why I did it. Both men's bath room was filled and I had to go real bad. He told me that is not the point. I should've waited. So he fired me for that.

Kevin says well Ben I am sorry for what happened. But it was inappropriate for you to use the women's bath room. I am sorry but Joe is right. So there is nothing I can do about it. I have to agree with Joe on that. You are fired.

Ben says but Jennifer went into the men's bath room and he did not fire Jennifer.

Kevin says I'm sorry Ben I agree with Joe. Since you are fired you have to leave now.

Ben leaves the bank and gets in his car and drives home.

Now Bill goes to Joe's office.

Bill says excuse me Joe. Ben told me he was fired.

Joe says yes he is.

Bill says I will like to keep in touch with him. Could I have his phone number?

Joe says yes.

Then Joe looks in his desk drawer and pulls out a pen and note pad paper, then looks in his file cabinet with employee names and numbers then writes down Ben's number and hands it to Bill.

Bill says thank you.

Joe says you are welcome.

Bill leaves the office and goes back to his teller window.

Now when Ben gets home, Mary look at Ben.

Mary says honny you are home early again. What happened this time?

Ben says my boss just fired me.

Mary says WHAT! What for?

Ben says I had to go to the bath room real bad. Both men's bath room was filled up. So Orletta made sure the women's bath room was clear, then told me to go in there. Because I almost went in my clothes. So my boss fired me for it. I even tried going to the administrator about it and Kevin just agreed to it. So now I am going to call the district manager.

Mary says I don't blame you.

Now Ben gets the phone book and phone and sits them on the table and looks up the banks corporate phone number. When he finds it then picks up the phone and dials the number.

The phone rings to the secretary of the district manager. Her name is Becky. Becky picks up the phone.

Becky says thank you for calling Sonny Bank Corporation. This is Becky speaking. How may I help you?

Ben says this is Ben Cloud I work at 1 of your branches. Branch 101. I need to speak to the district manager I have a complaint.

Becky says ok let me transfer you to his office.

The district manager's name is Buddy.

Buddy's phone rings and he picks it up.

Buddy says Buddy speaking how may I help you?

Ben says this is Ben Cloud. I worked at branch 101. I was a teller. I have a complaint about your administrator.

Buddy says ok what is the complaint?

Two Women Are Opposite Sex

Ben says I had to go to the bath room real bad and sit on the toilet. Both men's bath room were filled up. So a lady staff named Orletta made sure the women's bath room was clear, then told me to go in. When I came out my teller manager Joe was standing there by the bath room and later pulled me into his office and told me it was inappropriate for me to go in there. I told him why I did it. And he still fired me for it. Plus a week earlier a lady staff named Jennifer went into the men's bath room and Joe knew about it and did not fire Jennifer.

Buddy says well Ben if a female customer was in a hurry to go to the bath room that would've made the bank look real bad. We don't want customers to think we hire gay people to work in our bank.

Ben says I am not gay.

Buddy says I trust you're not but we don't want people to think that. Plus it was inappropriate for you to go in there.

Ben says I told you Orletta made sure the bath room was clear. Does it matter that I almost messed in my pants?

Buddy says sorry Ben but it still was not right. Sorry but you are fired. Bye Ben.

Ben says bye.

Then they both hang up their phone.

Ben looks at Mary and in a mad voice Ben says I can't believe this. This is a bunch of bull. I talked to the administrator and the district manager and they both agreed with Joe.

Ben's phone rings and he picks it up.

In a normal voice Ben says hello.

Bill says hi Ben this is Bill. Your ex-co-worker.

Ben says hi Bill how are you doing?

Bill says I am ok.

Ben says Bill I am glad you called me and it is fine that you have my number. But how did you get it?

Bill says Joe gave me your number after you left.

Ben says thank you for telling me.

Bill says I am very sorry about what happened.

Ben says thanks but it is not your fault. It just ticked me off that when I went to the administrator and the district manager they both agreed with Joe.

Bill says let me know if you need me to defend you in any thing that I seen and I will. Because I know they did you wrong.

Ben says they haven't won yet. I know what I am going to do. I am going to call the owner. Just like they were my boss. The owner is still their boss. Bill I am enjoying talking to you but I need to call the owner. So I will call you later.

Bill says ok bye.

Ben says bye.

Then they both hang up their phone.

Ben picks up the receiver again and dials the district manager's secretary again.

Becky's phone rings and she picks it up.

Becky says Becky speaking how may I help you?

Ben says may I please have Josh's phone number?

Becky says sure and tells Ben the number. When they finish talking Becky hangs up her phone.

Ben holds his receiver and pushes the button to disconnect with Becky. Then Ben releases the button and dials the owner's number.

Josh's phone rings and he picks it up and says Josh speaking how may I help you?

Ben says Josh this is Ben Cloud I was working at 1 of your branches. At branch 101 as a teller. I have a complaint about the district manager.

Josh says ok what is the complaint?

Ben says I was a teller. And I needed to go to the bath room real bad. I don't mean to talk nansty but I had to move bowels. Both men's bath rooms up stairs and down stairs were filled up. Men were standing in line to use the toilet. I couldn't bear the smell so I waited in the hall way for a few minutes. While I was in the hall way a lady staff named Orletta came out of the women's bath room and I told her I had to go and I couldn't hold it any longer. I asked her could she please check , make sure no one was in the women's bath room. Orletta checked and came back out and told me to go in. While I was in there my teller manager Joe came walking toward the bath room and she told Joe she is guarding the door because a male staff is in there. She also told him why. When I came out I told Orletta thank you I barely made it. Orletta and I both told Joe why I was in there and he still pulled me into his office and told me that's no excuse it was still inappropriate for men to go in there. And he fired me for going into the women's bath room. A week earlier a lady staff named Jennifer went into the men's bath room and Joe knew about it and did not fire Jennifer for the same thing. So after Joe fired me then I went to the administrator Kevin Firm and the administrator agreed with Joe. Then I went to the district manager Buddy Long. Buddy agreed with Kevin. Since Buddy didn't do right. Now I am coming to you the owner. Because I know this is not right.

Josh says let me make sure I heard you right. You had to go to the bath room real bad and the men's were filled up and you went to the women's and Joe fired you for it?

Ben says yes.

Josh says thanks for telling me. Meet me at branch 101 at 5:30pm in the conference room.

Ben says ok.

Josh says bye.

Ben says bye.

Then they both hang up their phone.

Ben says honny I just talked to the owner of the bank. He wants me to meet him at branch 101 at 5:30pm in the conference room.

Mary says ok.

Now in Josh's office Josh picks up the phone and dials Buddy's number.

Buddy's phone rings and he picks it up.

Buddy say thank you for calling Sonny Bank Corporation. This is Buddy how may I help you?

Josh says Buddy this is Josh. Do you have any thing planned at 5:30 pm this evening?

Buddy says no.

Josh says good meet me at branch 101 at 5:30 pm in the conference room.

Buddy says ok.

Josh says bye.

Buddy says bye.

Then they both hang up their phone.

Now Josh dials Kevin's number and the phone rings and Kevin picks it up.

Kevin says this is Kevin speaking how may I help you?

Josh says Kevin this is Josh. Do you have any thing planned at 5:30 pm for today?

Kevin says no.

Josh says good meet me at branch 101 at 5:30 pm in the conference room.

Kevin says ok.

Josh says bye.

Kevin says bye.

Then they hang up their phone.

Now Josh dials Joe's number and the phone rings.

Joe picks up the phone and says Joe speaking how may I help you?

Josh says Joe this is Josh. Do you have any thing planned at 5:30 pm for today?

Joe says well around that time I am usually just finishing helping my tellers balance their cash drawer. Plus when I get off at 5:30 I did plan to run to the store.

Josh says well when you finish balancing your cash drawers cancel your arron. Meet me at branch 101 at 5:30 pm in the conference room.

Joe says ok.

Josh says bye.

Joe say bye.

Then they both hang up their phone.

It is nw 5:15 pm and Kevin leaves his office and walks to the conference room and waits for Josh.

It is now 5:20 pm and Buddy walks into the conference room. Kevin puts a shocked look on his face.

Kevin says what happened? You did not tell me you were going to be here today.

Buddy says well I got a call from Josh today and he told me to meet him at branch 101 at 5:30 in the conference room.

Kevin says Josh called me and told me the same thing.

It is now 5:23 and Joe walks into the conference room.

Kevin and Buddy look at Joe with a surprised look on their face.

Kevin says Joe what are you doing? I did not call a department manager meeting.

Joe says Josh called me and told me to meet him in the conference room at 5:30.

Kevin says that is strange. I wonder how come the owner told the department manager to meet him in the conference room. He did not tell me he was going to have 2 other people in the meeting with me. Well if some one is getting promoted maybe he just wanted to make us all aware of it. That is the only thing I can think of.

It is now 5:25 and Josh the owner of the whole bank walks into the conference room. Josh walks to a chair on the side of the table where he can see every one in the room and sits down.

Kevin says Josh is some one getting promoted?

Josh says you will see. I am just waiting on 1 more person then we will get started.

It is now 5:29 and Ben walks into the conference room.

Then Joe and Kevin and Buddy all 3 at the same time look at Ben with a shocked look on their face.

Buddy says why are you here?

Kevin says you were fired.

Joe says I fired you.

In a loud and firm voice Josh says GENTLEMEN QUIET! I told him to come.

In a normal voice Joe says did you know I fired him?

Josh says excuse me 1st of all I do know. He told me. Second of all I am your boss. I don't care what you did to him. I told him to be here at 5:30.

Ben says Josh may I please bring a bank witness in here.

Josh says yes you may.

Ben leaves the conference room for a few minutes and walks to Jennifer's teller window and gets her attention.

Ben says Jennifer Josh is having an important meeting in the conference room. And he gave me permission to invite a bank witness in the conference. Can I invite Bill in there?

Jennifer says yes you 2 can go.

73

Then Ben walks over to Bill and says Bill Josh is in the conference room for an important meeting about me getting fired. Do you remember when you said you would be willing to defend me in any thing you seen?

Bill says yes I remember.

Ben says Josh says I could bring a bank witness into the conference. Plus I told Jennifer about it. So she knows you are coming.

Bill says ok lets go.

Now Ben and Bill both walk to the conference room and sit down.

Josh says well I guess we will get started. I will speak first. I got a call today from Ben. And he told me that earlier today he had to go to the bath room real bad. When he went to the men's bath room both up stairs and down stairs were filled up. Men were standing in line to use the toilets. So Orletta made sure the women's bath room was clear and told him to go in. Then Joe fired him for it. Joe is that true?

Joe says I did fire him.

Ben says Josh a week earlier Jennifer went into the men's bath room and Joe knew about it and did not fire Jennifer.

Josh says Joe why did you fire Ben and not Jennifer? She did the same thing.

Joe says because I know it looks bad for a man to go into a women's bath room.

Josh says it looks just as bad for a woman to go into a man's bath room. Why did Jennifer go into the men's bath room?

Joe says she was looking for a male staff he was late coming back from his break.

Josh puts a firm look on his face and in a firm voice he says you think it is more important for a female staff to go into a men's bath room because she is looking for a male staff who is late coming back from break than for a male staff to go into a women's bath room because the men's is filled up and he has to go real bad. Joe that doesn't make any sense.

Joe says I thought it made sense.

In a mad voice Josh says you thought wrong!

Ben says before this happened. Amy told a female customer she is cute. Later I told a male staff he is cute. Joe gave me a written warning but he did not give Amy a written warning.

Two Women Are Opposite Sex

Bill says later Amy gave a female customer a hug and kissed her on her cheeks. Then later Ben's friend came to his window and Ben gave him a hug and kissed him on his cheeks. Joe suspended Ben for a week without pay. But did not suspend Amy.

Josh says Joe you were letting the women get away with these things but disciplining the men. Joe you are discriminating. Ben even went to the administrator and district manager and Kevin and Buddy you 2 did nothing about it. Just discriminated along with Joe. What kind of department manager and administrator and district manager do you call your selves? This makes me wonder. How are you treating my customers? Are you treating the male customers with the same kindness that you treat the female customers with? And are you treating the female customers with the same kindness that you treat the male customers with? Or are you discriminating against my customers too? This is some thing I do not tolerate in my business. You treat every body the SAME REGUARDLESS. Now Joe and Kevin and Buddy since all 3 of you were discriminating. You are fired. Take all your things out of your desk and leave.

Joe and Kevin and Buddy leave the conference room.

Josh says Ben I am very sorry about what they did to you. As the owner of this bank I am now asking you would you like your job back?

Ben says yes.

Josh says ok by my authority you are still employed here. Now how would you like to be promoted to being the manager of the teller department?

Ben says does that mean a raise too?

Josh says it sure does. As teller manager you will be the boss of the whole department.

Ben says sure I will be the teller manager.

Josh says well congratulations. You are now the teller manager. I will have the accounting manager to train you.

Ben says thanks for the promotion.

Josh says you are welcome. And you still have all your same seniority. And you now have manager benefits. The termination papers that Joe did I will tear them up.

Ben says Bill thanks for being my witness.

Bill says you are welcome.

Josh says Bill thanks for being here.

Bill says you are welcome too.

Josh says now every body is dismissed.

Josh leaves the conference room and walks to Kristine's office the assistant administrator. Josh knocks on the door.

Kristine says come on in Josh.

Josh walks in and says I hate to tell you the bad news but I just fired Joe and Kevin and Buddy for discriminating.

Kristine says ok you are the boss.

Josh says now until I get some one hired as administrator temporary I will have some one from the corporate level to act as administrator. And temporary I will also do the district manager's job. I want you to tell the accounting manager to train Ben Cloud to be the teller manager. I just promoted Ben this evening.

Kristine says ok I will tell the accounting manager.

Now Josh leaves the bank.

Now Ben gets into his car and drives home. When he gets home Mary is in the kitchen taking dinner out of the oven. Ben walks into the kitchen with a smile on his face.

Ben says honny guess what happened at the bank.

Mary says what?

Ben says I am so glad I went to the bank owner. He had a conference with me and Joe and Kevin and Buddy and even allowed Bill to be there as my witness. Josh fired Joe and Kevin and Buddy for discriminating. Josh also gave me my job back.

In an excited voice Ben says plus promoted me to being the teller manager. I am now the boss of the whole department.

Mary puts a big smile on her face and in a happy voice says all right.

Then they give each other a hug and kiss.

Ben sits at the table while Mary sits the dishes and food on the table.

Mary puts a smile on her face and says oh I am so happy for you.

Now at a retail store called Good Quality. Larry the general manager is leading and walking all the Good Quality staff to the break room.

Two Women Are Opposite Sex

Larry says ok have a seat every one.

Every one sits down.

Larry says it is manager appreciation day. And all the Good Quality staff here today has to vote for the department manager who they think is the best manager. At the same time they cannot vote for the manager of the department they work in. It has to be a manager you do not work for. I am doing it this way so people won't feel pressured to vote for their department manager. Plus in a department where there is only around 6 staff. That manager will only get 6 votes. But in a department where there is around 30 staff. That manager will automatically get 30 votes. This way all managers can get a high number of votes no matter what department you work in. I am now giving each staff a piece of paper and pen and you write down what manager you are voting for and why you voted for that manager. Which ever manager gets the most votes wins a 1 week paid vacation and $300.00 in cash. When I am finished passing out the paper and pen I will give you 15 minutes to write. Now Larry sits down.

Now the 15 minutes is over.

Larry stands up and says it is now time to stand up and read what you wrote. We will start at the rows up here in front of me from my left to my right until we get all the way to the back. I will keep count of all the votes. One person at a time please stand and read what you wrote.

Katrisha stands up and says I voted for Don Stream because I have always heard from his staff that he is very nice and always helping his staff and helping his customers. He is willing to be here when he is needed. Rather it is for the morning hours or day hours. He comes in on his day off. And that is why I voted for Don Stream.

Larry says thank you. Next.

Now Tina is wearing men's clothes and stands up and says I voted for Denise Round. Because her staff says she gives time off when requested. She bought new equipment for her staff. She bought her staff lunch with her own money. She is beautiful.

Every one laughs for 2 seconds.

Tina continues saying she never calls in. She is nice and expects you to do your work. That is why I voted for Denise Round.

Doug doesn't say a word, just looks at Tina for 1 second then looks back at Larry.

Denise says Tina you said I am beautiful. Are you trying to come to my department?

Every one laughs for 2 seconds.

Larry says thank you. Next.

Derek stands up and says I voted for Greg Crave. I have always heard from his staff that he bends over backwards for his staff. He is more married to his job than he is to his wife. He never calls in. He does every thing that he tells his staff to do. He doesn't think he is too good or too high up to help his staff on the floor. And that is why I voted for Greg Crave.

Larry says thank you. Now since every one has voted, I am going to count and see who has the most votes.

After Larry finish counting he says the winner is Denise Round. Congratulations you win 1 week paid vacation plus $300.00 in cash.

Now it is 2 hours later and the store is busy and crowded with customers. Tina Styles always wears men's clothes and working in the men's department. Shirley Eater is a close friend of Tina's. Shirley comes into the store and walks over to the men's cash register where Tina and Doug Styles and customers are standing close around looking for clothes. When Shirley gets to the cash register Tina is looking down at a sales ad she has lying on the counter.

Shirley says hey girlfriend.

Tina looks up at Shirley and puts a surprised look on her face and says hi girlfriend. How are you doing?

Shirley says I'm fine I'm just looking for a part-time job. Are they hiring here?

Tina says I don't know let me call my boss. His name is Greg Crave. If he is hiring he would know for sure a lot better than I would.

Tina gets on the pager and says Greg Crave please come to the men's cash register?

Tina repeats the page and says will Greg Crave please come to the men's cash register?

Greg is in the men's department behind 1 of the shelves folding the pants and putting them back on the shelf. When Greg hears the page he walks over to the register.

Greg says did some one page me to the men's cash register?

Tina says yes. I did. I need you to meet some body.

Tina points to Shirley and says this is my girlfriend Shirley Eater. She wants to know are you looking for part-time help here?

Greg says yes I am. Fill out your application and get back with me after 2:00pm that is usually when we are not busy with customers.

Shirley says ok thank you. I will see you later.

Greg says ok.

Greg says Doug I am sorry I almost for got your evaluation. It is due today. I need you to come to my office.

Doug says ok.

Then they both start walking toward Greg's office. When they get to the office Greg closes the door behind him and sits at his desk. And Doug sits on the side of the desk. Greg opens the desk drawer and pulls out the evaluation form.

Greg says I already have it filled out. I just have to put today's date on it and let you read it. If you agree with what I wrote then you just have to sign it. And I'll sign it.

So Greg puts the date on the evaluation and Doug reads it out loud.

The form says Doug is a good worker and he never calls in. He is never late. Doug is good with customers. Doug follows the dress code by always having a neat appearance. As a cashier he is always honest with the way he handles cash. As his boss Greg Crave is happy to have Doug Styles as my employee. And I recommend Doug for a raise.

Doug says thank you Greg.

Greg says you are welcome.

Then Greg tears off the original form and gives it to Doug.

Greg says as the employee you get to keep the original form. As the boss I keep the carbon copy in your file. Ok that's all you may go back to your register now.

Doug says ok and gets up and opens the door to leave the office. When Doug opens the door Tina is standing right out side of Greg's office waiting to talk to Greg.

Doug sees Tina and says we're done now.

Doug goes back to his register.

Tina goes into Greg's office and says may I please talk to you?

Greg says sure have a seat.

Tina sits in front of Greg's desk and says even though I am on your schedule to work in the men's department. Am I at times going to have to work in the women's department?

Greg says well if they get short of help over there. With you being a woman. You will have to work over there some times. Because they don't want men in the women's department. Most definitely don't want men in the women's dressing room. That would be very inappropriate.

Tina says I think women's clothes are so complicated to work with. Because there's so much more to dressing a woman. Than there is to dressing a man. Plus I hope I do not offend you by what I am about to say but to be honest with you I am gay. I like being around men things better. I don't like being around women things. I like being around men clothes.

Greg says I have noticed that you always wear men's clothes. I've never seen you wear anything of women's clothes. Strictly men's.

And I have no problem with that. And I have no problem with you being gay. Your sexual preference is your business. As far as I am concerned. But now I have a problem with gay men. Because I am a man. And very straight too. I also noticed that you called Shirley Eater your girlfriend.

Tina says well in her case Shirley is my female friend girlfriend.

Not my gay partner girlfriend.

Greg says I have noticed gay women call their female friend their girlfriend and also their gay partner their girlfriend. So how would you describe them differently?

Tina says I don't know. I have never thought about it like that.

Greg says plus an employer is not supposed to judge their employees by their life out side the job. But strictly by their work performance.

Two Women Are Opposite Sex

So like I said there will be times when you will have to work in the women's department. Ok.

Tina says ok.

Greg says do you have any other questions?

Tina says no.

Greg says ok. Go back to work.

Tina leaves the office and goes back to her register.

WEEK LATER

It is now 1 week later at Good Quality. Shirley and Tina and Doug are all in the men's department straightening the clothes at 1 of the tables and Greg walks to the table where they are.

Greg says Tina and Doug your names are on the list to watch a mandatory video about straightening the clothes. The general manager has noticed that some of the clothes are not being straightened right. You have to go to the break room to watch the video. Some employees from all departments have to watch the video.

Greg says Shirley you have already seen the video. So you don't have to go. You can stay at the register. Tina and Doug I have already told the other store staff about the video. So you 2 come with me.

Greg and Tina and Doug walk to the break room. When they get there every one sits down. Tina sits on Katrisha's lap. Greg is standing at the television and looks around the room at all the staff.

Greg says well it looks like every one is here so I'll go ahead and get started. I am passing around the sign in sheet. Make sure you sign the sheet to show that you did see the video. Greg pushes the button on the television to turn it on. Then Greg pushes the button on the VCR to turn it on. When the television comes on then Greg puts the video in the VCR and pushes the play button. Then Greg looks around at all the employees in the break room.

Greg says can every one see the television?

Every one says yes.

Greg says Katrisha can you see the television with Tina sitting on your lap?

Katrisha says yes I can.

Greg says ok. Tina are you comfortable with sitting on Katrisha's lap? There are still 9 other chairs left.

Tina says yes I am comfortable.

Greg says ok.

Derek doesn't say any thing. For 5 seconds he just looks at Tina sitting on Katrisha's lap when there are 9 empty seats left.

Greg says when the video is over then every one may go back to their department.

Now the video is over and all the staff is back in their department.

In the furniture department in Don's office Don is evaluating Derek Styles. Derek is reading the evaluation form out loud.

The form says Derek is a good worker. He is good with customers. Derek is always willing to be here when he is needed, rather it is to open or close the store. Derek keeps the furniture polished and looking real pretty. Allways will to help where ever he is needed. As a cashier he is very honest with money. He gives the customers the right amount of money and keeps the right amount of cash in his drawer. As his boss Don Stream is happy to have Derek Styles as my employee. And would recommend Derek for a raise.

Derek says thanks Don.

Don says you are welcome. Hey you've earned it. Thanks for doing a good job.

Now back in the men's department. Greg is on the sales floor around other customers and folding some shirts and Doug Is at the register putting a customer's order in a bag. When the customer leaves then Doug walks over to the table where Greg is.

Doug says Greg do you work this coming Saturday evening?

Greg says no I am off at 2pm.

Doug says good because I am inviting all my boyfriends to my house to watch the football games on television. And I am offering free food and beer. So I want you to come since you are 1 of my boyfriends.

Greg says ok. Thanks for the invitation.

Doug says you are welcome.

Two Women Are Opposite Sex

Then a customer comes up to Doug and says will you please help me to find my size?

Doug says sure.

Greg finishes folding the shirts on the table he is working on. Then Greg goes to his office. When he gets to his office he gets on his desk phone and dials the men's department extension. Then the men's department phone rings.

Shirley picks up the phone and says thank you for calling the men's department. How may I help you?

Greg says Shirley this is Greg. Shirley says ok.

Greg says is Doug still helping a customer with pants? Shirley says no. Looks like he's straightening some pants. Greg says will you please call him to the phone?

Shirley says sure.

Loud enough so Doug can hear her Shirley says Doug. Doug looks at Shirley and says what?

Shirley says Greg wants you on the phone.

Doug walks over to the phone and puts it on his ear and says this is Doug speaking.

Greg says Doug this is Greg will you please come to my office. I need to talk to you.

Doug says sure I will be there in a minute.

Greg says ok I will see you when you get here.

Now they both hang up their phone and Doug walks to Greg's office.

When Doug gets to the office Greg says will you please close the door?

After Doug close the door Greg says when I was on the sales floor you came over to the table where I was and called me your boyfriend. Please do not do that again. I am not your boyfriend. I am your employer. I am not gay.

Doug says I am not gay either. I am straight too.

Greg says well when you said that you gave people the impression that you and I are in some kind of gay relationship. And we are not. We are just employer and employee. Plus by saying that you could cause me to loose my position as a manager. Because managers are not

83

allowed to date their employees. Most definitely not allowed to marry their employees. The way the company sees it. It keeps managers from showing favoritism to employees because of being involved in romantic relationships.

Doug says I see what you are saying about favoritism through relationships.

In a frustrated voice Doug says but as for marriage how in the world could you and I marry each other when we both are men?

Greg says well in some states same sex marriage is legal. That is why I said please do not call me your boyfriend again. Because I am not your boyfriend ok.

Doug says ok. But I told you I am straight too just like you are. Plus a week ago Tina called Shirley her girlfriend. And you did not say a word to Tina about it.

Greg says Tina meant a female friend girlfriend.

Doug says I meant a male friend boyfriend as well. Plus how would you know for sure Tina meant female friend. I know my sister is gay.

Greg says ok Doug since you want to argue with me about it take this as a verbal warning.

Doug says verbal warning for what?

Greg says for arguing with me. You may go back to your register now.

Doug takes a deep breath and leaves the office and goes back to the men's department.

Now Denise is in the women's department and a male customer named Aaron walks up to Denise.

Aaron says will you please help me find a dress shirt and tie?

Denise says sure just follow me.

Denise and Aaron walk over to the dress shirts, when they get there Doug is straightening the shirts and Aaron notices Doug.

Aaron says hi Doug.

Doug says hi Aaron.

Aaron says how are you doing?

Doug says fine and you?

Aaron says I am fine.

Doug says boy we haven't seen 1 another in years.

Aaron says I know.

Two Women Are Opposite Sex

Denise says Doug will you help Aaron find a dress shirt and tie?
Doug says sure.

Aaron says excuse me mam what is your name? Denise says Denise.

Aaron says I like Doug he is a nice guy. But will you please help me? For my opinion I think a woman dresses a man better than most men. Because a woman knows what makes a man look good to a woman. And that is why I asked you to help me. It is a part of good customer service.

Denise says ok I will help you.

Denise stays close to Doug and Aaron, while she is looking for a stylish shirt Aaron and Doug start talking.

Aaron says Doug since we finished high school have you gotten married yet?

Doug says no I want to go back to school first and learn a skill that pays more money.

Aaron says boyfriend you sound like me.

Denise looks at Aaron with a strange and curious look on her face.

Doug says though I work full time here, because I am the lead worker. But still the hourly pay isn't much at all. Only $8.00 an hour. Have you got married yet?

Aaron says no. In my situation it is hard to find a wife.

Doug says what is hard about your situation?

Aaron says well I don't make much money. I work in a restaurant washing dishes for $6.50 and hour. Most women want their men to make more money. I am looking for a better job. Untill I get one. I live in an efficiency apartment. I can't even afford a car right now. I have to walk or take the bus every where I go.

Doug says well some women don't look at money or material things. Some women will look at the fact that you are a nice person. And you have a good heart on you.

Aaron says thank you Doug.

Doug says some women look at the inside rather than the outside. I like the good heart you have that is why I chose to be your boyfriend.

Denise gives Doug a strange look on her face. And in her mind she is saying oh my god.

Doug says plus you are cute. Plus you want to make things better that is why you are looking for a better job.

Aaron says thanks Doug I've never thought about it in that way.

Denise says Aaron look at this shirt. Look in the mirror and see what you think.

Aaron says lets 1st look at a nice tie to go with it. Then I will look in the mirror with them both together.

Denise says ok.

Aaron looks at Doug and says well boyfriend I enjoyed talking to you. But we're going over to look at the ties now. I will talk to you later.

Doug says ok.

Aaron and Denise walk over to the ties, when they get there Denise points to a sharp looking tie.

Denise says Aaron how about this tie here? It is a nice color to go with the shirt and has a stylish design in it.

Aaron puts the tie in front of the shirt at the neck part and says where is the nearest mirror?

Denise points to the mirror and says right here. Just a few steps away.

Aaron walks to the mirror and puts the neck part of the shirt up to his neck and puts the tie in front of the shirt.

Aaron says do you think this would make me look good to a woman?

Denise says of course it does. Boy too bad I am married.

Aaron says see I told you. You know what makes a man look good to a woman. Doug being a man he does not know that. Well I will take this shirt and tie. Thank you for all of your help. You gave me very good customer service.

Denise says you are welcome.

Aaron says where is the cashier?

Denise points to the direction and says that way.

Aaron says you have a good day.

Denise says you too.

Aaron walks to the cashier and Denise walks to Greg's office. When she gets to his office she knocks on his door.

Greg says hi Denise come on in.

Denise walks in the office and stands in front of his desk and says I need to talk to you about some thing I heard 1 of your staff say to a customer that was very wrong.

Greg says ok have a seat.

Denise sits down and says a male customer named Aaron asked me to help him to find a dress shirt and tie. So I took him to the men's department where the dress shirts are and Doug was there folding the shirts. I was going to let Doug help him but the customer wanted me to help him. So that's how I heard the conversation. I was looking through the dress shirts and Aaron started talking to Doug about why Aaron wasn't married. Doug mentioned the good things about why Aaron should be able to find a wife. Doug told Aaron he is cute. Then later Doug told Aaron because he has a good heart that's why Aaron chose to be his boyfriend. I am sorry to bring this kind of news to you.

Greg says that's ok. I am glad you did. When you see staff do something wrong and if they are not in your department. Then you are supposed to tell their department manager. I will take care of it. Is there any thing else you wanted to tell me?

Denise says no.

Greg says ok.

Then Denise leaves Greg's office.

Greg gets on his phone and dials the extension to the men's department. When the phone rings Shirley picks it up.

Shirley says thank you for calling the men's department this is Shirley. How may I help you?

Greg says Shirley this is Greg.

Shirley says ok.

Greg says is Doug on the sales floor?

Shirley stays on the phone and looks around the sales floor and sees Doug folding at 1 of the tables.

Shirley says yes Doug is on the sales floor.

Greg says will you please call him to the phone?

Shirley says sure.

Then Shirley speaks just loud enough for Doug to hear her and says Doug.

Doug says yes.

Shirley says Greg wants you on the phone.

Doug says ok.

Now he walks to the phone and puts it up to his ear and says this is Doug speaking.

Greg says Doug I am sorry to bother you. But will you please come to my office?

Doug says sure.

Greg says ok. I will see you in a minute.

When Doug gets to Greg's office Greg says please close the door and take a seat.

Doug closes the door and sits down.

Greg says Denise came to my office and told me that you were on the sales floor talking to a male customer named Aaron and made him feel uncomfortable by telling him that he is cute. People got the impression that you were trying to come on to him.

Doug says I wasn't trying to come on to him. If Aaron had thought that he would have told me. Remember when we were all in the break room to vote for the best manager? Tina said Denise is cute. You did not say a word to Tina. Nobody thought Tina was coming on to Denise. Tina was talking about the same sex.

Greg says later you told Aaron because he has a good heart that's why you chose to be his boyfriend.

Doug says Denise only told you part of the story. She did not tell you the whole story. Aaron was telling me the reason why he wasn't married yet. He feels it is because he doesn't make much money. Plus since he only lives in efficiency. Plus he can't afford a car right now. A woman is not going to want him. So I told him some women don't look at money or material things. Or any thing on the outside. They look at what is on the inside. I told him he is cute to help him see some good in his self. And not just looking at negative things. I told him some women will look at the good heart he has on him. When I told him I like the good heart he has on him that is why I chose to be his boyfriend. I meant his male friend boyfriend. A friend of the same sex. Not a gay partner.

Greg says well you made him feel uncomfortable when you told him he is cute. It is not a masculine thing for a man to tell another man he is cute. Plus you embarrassed him when you said that's why you chose to be his boyfriend. In front of other people you made it sound like you 2 are a gay couple.

Doug says Aaron did not tell me I made him feel uncomfortable. Nor did he say I embarassed him. If I had've done some thing like that he would have told me.

Greg says if the staff makes the customer feel uncomfortable then we could cause the store to loose business. Then the company can't make money to pay us.

Then Greg reaches into his desk and pulls out a write up form.

Doug says what is that?

Greg says I am writing you up.

Doug says for what?

Greg says I told you in the past you don't call other men your boyfriend. And you still did it any way.

Doug says you told me don't call YOU my boyfriend. Because it can cause you to lose your position.

Greg says you shouldn't call any man AT ALL your boyfriend.

Doug says you are not right. Tina did the same thing and you did not write her up. She got away with it. Oh but I get wrote up. You are discriminating.

Greg says excuse me. Are you accusing me of discriminating?

Doug says that's what you are doing?

Greg says that's another reason why I am writing you up. I am tired of your mouth arguing with me.

Greg continues doing the write up form. When he finishes he turns the sheet around and points to the signature line so Doug can see the line.

Greg says please sign here.

Doug signs the form.

Greg says you may go back to the department.

Doug leaves the office. On his way back to the department Doug and Katrisha are walking toward each other. When they meet up Katrisha notices the ticked off look on Doug's face.

Katrisha says Doug are you ok?

Doug says no.

Katrisha says what's wrong?

Doug says Greg just wrote me up.

Katrisha says for what?

Doug says for calling my men customers friends my boyfriend.

In a mad voice Katrisha says what? I call my women customer friends my girlfriend. For him to write you up for that was not right.

Doug says I know. Well I want to continue talking but I don't want him to see us just standing here talking. So I will get back to my department.

Katrisha says ok.

Then they both go back to the department they work in. When Doug gets back to the men's department Tina notices the same ticked off look on Doug's face.

Tina says what is wrong Doug?

Doug says Greg just wrote me up for calling my men customers my boyfriend. And telling them they are cute.

Tina says oh my goodness. I can't believe what I am hearing. That is not right.

THE NEXT DAY

It is now the next day at Good Quality and it is 45 minutes before the evening shift starts. Greg and most of the evening staff is in the break room. The chairs are all being used and Doug walks in with a pot of food in his hands to put on the food table.

Greg says hi Doug.

Doug says hi Greg.

Greg says I am glad you made it for the free food day.

Doug says I wouldn't miss free food for any thing.

Greg says well help your self and enjoy.

Doug says thank you Greg.

Doug puts his pot of food on the table and picks up a paper plate and silverware and puts food on his plate and when the plate is filled

Two Women Are Opposite Sex

Derek and Greg see Doug looking around the break room for an empty seat and Doug notices all the chairs are being used.

Derek says Doug do you need a place to sit?

Doug says yes.

Derek says you can come over here and sit on my lap. It is crowded in here right now.

Doug walks his food over to Derek and sits on Derek's lap and says thank you Derek.

Derek says you are welcome.

Then Doug starts eating his food.

It is now 30 minutes after the shift has started and Greg is in the men's department with his staff talking to the staff about focusing on good customer service. When Greg is finished talking to the staff he looks at Doug.

Greg says Doug will you please follow me?

Doug says sure.

They both walk to the men's department stock room. When they get there Greg says earlier when you were in the break room and sat down to eat your food. You sat on Derek's lap. Do not do that again. I know Derek is your brother but it is not proper for a man to sit on another man's lap. Now this time I am not going to write you up. In the past you have been a very good employee. So deep within I really don't want to discipline you. So please don't sit on another man's lap again.

Doug says Greg I promise you I am not arguing. It is something I just don't understand. But when we were in the break room to watch the videos about straightening the clothes Katrisha was sitting on Tina's lap and that was during the shift and there was 9 other seats left for her to sit on. And I noticed nobody said a word to Karisha or Tina about it. They just got away with it. When I sat on Derek's lap it was before the shift started and there was no other place to sit. But I still get talked to about it.

Greg says you should have got a chair from another room.

Doug says all the chairs were taken from other rooms. I could tell because there were people sitting in chairs that weren't at the table. Plus some desk chairs were in there.

Greg says you should have just stood up and ate. I am sorry but that is just the way it is. Now go back to the sales floor.

Doug walks back to the sales floor and Greg walks to his office.

When Greg gets to his office he sits at his desk and dials the extension to the furniture department.

Don Stream is in his office and the phone rings and he picks it up.

Don says the furniture department. This is Don. How may I help you?

Greg says this is Greg from the men's department.

Don says ok.

Greg says something I have to tell you. Earlier today in the breakroom your staff Derek told Doug to sit on Derek's lap to eat his food. And Doug did it.

Don says ok. Thank you for telling me. I will take care of it.

Greg says ok bye.

Don says bye.

Then they both hang up their phone.

Don walks to the sales floor and sees Derek polishing the furniture.

Don says Derek.

Derek says yes.

Don says may I please see you in my office?

Derek says sure.

When they get in to Don's office Don says I was told that earlier today you and Doug was in the break room and you told Doug to sit on your lap to eat his food. That is not masculine for a man to sit on another man's lap. Don't do it again.

Derek says the only reason why I did It is because the break room was crowded and Doug needed a place to sit so he could eat his food.

Don says you should've got chairs from other rooms.

Derek says we already had chairs from other rooms and there still was no place to sit.

Don says that's not a good enough excuse. He could have stood up to eat. This is a verbal warning for you. Now go back to the sales floor.

Derek says ok.

Later that evening at Doug's house Doug is sitting on his couch watching television and he turns it off and picks up the phone and dials

Derek's number. When the phone rings at Derek's house he is sitting down reading a book and picks up the phone.

Derek says hello.

Doug says Derek this is Doug.

Derek says hi.

Doug says at work today when we were in the break room eating our food. I told you to sit on my lap because there was no other place to sit. Greg had the nerve to talk to me about that.

Derek says Don talked to me about letting you sit on my lap. He told me I should have just let you stand up and eat. Because it is not masculine for a man to sit on another man's lap. Don gave me a verbal warning for that.

Doug says it is discriminating because when we was in the break room to watch the videos Katrisha was sitting on Tina's lap and nobody said a word about it. They just got away with it.

THE NEXT DAY

It is now the next day at Good Quality and during the day hours and a cute male customer named Scott came into the store and goes to the men's department where Doug and Tina and Shirley are. Scott walks up to Tina.

Scott says I am trying to find some bikini underwear. Could you please help me find a pair I like and can fit?

Tina says sure.

When they get to the men's underwear section Tina says we have different kinds of bikini underwear. To name just a few kinds we have string bikini and performance bikini and intimo bikini and cotton bikini. What kind do you wear?

Scott says I wear the string bikini.

They walk over to the string bikini.

Tina says what size do you wear?

Scott says I wear size 32.

Then they look in the 30s and go 2 more sizes up and find size 32.

Tina says what color do you like?

Scott says I like red and gray and white.

Tina says here they are string bikinis in size 32 in red and gray and white.

Scott says thank you.

Tina says you are welcome.

Scott says also my wife and I just got married and we plan on having sex. We are crazy about other people's kids but we don't want any kids of our own. So could you please help me find some condoms and viagra?

Tina says sure.

Tina and Scott walk over to the shelf where the condoms are.

When they get there Tina says just to name a few of the kinds of condoms we have. We have extra strength condoms and extra strength lubricated condoms and assorted colors with extra strength and assorted flavors extra strength. Which 1 would you like?

Scott says I will take the 1 that just says extra strength. Because when we have sex all I am concerned about is that she don't get pregnant.

Then Tina picks up the box that says extra strength and gives it to Scott.

Scott says thank you.

Tina says you are welcome.

Scott says 1 more thing.

Tina says ok.

Scott says just so my penis can grow longer can you show me where the Viagra pills are?

Tina says sure just follow me.

Tina walks Scott over to the shelf where the packages of Viagra are and shows Scott the package that has the most amount of pills in the container.

Tina says right here. This package is your best offer.

Tina pulls the package off the shelf and shows Scott what the label says about what all comes in the package.

Tina says this package cost more but this package has a container for the most amount of pills in it. Plus the pills in this container will

Two Women Are Opposite Sex

help you grow longer than any other pills here. Plus these pills will get you more erected than any other pills and you will stay erected for 4 long hours. Plenty of time to enjoy sex with your wife. Plus this container has female Viagra as well, with the same amount of pills as for the men. So this package will be your best buy.

Scott says I will buy it.

Tina says ok would you like to look for any thing else?

Scott says no thank you this is all I need. Are you a cashier?

Tina says yes.

Scott says where is your register?

Tina says follow me.

Tina and Scott walk to the cash register and Tina rings the order, when she has finished she tells Scott the total and Scott hands Tina the money. Tina puts the money in the drawer and then counts out Scott's change from the drawer and then recounts Scott's change while giving it to him.

Tina says you have a nice day.

Scott says you too.

LATER THAT EVENING

It is now the evening time and we are at Scott Eter's house and his wife's name is Tonya Eter. Scott and Tonya are in their bedroom standing up and wearing their day clothes and they are hugging each other and just finished kissing.

Scott says do you want to make love?

Tonya says yes I do. Let me look in my drawer for my birth control pills.

Scott says I bought some condoms from Good Quality today. So you don't have to take your birth control pills.

Tonya says I don't like using condoms.

Scott says why not.

Tonya says when we have sex the texture of the condom does not feel any thing like the skin on the penis. So I'd rather use birth control pills. I can enjoy sex better in that way.

While Tonya is looking in her dresser drawer she notices she can't find her birth control pills.

Tonya says since I can't find my pills. I will go to the store and buy some more. There are other things I need as well. The condoms you just bought let me take those back to the store and get a refund.

Scott looks in his bag and pulls out the box of condoms and the receipt and says here you go. He hands them both to Tonya.

Tonya takes the box and receipt and says ok I will be right back.

Scott says ok.

Now at Good Quality the evening shift has started and ALL the female staff including managers has called in or they were scheduled off. There is ONLY MEN staff including managers in the whole store.

Greg is in the men's department and he is explaining to the staff what is going on.

Greg says gentlemen we are extremely short of help today. Unfortunately this evening by mistake ALL the women staff called in or they were scheduled off. This just got noticed a few minutes ago. So for the ones who were scheduled off the managers are going to call them to see if they can come to work today. If a customer gets a product from the women's department tell them they have to pay for it in another department. Because unfortunately there are no women staff here right now. And the male staff is not allowed to work in the women's department.

Now Tonya comes into the store and she 1st walks to the women's department and looks for a cashier so she can get a refund. When she notices there is no cashier over there. Then she walks to the men's department cash register and sees Doug.

Tonya says where is the cashiers in the women's department?

Doug says mam I am sorry but unfortunately all the women staff called in or were mistakenly scheduled off today. The managers are trying to call some women staff to come in.

Tonya says I 1st want to get a refund on this box of condoms.

Tonya reaches into her bag and pulls out the receipt and gives it to the cashier, then she reaches into her bag again and pulls out the box of condoms.

Doug does the refund transaction on the register and puts the receipt in the drawer and puts the box of condoms behind the counter. Then gives Tonya her money.

Tonya says thank you.

Doug says you are welcome.

Tonya walks back over to the women's department and starts looking for birth control pills. After 3 minutes of searching she notices she can't find the pills. Then Tonya looks around and the 1st staff that she sees from a distance is Derek in the furniture department. So Tonya walks over to the furniture department and gets Derek's attention.

Tonya says excuse me sir

Derek says yes.

Tonya says will you please help me in the women's department?

Derek says if it does not bother you for a man to help you with women's items then I will be glad to help you.

Tonya says well 1st of all the way I see it. Even on the job. In a respectful way at times a man has to work with women items. Just like at times a woman has to work with men items. So if you can do it in a respectful way then it won't bother me.

Derek says ok I will help you.

Tonya and Derek walk to the women's department and when they get there.

Tonya says I was trying to find the birth control pills. But I couldn't see where they are.

Derek walks Tonya over to the birth control pills and says here they are. Right here mam.

Tonya says which package is the best?

Derek picks up the best package and points to the label and says well according to what is written on the label this package here is the best. This package has 90 pills in it. Plus the protection last 24 hours. It may cost you more, but you won't have to buy pills for 3 months.

Tonya says I will take that one.

Derek says ok.

Tonya says now could you please help me find my size in panties?
Derek says sure. Follow me.
They walk over to the panties.
Derek says do you like the fancier styles or the regular styles?
Tonya says I like the regular styles better.
Derek says these here are our regular style of panties. What size do you wear?
Tonya says I wear 30.
Derek says ok now let me look for size 30.
Derek flips through the panties looking for size 30 and says here they are I found size 30. Now what colors do you want?
Tonya says I just want 3 white ones.
Derek sees 3 white ones and says here they are 3 size 30 in white. Here you go.
Derek hands the panties to Tonya.
Tonya says now could you please help me find some tampons? Derek says sure.
Derek walks Tonya over to the sanitary napkins and when they get in front of them Derek points to the biggest box.
Derek says these here will last you the longest. This name brand is the thickest and has the most sanitary napkins in them.
At the same time the furniture manager Don walks up to them and has a mad look in his face.
Tonya says what is the price?
Don says Derek what are you doing over here in the women's department?
Derek says I am trying to help a customer find what she wants.
Tonya looks at Don and says excuse me sir who are you to interrupt the service here?
Don says I am Don the furniture manager and Derek here is supposed to be working in the furniture department. Not in the women's department.
Tonya says he was in the furniture department. At the same time have you forgotten? You have no female staff here today. I walked over to the furniture department and asked him to come over here and help me because we had no other choice.

Don says I am sorry mam but it is the company's law that men do not work in the women's department.

Tonya says well you need to break the rule because I need help. And he was kind enough to help me. He was even being respectful about it by telling me if it does not bother me for a man to help me with women's things then he would be glad to help me out. Then I told him even on the job sometimes in a respectful way men have to work with women items. Just like women have to work with men items.

Don says I am not willing to lose my job because I am letting employees break company laws.

Tonya says well since you have no female staff here today what is a female customer supposed to do when she needs help in the women's departments?

Don says you need to just do the best you can to help your self or come back on another day when there is women staff here or go to another store.

Don says Derek I want you to go back to the furniture department now.

Derek walks back to the furniture department.

Don says as for you miss since you are causing my staff to break company laws I want you to leave the store right now. Or I will call security and have you taken out of here.

Tonya says I need help with other items as well.

Don says I told you help your self or leave.

Tonya says I am first going to pay for my things I have already got here then I am getting out of here.

Tonya starts walking towards the men's department and Don walks toward his office.

When Tonya gets to the men's department Doug rings her order and tells her the total amount.

Tonya hands Doug the money.

Doug puts the money in the drawer and gives Tonya her change back.

Doug says you have a good mam.

Tonya says thank you sir you too.

Tonya leaves the store ticked off.

Don is in his office and walks to the sales floor and sees Derek and gets his attention.

Don says Derek I need to see you in my office.

Derek says ok.

They both walk to Don's office.

When they get to his office Don says you know the company law that men do not work in the women's department.

Derek says I thought with the situation of no women here today and since she did come to me and ask for help it was ok.

Don says Derek you should've asked a manager 1st. You can't just break company laws. If some one from the corporate office came in here unexpected and seen a male staff working over there. Me and Larry would have been in big trouble.

Now Don opens his desk drawer and pulls out a write up form.

Derek says what is that?

Don says it is a write up form.

Derek says are you writing me up for helping a female customer?

Don says no I am writing you up for working in the women's department and working with women's personal items. That's why I am writing you up.

When Don finished with filling out the form he says now read and sign here.

Derek reads the form. When he finished reading he signs it.

Don says now go back to the sales floor.

Derek goes back to the sales floor with a mad look on his face Greg comes to the men's department.

Greg says Doug go ahead and take your break now.

Doug says ok.

Doug walks over to the furniture department and sees Derek.

Doug says are you going on your break?

Derek says let me ask Don.

Derek goes to Don's office and says Don may I take my break now?

Don says sure I will come out there while you take your break. Go ahead.

Derek says ok.

Derek and Doug walk to the break room and sit down.

Doug says Derek why did you ask to take a break?

Derek says well since we are short of help today I wanted to let Don know I was on break. Plus I am trying to be careful. I don't trust Don any more.

Doug says why what is wrong?

Derek says 1st he gives me a verbal warning for letting you sit on my lap. Plus about a minute ago he wrote me up for helping a female customer in the women's department with personal items. He did not care about having no female customers here today.

Doug says that is not right because Tina helped a male customer look for men personal items. And she did not get wrote up. I feel it is not fair that a woman staff can work in the men's department but a male staff can not work in the women's department. What is the difference?

Derek says I agree.

THE NEXT DAY

It is the next day at Good Quality and Greg is in the men's department folding some shirts and an elderly man named Jarred is walking with a walker and walks up to Greg.

Jarred says excuse me sir. My wife is shopping for me and her. And I don't want to embarrass her by asking her to take me to the bath room in a public place. Could you please tell me where the bath room is?

Greg says just to be courteous I will do more than tell you I will walk you all the way up to the men's bath room.

Jarred says thank you.

Greg says you are welcome.

When they get 2 feet away from the men's bath room door Jarred and Greg sees Tina come out of the women's bath room. At the same time Tina and Greg and Jarred sees Katrisha come out of the men's bath room. Jarred puts a shocked look on his face.

Jarred looks at Greg and says why in the world are you taking me to the women's bath room? Are you trying to call me a woman or gay?

Greg says oh no sir. I did not know that a woman was in the men's bath room.

Jarred says is the woman gay or half man and half woman?

Greg says sorry sir. I don't ask people questions about their personal life. I promise you this is the men's bath room. When you get in there you will see the urine bowl for men.

It is now 4 hours later in the furniture department and Don has just hired Ron a new cashier to work with Derek. Don walks Ron out to the sales floor to introduce him to Derek.

Don says Derek this is Ron a new cashier. He's been with another branch of Good Quality for 4 years, so he is only new to this store. The registers in all the stores operate the same, so you don't have to train him on the register. You just have to give me time to memorize where every thing is in this store.

Derek says ok. It will be nice to have some one to work with. We have been short of help. I will show him where the returned merchandise is.

Don says ok.

Then Don goes back to his office.

Now Derek walks Ron to the returned stock room.

When they get in there Derek says this is the room for all the returned furniture. It was returned because customers could not finish making their payments so now managers have to put a reduced price on it. So hopefully we can sell the product.

Now Derek walks Ron back to the sales floor and shows Ron where the registers are.

Derek says all the registers are right here. During slow periods you can dust the wood parts of the furniture and clean the glass parts. Do you think you can handle working the floor by your self for a few minutes? I need to go to the bath room.

Ron says since I don't need training on the registers. I can handle it by myself for a few minutes.

Derek goes to the bath room and when he gets to the men's bath room there is a sign on the outside of the bath room door saying out of order. Toilets and urinals are not flushing. So then Derek goes to the bath room down stairs. When he gets there he notices the house keeping cart right out side of the bath room. Plus all the water all over the floor.

The house keeper Joice says sorry Derek nobody can use this bath room right now. Because it is flooded. Maintenance men are coming to fix the toilets and urinals. Would it bother you to use the ladies bath room?

Derek says since I have to go real bad it won't bother me. Joice says I will go check to make sure no body is in there.

Joice goes inside of the women's bath room and when she sees nobody is in there, she comes out.

Joice says nobody is in there. You can go in now.

Derek goes in to the women's bath room.

Then Joice puts a note on the women's bath room door.

The note says THERE'S A MAN IN HER PLEASE WAIT.

Now back in the furniture department 4 married couples have come in to the department to look for furniture and Ron is helping 1 of the couples.

Don is in his office and decides to walk to the furniture department to see how things are going. When he gets to the furniture department he sees the couples walking around. Then he sees Ron helping 1 of the couples.

Don gets Ron's attention.

Don says excuse me Ron I hate to interrupt you with the customers but where is Derek?

Ron says Derek told me he had to go to the bath room so I told him I could handle it by my self for a few minutes.

Don goes to the 2nd couple and says may I help you?

The 2nd couple says we are just looking thank you.

Don says ok.

Then Don goes to the 3rd couple and says may I help you?

The 3rd couple says no. Thank you.

Don goes to the 4th couple and says may I help you?

The 4th couple says yes.

Then tells Don what they are looking for.

Now Denise has to go to the bath room. When she gets to the women's bath room door she sees the sign saying THERE'S A MAN IN THE BATH ROOM. PLEASE WAIT. After she waited for a minute then Derek comes out of the bath room.

Denise says hi Derek.

Derek says hi Denise.

Then Denise goes to the women's bath room and Derek goes back to the furniture department.

When Denise comes out of the women's bath room she goes to her office and sits at her desk and gets on her phone and dials Don's extension. When the phone rings Don's answering machine comes on and Denise leaves a message.

Denise says Don this is Denise from the women's department will you please call me when you get this message?

Then Denise hangs up the phone.

Now back in the furniture department on the sales floor Don is finishing with his last customer for now.

Don looks at Ron and says you are doing a good job.

Then Derek comes back into the department.

Derek says I am sorry it took so long.

Don says that's ok. We managed just fine. If you 2 need me I will be in my office.

Derek and Ron says ok.

When Don gets back into his office he notices the light flashing on his answering machine. Don pushes the button to see what the message is. When the message is done playing Don picks up the phone and dials Denise's extension.

Then Denise's phone rings and she picks it up and says Denise speaking how may I help you?

Don says Denise you left a message on my phone for me to call you.

Denise says will you please talk to Derek? As I was going into the women's bath room he was coming out of the women's bath room. It is not proper for a man to go into a women's bath room.

Don says ok. I will take care of it. Thank you for telling me.

Denise says ok bye.

Don says bye.

Then they both hang up their phone.

Now Don picks the receiver back up and dials the number to the furniture department sales floor.

When the phone rings Derek picks it up and says furniture department. Derek speaking may I help you?

Don says Derek this is Don will you please come to my office?

Derek says sure.

Don says I will see you when you get here. Bye.

Derek says bye.

Then they both hang up the phone and Derek walks to Don's office.

When Derek gets to Don's office then Don says Denise called me and says she seen you coming out of the women's bath room as she was going in. That was very improper for a man to go into the women's bath room.

Derek says well I had to go to the rest room and in the men's bath room up stairs the toilets were not working. They were not flushing. And then down stairs the men's bath room was flooded. No body could use either men's bath room. Before I went into the women's bath room the house keeper Joice made sure the women's bath room was clear. Then she put up a sign to alert women that a man was in there.

Don says in that case you should have waited until maintenance came to fix the bath room. That was no excuse to go into the women's bath room.

Don reaches into his drawer and pulls out a suspension form and fills it out. When he finishes he points to the signature line.

Don says sign right here.

Derek says what is this?

Don says I am suspending you. If you refuse to sign the suspension form then I will fire you.

Derek puts a mad look on his face and signs the form.

Don says Derek I am very sorry but you are suspended for a week without pay. Please clock out and go home.

Now Derek leaves Don's office and goes to the time clock and clocks out. Then Derek walks to the men's department and picks an item to buy. When Derek gets to the cashier he is the only person standing in line. Tina and Doug both are at the register talking.

Tina says come on up.

Derek walks up to Tina's register and Tina does the sale transaction. When she finishes the transaction.

Derek says well you guys won't see me at work for a week.

Tina says are you going on vacation?

Derek says no. Don just suspended me for a week.

Doug says what for?

Derek says because I had to go to the bath room and both of the men's bath room were out of order. So Joice made sure the women's bath room was clear and I went in there. Later Don was told about it. And so he suspended me for it.

Tina says boy I promise there is so much discrimination going on in this place it is pathetic. Earlier when I came out of the women's bath room me and Greg and a customer seen Katrisha come out of the men's bath room. And I promise you Katrisha did not get in trouble for it either. Derek I am sorry about what happened.

Doug says I am sorry about that too.

Derek says thanks Tina and Doug. Well I will see you guys in a week.

Doug and Tina says ok.

Derek leaves the store.

30 MINUTES LATER

Now Greg and Tina are both standing in the isle talking to an ex-employee name Vernitta. Vernitta and Katrisha were close friends. Now Katrisha is standing from a distance and sees Vernitta and walks up to her and puts 1 arm around her.

Katrisha says hi honny bun.

Vernitta says hi sweetie.

Katrisha says are you coming back to work here?

Vernitta says no. I am sorry. I am just visiting and saying hi.

Katrisha says well we do miss you. And that's speaking from the heart.

Tina says that's right.

Greg says that's right. I miss you too. You were a good worker. If you ever want to come back to work for me I will be glad to take you back.

Vernitta says thanks Greg I really appreciate the complement.

Greg says you are welcome.

Vernitta says well I better get home now so I can cook and get ready for bed. Bye you all.

Greg says ok bye.

Tina and Katrisha says bye.

Now in the men's department Doug is standing behind the checkout counter getting things organized. While Doug is organizing things his male neighbor Russle comes up to the front of the counter.

Russle says good to see you Doug.

Doug looks up at Russle and puts a shocked look on his face.

Doug says good to see you too Russle.

At the same time Greg walks up to the front of the register with a green money bag and does a money pick up. Greg counts $300.00 out of the register.

At the same time Doug says Russle how are you doing man?

Russle says I am fine. I just got some money in the mail. So you know I am fine. How has things been going for you?

Doug says other than going to a funeral tomorrow. I am fine.

Russle says who died?

Doug says an aunt of mine that I was real close to. Since she never had any kids of her own she's always treated her nieces and nephews like her own kids. So I want to get this over with.

Russle says you have my symphathy.

Then Russle raises up both of his arms and gives Doug a hug. And Russle raises both of his arms and gives Russle a hug.

Doug says thank you.

Russle says you are welcome.

Then Greg looks at Doug and says just to make sure I counted right will you please count this $300.00?

Doug turns around and says sure.

When Doug finish counting the money then he hands it back to Greg and Greg puts the money in the money bag. Then Greg signs his signature on the pick up sheet. Then Doug signs his signature on the pick up sheet.

Greg says I take it you 2 are related to each other.

Doug says no we are neighbors. Greg this Is my neighbor Russle. Russle this is my boss Greg.

Greg and Russle say to each other hi.

Greg says good to meet you.

Russle says good to meet you.

Then they both shake each other's hand.

Russle says Doug I don't want to keep you from your work. I will see you later bye.

Doug says bye.

Russle leaves the counter.

Greg says Doug will you come with me?

Doug says sure.

First Greg takes the money to the security department. When Greg and Doug get to the security department Greg hands the money to Steve the security guard. Then Greg signs the sheet that says he did turn the money in to security. Then Steve puts the money in the safe then Steve signs the sheet saying he put the money in the safe. Now Greg and Doug walk to Greg's office.

While in the office Greg says have a seat.

Doug sits down.

Greg says you know what you did with the customer was inappropriate.

Doug says what did I do with a customer that was inappropriate?

Greg says when you gave the customer a hug. That is considered as sexual harassment to hug a customer.

Doug says how could it be sexual harassment when he first raised his arms and hugged me? Plus he was only showing sympathy when he hugged me. He was not trying to be sexual.

Greg says you should have told him the staff is not allowed to hug on the job.

Then Greg reaches into his desk drawer and pulls out a suspension form.

Doug says what is that?

Greg says it is a suspension form. I am going to suspend you for a week with out pay because it is not proper for a staff to hug on the job.

Greg continues filing out the suspension form and when he finishes he points to the signature line.

Greg says sign right here.

Doug says this is not fair the women staff don't get suspended for hugging on the job.

Greg says if you refuse to sign and take the suspension. I will just fire you.

Doug puts a mad look on his face and signs the suspension form.

Greg says now please leave for a week.

Doug leaves the office, when he gets home he gets on his telephone and dials Derek's number.

Now at Derek's house the phone rings and he picks it up.

Derek says hello.

Doug says Derek this is Doug. You will never guess what just happened to me at work.

Derek says what happened?

Doug says Greg just suspended me for a week without pay. Now I am in the same situation that you are in. If this mess continues then I am going to the administrator. Because this is not right.

Derek says I am too because we are not being treated right.

Doug says I am not going to hold you long. I just wanted to let you know that I am in the same situation that you are in. I will talk to you later.

Derek says ok bye.

Doug says bye.

Then they both hang up their phone.

Then Doug picks up his phone again and dials Tina's number.

At Tina's house the phone rings and she picks it up.

Tina says hello.

Doug says Tina this is Doug.

Tina says ok.

Doug says guess what happened to me at work today.

Tina says what?

Doug says Greg suspended me today.

Tina says hold it. You and Derek got suspended in the same day. What in the world is going on? Why did he suspend you?

Doug says my neighbor came into the store and I told him about the funeral tomorrow. Then the neighbor gave me a sympathy hug and I hugged him back. So Greg suspended me for it.

Tina says that is not right. Earlier today Katrisha was hugging a customer. Since Vernitta is now a customer she came into the store and Katrisha went up to her and called her honny bun. And even put her arm around her. And Katrisha did not get suspended for it. If this keeps up go to the administrator.

Doug says I already have that planned. Well I am not going to hold you. I just wanted to let you know why you won't see me at work for a week. I will talk to you later. Bye.

Tina says bye.

Then they hang up.

Now Doug picks up his phone again and dials his dad's number.

At Jeff and Grace's house the phone rings and Jeff picks it up. Jeff says hello.

Doug says dad this is Doug.

Jeff says hi son.

Doug says dad how are you doing?

Jeff says I am fine.

Doug says dad I am sorry to bother you. But I may need your help with a weeks worth of grocery money.

Jeff says that is fine son.

Doug says on my job I just got suspended for a week without pay.

Jeff says what happened?

Doug says my neighbor came to my job and I told my neighbor about the funeral tomorrow. And my neighbor gave me a sympathy hug and I hugged him in return and my boss seen it. And my boss told me it is not right to hug on the job. I should've just told him thank you. He told me that was sexual harassment to hug. So he suspended me for it with out pay. If this continues I am going to the administrator about it.

Jeff says and if the administrator doesn't do any thing about it. Then you go all the way to the top to the district manager or even to the owner.

Doug says I already have that planned.

Jeff says son when you need grocery money you let me know and I will be glad to help you.

Doug says thanks dad.

Jeff says you are welcome son.

Doug says bye.

Jeff says bye.

Then they both hang up.

ONE WEEK LATER

It is now a week later at 6:00 am at katrisha'a house and Katrisha is lying in her bed sleep and her phone ring and she picks it up.

Katrisha says hello.

Denise says hello Katrisha this is Denise Round from Good Quality.

Katrisha say ok.

Denise says Katrisha my husband had an asthma attack real early this morning. So I am with him now at the hospital. I have already called Larry Good and told him about what happened. I was scheduled to open the store this morning. Could you please open for me?

Katrisha says sure.

Denise says I will be at work as soon as the doctor finishes his breathing treatment.

Katrisha says ok.

Denise says thank you Katrisha.

Katrisha says you are welcome.

Then they both hang up the phone.

Now Katrisha gets out of her bed and goes to the bath room and does her hygiene

At the same time at Doug's house. Doug gets out of his bed and goes to his bath room and does his hygiene.

At the same time at Derek's house. Derek gets out of his bed and goes to his bath room and does his hygiene.

Now back at Katrisha's house Katrisha has finished her hygiene. Now she goes to her kitchen and looks in her freezer and pulls out a frozen breakfast and puts it in the microwave to cook. When it has finished cooking then she eats it.

Now back at Doug's house. Doug is finished with his hygiene. Now he goes to the kitchen and looks in the freezer and pulls out a frozen breakfast sandwich and puts it in the microwave to cook. When it is finished cooking he takes it out and eats it.

Now back at Derek's house. Derek is finished with his hygiene. Now he goes to the kitchen and looks in the freezer and pulls out a frozen breakfast sandwich and puts it in the microwave to cook. When it is finished cooking he takes out and eats it.

Now back at Katrisha's house. Katrisha has finished eating her breakfast and goes to her bedroom and starts getting dressed for work. First she puts on men's dress pants then she puts on a men's dress shirt then she puts on a tie then she puts on men's dress socks then she puts on men's shoes.

Now back at Doug's house. Doug is finished with his breakfast. Now Doug goes to his bedroom and starts getting dressed for work. First Doug puts on a women's stockings then Doug puts on a women's dress pants then puts on a women's dress shirt then puts on a women's dress shoes.

Now back at Derek's house. Derek is finished eating his breakfast. Now he goes to his bedroom and starts getting dressed. First Derek puts on a women's stocking. Then he puts on a skirt then he puts on a women's dress top. Then he puts on a women's dress shoes.

Now at the same time all 3 Katrisha and Doug and Derek get in their car and drive to work. All 3 arrive to work at the same time. First Katrisha pulls into her parking spot. Second Doug pulls into his parking spot next to Katrisha. Third Derek pulls into his parking spot next to Doug. Then at the same time they all get out of their car.

Doug says where is the opening manager?

Katrisha says Denise called me this morning and said she is going to be late and asked me to open the store for her.

Now Doug and Derek follow Katrisha up to the door.

Katrisha says both of you wait here until I turn off the alarm.

Doug and Derek say ok.

Katrisha goes inside the store and turns off the alarm and then opens the door.

Katrisha says come on in.

Then regular employees from other departments come to work.

It is now 4 hours later and Doug is in the men's bathroom and Derek is in the back return room dusting the return furniture.

Now Denise and Greg and Don come to work and immediately go to their office and get settled in. When they are settled in Greg and Don walk to the women's department and sees Denise and Katrisha standing close to the register talking.

Greg says Denise I heard about your husband. How is he doing?

Denise says he has asthma real bad. So he had an asthma attack. And the doctor gave him a breathing treatment. So now he is doing fine. Thanks for asking.

Now Greg and Don go back to their department to make sure their staff is here.

When Greg gets to his department he sees Tina and Shirley and Doug building a seasonal display. He notices Tina wearing men's clothes as usual.

Greg says Tina you love the men's clothes don't you?

Tina says oh yes.

Then he looks at Doug and notices Doug is wearing a women's shirt and women's shoes and women's pants.

Greg says Doug your clothes are not appropriate. Will you please go to the conference room? And wait for me I will be coming soon.

Now Doug goes to the conference room and Greg goes to his office and looks in the employee file cabinet for Doug's file. When he finds Doug's file he makes sure the write up form and suspension form are in there and takes the file out of the cabinet. Then Greg opens his desk drawer and pulls out a firing form. Then Greg puts the firing form in Doug's file.

Now when Don gets to his department he sees Ron and Derek both dusting off the furniture. Then Don notices the clothes Derek is wearing.

Don says Derek your clothes are not appropriate. Will you please go to the conference room? And wait for me I will be coming soon.

Derek says do you mean go to your office?

Don says no I mean go to the conference room.

Now Derek goes to the conference room. When he gets there he sees Doug.

Derek says what are you doing in here?

Doug says Greg told me to come to the conference room and wait for him.

Derek says Don told me the same thing.

Now Don goes to his office and looks in the employee file cabinet and looks for Derek's file. When Don gets to Derek's file he makes sure the write up form and suspension form are in there. Then he takes the file out of the cabinet and looks in his desk drawer and pulls out a firing form.

Now Don and Greg both walk to Larry's office with the files in their arms and they both arrive at the same time. Then Greg knocks on the door.

Larry says hi gentlemen come on in.

Greg says will you please come to the conference room it looks like we have to fire Doug.

Larry says fire Doug for what?

Greg says for cross dressing on the job.

Don says I need you for the same reason. To fire Derek for cross dressing on the job. You won't believe your eyes when you walk in the conference room for 1 minute.

Larry says excuse me gentlemen I will be right back.

Larry walks to the conference room, when he gets in there he says excuse me Derek and Doug will you both step away from the table so I can see you from head to toe.

Derek and Doug step away from the table so Larry can see them both with his own eyes.

Larry says you both know this is not appropriate. Please sit back down.

Then they both sat down. And Larry went back to his office and sat in his chair.

Larry says I can't believe they did this. Just making the store look bad. I agree they need to be fired. But you know I have to first call the district manage Cory and call the owner Vern. So they can see what is going on. Then Vern has to make the decision to fire not me.

Don and Greg says we know.

Larry says ok. You gentlemen go in the conference room and I will be there as soon as I call Cory and Vern.

Don and Greg says ok.

Then they both walk to the conference room with their files in their arm.

Now Larry picks up his phone and dials Cory's number. When Cory's phone rings he picks it up.

Cory says thank you for calling Good Quality's Corporate office this is Cory may I help you?

Larry says this is Larry Good from branch 14. I just got informed by 2 of my department managers that we need to fire 2 of our staff.

Cory says for what?

Larry says for cross dressing on the job. I need you to come and see this so Vern can make the decision to fire.

Cory says did you see this with your own eyes?

Larry says yes I did.

Cory says ok I will be there in 20 minutes.

Larry says ok thanks Cory. Bye.

Cory says bye.

Then they both hang up their phone.

Now Larry picks up his phone again and dials Vern's number.

When Vern's phone rings he picks it up.

Vern says thank you for calling Good Quality Corporation. This is Vern speaking. May I help you?

Larry says Vern this is Larry from branch 14. I just got informed by 2 of my department managers that we need to fire 2 of our staff.

Vern says for what?

Larry says for cross dressing on the job.

Vern says did you see this with your own eyes?

Larry says yes I did.

Vern says I will be there in 20 minutes.

Larry says ok thank you Vern. Bye.

Vern says bye.

Then they both hang up their phone.

Now Larry gets up and walks to the conference room.

It is now 20 minutes later and Cory and Vern walk into the conference room and they both look at Derek and Doug.

Vern says will you both step away from the table so I can see you form head to toe?

Again Derek and Doug step away from the table. Vern and Cory look at Derek and Doug from head to toe.

Vern says you may sit back down.

Then Vern sits at the end seat where he can see every one. And Cory sits at the other end seat where he can see every one.

Vern says Derek and Doug I invited Cory here because when an administrator calls me to a store to discipline the staff I also like the district manager to be there so he can know what is going on in all the stores he is responsible for. At the same time If an administrator thinks a staff should be fired then I like to know what is going on and me make the decision to fire that way I don't have managers firing my employees for unfair reasons and at the same time I don't have regular employees getting managers fired for unfair reasons. Because it works both ways. Now Greg may I please see Doug's folder?

Greg says sure.

Greg hands the folder to Vern.

Vern opens the folder and says well I see you got evaluated.

Then Vern reads the evaluation. When he finished reading.

Vern says I like what I see in your evaluation. You never call in plus you are good with customers. And you are honest with money. You got a very good evaluation here.

Vern finished looking at the evaluation form and lays it next to the folder.

Vern looks at the next form and says oh my goodness I see you got wrote up.

Vern reads the write up form. When he finish reading he says you got wrote up for making a male customer feel uncomfortable by calling him your boyfriend.

Doug says the women staff call the women customers their girlfriend and the women staff don't get wrote up for it.

Vern says on the job it is acceptable from. Not from men.

Now Vern reads the suspension form. When he finish reading it Vern says unfortunately you also got suspended for hugging customers on the job.

Doug says women staff hug customers on the job and they don't get suspended for it.

Vern says on the job it is acceptable from women not from men. In this kind of business you are working directly with customers. You can not make customers feel uncomfortable rather it is by what you do to them or by what you call them. Because that can cause the store to loose business.

Now Vern puts all of Doug's papers back in his folder and hands the folder back to Greg and says put it back into your employee file after this conference.

Greg says ok.

Vern says Don may I see Derek's folder?

Don says and hands the folder to Vern.

Vern opens Derek's folder and reads the papers.

Vern says I see you have been evaluated too.

Vern reads the evaluation. When he finished reading.

He says according to your evaluation you are a good worker and good with customers too. You are always willing to be here when needed. You are very honest with money.

Vern lays the evaluation form next to the folder. Vern looks at the next form.

Vern says oh no looks like you were wrote up too.

Then Vern reads the form. After reading it he says it looks like you were wrote up for working in the women's department.

Derek says women staff work in the men's department. Why can't the men staff work in the women's department?

Vern says it is acceptable on the job for women to work with men things but not for men to work with women things.

Then Vern looks at the suspension form.

Vern says you were also suspended for going into the women's bathroom.

Derek says there are times when women staff will go into the men's bathroom and they don't get suspended for it.

Vern says on the job it is acceptable for a woman to go into a men's bathroom. But never for a man to go into a women's bathroom.

If a female customer walked in there that would make her feel very scared to use the bathroom.

Now Vern puts Derek's papers back into his folder and hands the folder to Don and says put it back into your employee file.

Don says ok.

Katrisha walks into the conference room and Vern sees her wearing men's clothes.

Vern says who are you?

Katrisha says I am Katrisha Cloud. I work in the women's department. Some body accidently dialed the wrong department number looking for Don Stream. Don has a phone call.

Vern says I am the owner. Will you please tell them Don is in a very important meeting? And to please call back or leave a message.

Katrisha says sure.

Then she leaves the room.

Now Tina steps in the conference room and Vern sees Tina wearing men's clothes.

Vern says who are you?

Tina says I am Tina Styles. I work in the men's department. I just wanted to ask Greg could I take my break now?

Vern looks at Greg.

Greg looks at Tina and says go ahead.

Tina says thanks and leaves the room.

Two Women Are Opposite Sex

Now Vern says Doug and Derek I wanted to see both of your files so I could see what happened when I was not here. Now both of you got very good evaluations but later the things you got wrote up and suspended for. I don't like what you did. And now my eyes see both of you wearing women's clothes. At the beginning of the conference I told you before someone is fired I like to see what is going on to make sure my managers are not firing my regular employees for unfair reasons and at the same time regular employees are not getting managers fired for unfair reasons. Because it happens both ways. With the things my eyes have seen in your files and now my eyes seeing Doug and Derek both crossed dressed on the job. By my decision Doug and Derek you both are fired.

Doug says Vern I mean no disrespect but, but every thing we were disciplined for the women staff did the same thing and they were not disciplined for it. Now just today your eyes just seen Katrisha and Tina come in here wearing men's clothes. You just fired me and Derek for cross dressing on the job. But you did not fire Katrisha and Tina for cross dressing on the job. That is not fair. You are discriminating.

In a firm voice Vern says it is not discriminating. It just is not acceptable by society for a man to cross dress on the job. You have to accept that. That's just the way it is. This coming pay day Doug and Derek you 2 will be coming in here to pick up your last pay check. Please clock out and leave.

Now Derek and Doug leave the conference room and go to the time clock and clock out.

Then Doug says hold it Derek before we leave we are first going to the women's department and tell Katrisha what happened.

When they get there they see Katrisha standing by the register and they walk up to her.

Derek says Katrisha you won't see us at work any more.

Katrisha says why?

Derek says we both just got fired for cross dressing on the job.

Katrisha says that is not right. I am cross dressed on the job today and no manager said a word to me.

Derek says I know it is not fair.

Doug says we are going to tell Tina before we leave. See you later.

119

Katrisha says see you later.

Doug and Derek walk to the men's department. When they get there Tina and Shirley are standing behind.

Doug says Tina you won't be seeing me or Derek at work any more.

Tina says why?

Doug says we just got fired for cross dressing on the job.

Tina says that's not fair. I cross dress every day on the job and no manager ever says a word to me. To be honest with you it is discriminating.

Derek says I know. Women are allowed to cross dress on the job but men are not. Well we will see you when we all hang out together.

Tina says ok. Bye.

Now Doug and Derek leave the store.

Now Vern walks with Don to Don's office.

When they get there Vern says where are your firing forms?

Don opens the file cabinet and opens the file and pulls out a firing form then hands the form to Vern. Vern fills out the form then hands the form back to Don.

Vern says please put this form in Derek's file.

Don says ok.

Then puts the form in Derek's file then puts the file back into the file cabinet and closes the cabinet.

Now Vern walks to Greg's office

Vern says Greg where's your firing forms?

Greg gets out of his chair and walks to the file cabinet and opens the drawer and opens the file and pulls out a form and hands it to Vern. Vern fills out the form then hands it back to Greg.

Vern says please put this back in Doug's file.

Greg says ok.

Then Greg puts the form in Doug's file and closes the cabinet.

Later that evening at Katrisha's house. Katrisha and Angela and Tina and Doug and Derek are sitting in Katrisha's living room. They are talking about what happened to Derek and Doug.

Derek says I hope we soon find another job.

Angela says what happened at Good Quality?

Derek says Doug and I got fired today.

Two Women Are Opposite Sex

Angela says what for?

Derek says for cross dressing on the job.

Tina says that is not fair. I cross dress every day on the job. And no manager ever says a word to me about it.

Doug says the very same things we were doing the women were doing them too. And we were getting disciplined for it. Not the women.

Angela says to be honest with you that is discriminating. Because you are supposed to treat every body the same. And that is not treating every body the same. Plus you don't have to accept being fired for an unfair reasons. Since your manager fired you then you have a right to go to the administrator. You know the boss of the whole building. If he doesn't do any thing about it then go to his boss the district manager.

Derek says it wasn't the department boss that fired us. Nor was it the administrator that fired us. Nor was it the district manager. It was the owner that fired us. He came in and said after look at our files and seeing us cross dressed on the job. By his decision we are fired. Now the owner is the boss of the entire business. There's no boss over the owner. So unfortunately we do have to accept being fired for an unfair reason.

Angela says Derek and Doug you 2 have forgotten. I am a licensed lawyer. I know from law books that you don't have to accept being fired for an unfair reason. In a business you can take even the owner to court. Because even the owner may be discriminating. All you need is visible proof of what was done. Do you have a copy of the papers showing why you were fired?

Derek says no we don't.

Angela says you need to get the papers showing why you were fired and all the other papers showing why they disciplined you. When you get those papers and if you want to take them to court. I will be your lawyer since I know you have a good case and I know you are an honest person. And I know you well.

Derek and Doug says thank you Angela.

Angela says you both are very welcome.

Doug says only 1 problem.

Derek says what is that?

Doug says how do we get the papers without telling the owner or the managers why we want the papers?

Derek says I have an ideal. Friday of next week is payday. Doug do you have a back pack?

Doug says yes.

Derek says good. You and I will arrive at the same time at Good Quality with our back pack. When Larry has all the department managers in the department head meeting then we will get our check and our file. Because our file tells every thing the managers did to us. We will hide our file in our back pack.

Doug says that sounds like a good ideal. Because I know they won't give us the files especially knowing we want to use the files in a court against them.

Derek says Larry usually has the department head meeting at 1pm. So next Friday meet me at Good Quality at 1pm.

Doug says ok.

ONE WEEK LATER

It is now 1 week later at 1 pm and Derek and Doug arrive at Good Quality to pick up their paycheck and their file. They are in the men's department in the clothing aisle talking to Tina.

Doug says hi Tina.

Tina says hi Doug.

Then they give each other a hug.

Doug says has Larry started the department head meeting yet?

Tina says no. Larry cancelled the department head meeting.

Doug says oh my God.

Tina says what is wrong?

Real quick Doug shakes his head from side to side and blinks his eye and says how are we going to get our check?

Tina says since Greg made me the lead worker he made me a key to his office. I will open the door to his office and you can get your check.

Doug says won't Greg be mad if he comes by here and sees me in his office?

Tina says Greg called in today. So he won't see you in there. And since you used to work here and I know you are an honest person and I know you real well. I will give you the key to Greg's office and you can go in there by yourself and get your check.

Doug says what if Larry comes and sees me in there?

Tina says Larry just left for a late hour lunch. Here take the key and go in there and get your check.

Now Derek waits in the clothing aisle talking to Tina. At the same time Doug goes to Greg's office door and puts the key in and opens the door and walks over to the employee file cabinet and opens the drawer and flips through the checks and takes out his check. Then Doug flips through the employee files until he finds his file. When he finds his file then he looks at all the papers to make sure all the papers are there then he takes out the entire file folder with all the papers in it and puts the file in his back pack. Then he closes the drawer and walks out of the office and closes the door behind him then he locks the door back. Now Doug walks over to the clothing aisle where Derek and Tina are standing. When he gets there he hands the keys back to Tina.

Doug says here's your keys thank you for trusting me.

Tina says you are welcome.

Doug says Derek are you ready to go get your check?

Derek says yes I am

Doug says Tina it was good to see you again bye.

Derek says bye Tina.

Tina says bye guys. I'll see you later.

Now Derek and Doug walk over to the furniture department. Ron is dusting off the furniture and Derek and Doug walk up to him.

Derek says hi Ron.

Ron says hi Derek and Doug.

Derek says I need to get my check. Is Don in his office?

Ron says no Don took a vacation day.

Derek says so how am I going to get my check?

Ron says I used to work with you. So I know you are an honest person. Here I will give you the keys to Don's office and you can go In there and get your check.

Ron pulls the keys out of his pocket and hand them to Derek.

Derek takes the keys and goes to the Don's office and puts the key in the whole and turns it and pushes the door open and walks to the file cabinet and then opens the drawer with the checks in it and flips through the checks and finds his check and takes it out and puts the check in his back pack. Now he looks in the same drawer and flips through the employee files until he finds his file. Then he takes his whole file out and makes sure all the papers are in there and then puts the whole file in his back pack. Then Derek closes the file drawer and walks out of the office and locks the door behind him. Now Derek walks back to the aisle where Doug and Ron is.

Derek says Ron here are your keys. Thank you for trusting me.

Ron says you are welcome.

Doug says Ron we have to go cash our checks see you later.

Ron says bye guys.

Derek and Doug both leave the store.

Later that evening Katrisha and her boyfriend Jake and Derek are at Katrisha's house in the living room and talking about going out for entertainment.

Jake says Derek how would you like to go out with me and Katrisha to try to win some money?

Derek says thanks for inviting me. That is real kind of you. But since I just lost my job last week and I don't know how long it will be before I find another job. I can't afford to spend money on those machines.

Jake says since you are a good friend of Katrisha's and I want you to come with us. I will make a deal with you. This will start off as a gift. I will give you $100.00 to spend on the machines. And the only way you will have to pay me back is if you win at least $200.00. If you win less than $200.00 then you owe me nothing. Pay me back only if you win at least $200.00. I really want you to go. Do we have a deal?

Derek says yes we have a deal.

Jake says ok lets all get in my car.

Katrisha and Derek says ok.

Now all 3 ride to the casino and then Jake hands Katrisha 5-20 dollar bills. Then Jake hands Derek 5-20 dollar bills. Now they look for 3 machines together where nobody is sitting at the machines. Then Katrisha sees 3 empty seats together.

Katrisha says there's 3 empty seats.

They walk to the seats. Derek sits on the first seat then Jake sits on the second seat then Katrisha sits on the third seat.

Jakes says the only tough thing about these machines is that they only take 20 dollar bills.

Now after they finished playing all their games. Then all 3 walk outside to Jake's car and get in and ride home.

Katrisha says I can't believe I paid $100.00 and won $400.00.

Jake says I can't believe I only won $60.00. But my goodness Derek you were trying to get rich in there.

Derek is smiling and says I know. I actually won $200,000.00.

Katrisha says what are you going to do with all that money?

Derek says I don't know yet. For right now just put it in the bank. Jake since the cashier gave me 8-25,000 dollar bills I am going to have to wait until I get to the bank tomorrow and deposit this money. Plus make change so I can give you your money I owe you.

Jake says I know you will. I don't expect you to give me 1 of your 25,000 dollar bills when you only owe me $100.00.

THE NEXT DAY

It is now the next day at Doug's house. Doug gets on the phone and calls Derek's house. When the phone rings he picks it up.

Derek says hello.

Doug says Derek this is Doug.

Derek says ok.

Doug says Derek you and I need to meet at the court house today so we can file a discrimination charge against Vern.

Derek says ok. What time?

Doug says lets meet in 30 minutes.

Derek says ok.

Doug says bye.

Derek says bye.

Then they both hang up their phone.

It is now 30 minutes later and Derek and Doug arrive at the courthouse. They get out of their car and walks up to Peter the court clerk.

Derek says my name is Derek Styles and this is my brother Doug Styles. We both were discriminated against on our job. So we want to file charges of employment discrimination.

Peter says do you both work in the same place with the same boss?

Doug says when we were fired we worked for the same company in the same building but different departments. Plus it wasn't the department manager that fired us it was the owner of the business. So we want to file charges against the owner.

Peter says ok let me get the forms you need to fill out.

Derek and Doug says ok.

Peter walks over to the file cabinet and opens the drawer and flips through the files until he gets to the employment discrimination file then he pulls out 2 forms then closes the drawer and walks over to Derek and Doug.

Peter says here are the forms you need to fill out. I am giving you separate forms because on the forms there is only 1 line for the plaintiff. All information is needed. But most important make sure you write your name and address and phone number. And the name and address and phone number of the person you are filing against. And the discrimination that was done and the date of the discrimination. You will be surprised of how many people come in to file a complaint and don't have the most important information.

Derek and Doug says ok.

They both sit down and start filling out their form. After they got most of the information on their form Doug gets up and walks up to Peter.

Doug says I need to find the address of the owner. Do you have a phonebook I can borrow?

Peter says yes and looks under the counter for a phonebook then hands it to Doug.

Doug says thank you and walks back to his seat and flips through the pages of the phonebook looking for the address of the owner. When he finds the address then he writes it down and shows the same information to Derek. When Derek finish writing then they both take their form up to the counter and hands them to Peter.

Doug says thank you for all of your help.

Peter says you are welcome. I will give the forms to the sheriff.

Doug and Derek says ok.

And they both leave.

Now Peter walks to Sam's office the sheriff. Peter knocks on Sam's door.

Sam says come on in.

Peter walks over to Sam's desk.

Peter says I have 2 notices for you to deliver to someone.

Peter hands the notices to Sam then Peter leaves the office.

Sam reads the notices. After he reads them he notices they go to the same person. Sam walks to his police car and gets in and drives to Vern's house. When he gets there he walks up to Vern's door and rings the doorbell. Vern answere's the door.

Sam says may I please speak to Vern Find?

Vern says I am Vern Find.

Sam says Mr. Find I have 2 notices for you to appear in court.

Vern puts a shocked look on his face.

Sam hands the notices to Vern.

Sam says Mr. Find will you please sign the notices.

Vern takes the notices.

Vern says appear in court for what?

Sam says I don't discuss that sir. I just hand out the notices and get signatures.

Vern reads the names of the 2 plaintiffs and reads what he did to them.

Vern says you are allowing them to take that to court?

Sam says I have nothing to do with what is allowed. I just hand out notices and get signatures.

Sam hands Vern a pen.

Sam says will you please sign the form?

Vern signs both forms and hands them back to Sam.

Sam gives Vern his carbon copies and keeps the original forms.

Vern gives Sam his pen.

Sam says thank you sir.

Sam now leaves.

Now Vern closes door and gets on his home phone and calls Good Quality and dials Greg's office extension number. When Greg's phone rings he picks it up.

Greg says thank you for calling the men's department. This is Greg may I help you?

Vern says Greg this is Vern.

Greg says ok.

Vern says Greg I need to have a very important meeting with you and Don at Good Quality in the conference room in 30 minutes. Please don't leave the store until after the meeting.

Greg says ok.

Vern says bye.

Greg says bye.

Then they both hang up the phone.

Greg leaves the office and goes to the conference room.

Now Vern picks up the phone again and redials Good Quality and dials Don's office extension.

Don's phone rings and he picks it up.

Don says thank you for calling the furniture department this is Don may I help you?

Vern says Don this is Don.

Don says ok.

Vern says I need to have a very important meeting with you and Greg at Good Quality in the conference room in 30 minutes. Please do not leave the store until after the meeting ok.

Don says ok.

Vern says ok bye.

Don says bye.

Then they both hang up their phone.

Vern gets in his car and drives to the store.

Don leaves his office and goes to the conference room.

When Don gets in the conference room he sees Greg.

Don says Greg are you waiting in here for Vern?

Greg says yes I am.

Don says I am too. Vern just called me and told me he needs to have a very important meeting with me and you in the conference room. The last time he called a meeting with us 2 people got fired. I hope we are not in trouble.

Vern walks in the conference room and closes the door.

Vern says gentlemen it is good to see you.

Vern sits on the end seat so he can see Greg's face and Don's face.

Vern says gentlemen a police came by my house today with 2 notices to appear in court. One from Derek Styles and the other from Doug Styles. They filed a complaint against me for firing them because of cross dressing on the job. I was shocked to see that something like that was acceptable to file a complaint about. I need you gentlemen to be my witnesses in court. You know what they did wrong. Plus I am not going to let them win. When all this is over with they will be paying court cost.

Greg says what do we tell the judge that they did wrong?

Vern says well I will put it to you this way. Both of you have a wife and kids to support. Am I right?

Don and Greg both knod their heads up and down and verbally say yes.

Vern says ok. You both are going to rehearse with me on what to say to the judge.

Now when the meeting is over Vern opens the conference room door.

Vern says you gentlemen may leave now.

Vern stays in the conference room.

Greg and Don walk out of the conference room and they get far enough where Vern can't hear them.

Greg says I don't like this at all.

Don says I don't either.

Greg says the only reason why I am doing this is because I can't afford to be fired.

Don says that is the only reason why I am doing it too.

Now Vern is still in the conference room and he gets on the phone and dials the phone number to his lawyer Bob. Bob's phone rings and he picks it up.

Bob says this is Bob speaking how may I help you?

Vern says Bob this is Vern Find.

Bob says oh hi Vern what can I do for you?

Vern says it looks like I need you in court along with 2 other witnesses.

Bob says what happened?

Vern says I had to fire 2 of my male staff for cross dressing on the job. And later they filed a complaint against me. And now I have to go to court about it. So along with my 2 other witnesses are you able to defend me in court?

Bob says if they cross dressed on the job, they know that is not acceptable on the job nor off the job for a man to wear women's clothes. It sounds to me like you got a good case. Yes I will defend you.

Vern says thank you Bob.

Bob says you're welcome.

Vern says bye.

Bob says bye.

Then they both hang up the phone.

Now Vern picks up his phone again and dials and dials Doug's home phone number.

When Doug's phone rings he picks it up.

Doug says hello.

Vern says Doug this is Vern the owner of Good Quality. You know what you did was wrong. You are going to end up paying court cost. But if you win. I promise to make your life miserable.

Doug is playing with a mini tape recorder and holds it to the phone.

Doug says Vern what did you say?

Vern says don't forget if you win this case I promise to make your life miserable.

Doug says tell that to the judge. I am not going to argue with you. Bye.

Then Doug hangs up the phone.

Now Vern dials Derek's home phone number. When it rings Derek picks it up.

Derek says hello.

Vern says Derek this is Vern the owner of Good Quality. I wanted to tell you it was very inmature of you to file charges against me.

No judge is going to agree for a man to wear a skirt. If you win I promise to make your life miserable.

Derek says you tell that to the judge. I am not going to argue with you.

Derek hangs up the phone.

Later that evening at Angela's house Derek and Doug and Angela are sitting in the living room talking about going to court.

Doug says Angela you told us to get the papers that shows every thing that the managers did to discipline us. And now we have my whole file and Derek's whole file.

Angela says Doug let me take a look at your file.

Doug hands his file to Angela and she opens it and reads all the papers in it. When she finish reading all of them she puts all the papers back into the file and hands the file back to Doug.

Then Angela says Derek let me take a look at your file.

Derek hands his file to Angela and she opens it and reads all the papers in it. When she finish reading them she puts all the papers back into the file and closes it and hands it back to Derek.

Angela says from what I can see in your files you guys have a very good case. So I will be your lawyer. When do you have to go to court?

Derek says tomorrow at 8:00 am.

Angela says ok take your files with you to court. And I will be there with you tomorrow.

THE NEXT DAY

It is now the next day and Angela and Doug and Derek are at the courthouse in the courtroom as the plaintiffs and Derek and Doug have their employee files on their table. Also Bob and Vern and Don and Greg are in the courtroom as the defendants. Sam and the other courthouse sheriff are standing in front of the judges table. The judge Sherri walks from her chambers and opens the door to the courtroom.

Sam says every body please stand.

Every body stands.

Judge Sherri walks to her chair and sits down.

Alex says you may be seated.

Every body sits down.

Judge Sherri says ok this case is 2 plaintiffs Doug Styles and Derek Styles vs the defendant Vern Find.

Judge Sherri looks at Doug and Derek and says Doug Styles and Derek Styles what you wrote here is you both were discriminated on your job because you were fired for an unfair reason. For cross dressing on the job. Lets get started with the plaintiff.

Angela stands up and says Your Honor may I please call Doug Styles to the witness stand?

Judge Sherri says yes.

Angela says Doug will you please go to the witness stand?

Doug and Angela walk to the witness stand and Doug continues standing.

Angela picks up the bible and says will you please raise your right hand and put your left hand on the bible.

Doug does just so.

Angela says do you swear to tell the truth and the whole truth and nothing but the truth?

Doug says I do.

Angela puts the bible down and says thank you. You may be seated.

Doug sits down.

Angela says where was your last place of employment?

Doug says Good Quality retail store.

Angela says why aren't you still working there?

Doug says I was fired.

Angela says why were you fired?

Doug says because I was wearing women's clothes.

Angela says will you please be more specific as to the kind of women's clothes you were wearing?

Doug says I was wearing a woman's shirt and a woman's pants and women's shoes and women's stockings.

Angela says who fired you?

Doug says the owner Vern Find.

Angela says Your Honor I have no further questions for Doug at this time.

Angela continues standing at the witness stand.

Angela says may he go back to his seat?

Judge Sherri says yes.

Doug walks back to his seat.

Angel says Your Honor may I please call Derek Styles to the witness stand?

Judge Sherri says yes.

Derek walks to the witness stand and continues standing.

Angela picks up the bible and says will you please raise your right hand and put your left hand on the bible?

Derek does just so.

Angela says do you swear to tell the truth and the whole truth and nothing but the truth?

Derek says I do.

Angela puts the bible down and says thank you. You may be seated.

Derek sits down.

Angela says Derek where was your last place of employment?

Derek says Good Quality retail store.

Angela says why aren't you employed there any more?

Derek says I was fired.

Angela says why were you fired? Please be specific.

Derek says I was wearing a women's skirt and a women's stockings and a women's heels and a women's shirt.

Angela says when you and Doug filed your complaint you both said that firing you was discriminating. Why did you say Vern was discriminating against you?

Derek says because the women staff were allowed to wear men's clothes on the job but the men staff weren't allowed to wear women's clothes on the job.

Angela says did Vern actually see the women staff wearing men's clothes on the job?

Derek says yes in the conference room.

Angela says Your Honor at the present time I have no further questions for Derek.

Angela takes her seat.

Bob says Your Honor may I approach the witness?

Judge Sherri says yes.

Bob walks to the witness stand and says Derek you told the court you were discriminated against because you weren't allowed to wear women's clothes. Do you realize how bad you were making the company look before all the customers being on the clock and on the sales floor wearing a skirt and women's heels and a women's top?

Bob says Your Honor Derek was disgracing the company and his self. So when Mr. Find fired Derek and Doug Mr. Find was not discriminating. The Mr. Find was just not accepting something that was not right. The Mr. Find should not be disciplined when he did nothing wrong to Derek. Your Honor I have no further questions.

Now Bob goes back to his seat.

Angela stands up and says Your Honor may Derek come back to his seat?

Judge Sherri says yes.

Derek goes back to his seat.

Angela says Your Honor may I please call Vern Find to the witness stand?

Judge Sherri says yes.

Vern and Angela walk to the witness stand and Vern continues standing.

Angela picks up the bible and says will you please raise your right hand and place your left hand on the bible?

Vern does just so.

Angela says do you swear to tell the truth and the whole truth and nothing but the truth?

Two Women Are Opposite Sex

Vern says yes I do.
Angela says thank you. You may be seated.
Vern sits down.
Angela says Mr. Find will you please say what you do for a living?
Vern says I own my own business.
Angela says what kind of business do you own? Please be specific.
Vern says I own a retail store called Good Quality. Angela says did you fire Doug Styles and Derek Styles? Vern says yes I did.
Angela says will you please tell the court what you fired them for?
Vern says I fired them for violence on the job. Wouldn't you fire some one for getting violent on the job?
Judge Sherri puts a firm look on her face and in a firm voice says excuse me Mr. Find when you are on the witness stand, you don't ask the lawyer questions. The lawyer asks you questions. And then you just answer them. Now I want you to repeat your answer to the court.
Vern says I fired them for getting violent on the job.
Angela says how were they getting violent on the job?
Vern says I seen Doug going up to people thumping them with his finger and hitting and pushing them for no reason. And then when they would turn around to defend them self by trying to hit back then his brother Derek was trying to help him by holding their arms and kicking them so they could not hit back. Doug was hitting and pushing. Derek was holding and kicking.
Angela says how many times did you see them doing this?
Vern says I seen them do this 1 time.
Angela says you seen 1 act of violence and you fired them?
Vern says yes I did.
Angela says did you investigate the violence?
Vern says no I did not because they did other things wrong as well.
Angela says ok Mr. Find you said you fired the guys because they were getting violent on the job. Derek and Doug said you fired them because they were wearing women's clothes. Now we are going to say if wearing women's clothes was the case.
Vern interrupts and says they lied cross dressing was not the case.
Angela puts a firm look on her face and in a loud voice says don't interrupt me.

In a normal voice Angela says as I was saying. If cross dressing was the reason. Did you ever see female staff cross dressing on the job?

Vern says no I did not.

Angela says ok rather you fired them for cross dressing or for violence on the job. Your eyes seen them do 1 wrong thing and you fired them for it.

Vern says I was told by their department manager that they did other things wrong as well.

Angela say ok Your Honor I have no further questions for Mr.Find, may he go back to his seat?

Judge Sherri says yes.

Vern goes back to his seat.

Angela says Your Honor may I please call Doug Styles to the witness stand?

Judge Sherri says yes.

Doug walks to the witness stand and sits down.

Angela says you are still under oath.

Doug says ok.

Angela says Doug when you filed your discrimination charge was cross dressing the only thing you were disciplined for?

Doug says no I was disciplined for other things as well.

Angela says what other things were you disciplined for?

Doug says I was talking to a manager about an all men gathering I was going to have at my house. I told the manager since he's 1 of my boyfriends he could come too. Plus I told a customer since he has a good heart that's why I chose to be his boyfriend. I was meaning a male friend when I said boyfriend. It's just like when a female cashier named Tina Styles was talking to Greg about her female friend named Shirley Eater. Tina called Shirley her girlfriend. She didn't just say her friend. She said her girlfriend. Tina did not get a verbal warning for that but I did. Greg just let Tina get away with it.

Angela says ok did Greg see Tina call other women her girlfriend?

Doug says yes. Tina was talking to Greg when she called Shirley her girlfriend.

Angela says ok were you disciplined for any thing else?

Doug says yes. I was given a verbal warning for saying men are cute. I was talking to a boyfriend of mine who came into the store and I told him he is cute. Greg wrote me up for that. But earlier we were voting for the best department manager and the cashier Tina said in Denise's presence and around other people that Denise is cute. Tina did not get wrote up for it. She got away with it.

Angela says ok were you disciplined for any thing else?

Doug says I was talked to about sitting on another man's lap. We were having a free food day. Every body was asked to bring in a dish. I was the last to get there. So when I walked in I took my pot to the food table and sat it down. Then after I got my plate and put food on it I turned around and started looking for a place to sit. And I noticed how crowded the break room was. Every chair in there was taken they even were using chairs from the offices. There was no place to sit. So Derek and Greg seen me looking for a place to sit. They both seen there was no place to sit. So Derek got my attention and asked me do I need a place to sit? I said yes. Derek said come over here and sit on my lap. Greg seen me sitting on another man's lap and later that day he talked to me about it and said it is not proper for a man to sit on another man's lap. Bu t earlier in the break room the men and women staff were watching a video about good customer service and Tina sat on Katrisha's lap. And there were 9 other empty seats left. Greg seen it and did not say a word about it.

Angela says ok were you disciplined for any thing else?

Doug says yes. My neighbor came into the store and I told him that my aunt passed away and since I felt close to her I wanted to hurry and get the funeral over with. My neighbor's name is Russel. Russel first raised his arms and gave me a sympathy hug. Then in return I raised my arms and gave him a hug. So later Greg asked me were we related to each other. I told Greg no. Russel gave me a sympathy hug because my aunt passed away. Since I hugged Russel in return Greg suspended me for a week with out pay. Because of hugging on the job. But earlier a customer named Vernitta came into the store and another cashier named Katisha gave Vernitta a hug and even called her honny bun.

Angela says did Greg see it when Katrisha hugged the customer?

Doug says yes he did.

Angela says no further questions Your Honor.

Angela walks back to her seat.

Bob says Your Honor may I please question the witness?

Judge Sherri says yes.

Bob walks to the stand and says Doug you just told this court that you call your male friends your boyfriends. You are giving people the impression that you are in a gay relationship. And you think Greg should be disciplined for it. Let me ask you this. Are you in a gay relationship?

Doug says no I am not. Tina was calling her women friends her girlfriend and people did not think Tina was in a gay relationship.

Bob says later you said men are cute. Let me ask you this are you sexually attracted to men?

Doug says no I am not. Nobody thought Tina was sexually attracted to women.

Bob says you also said that you sat on another man's lap. When a woman sits on a man's lap that is a way of being romantic with him. When you sat on Derek's lap you were giving people the impression that you were being romantic with him. Do you get romantic with men?

Doug says first of all Derek is my brother. Second of all I would never get romantic with any man AT ALL. But most definitely not my own brother.

Bob says ok you've admitted to doing these things but when I ask you about your sexual feelings you say your sexual feelings are not toward men.

Doug says nobody thought the women had sexual feelings toward other women. And the women were doing and saying the same things that the men were doing and saying.

Bob says Doug let me ask you this. What would you do if you were the boss and your employees did things that society does not accept? Would you discipline the staff too?

Doug says I would treat every body the same. I would not let some do it but the others can't.

Bob says please answer the question.

Doug says I did answer the question.

Bob says for my opinion I think you are lying to your self and to this court. Because only gay men say the things you were saying to other men.

Bob says Your Honor I have no further questions.

Bob walks back to his seat.

Angela says Your Honor can Doug come back to his seat? And may I call Derek Styles to the witness stand?

Judge Sherri says yes.

Doug goes back to his seat and Derek goes to the witness stand.

Angela walks up to the witness stand and says Derek you are still under oath.

Derek says ok.

Angela says Derek when Mr. Find was on the witness stand he said the reason he fired you and Doug is because your department managers said you guys also did other things that were wrong. What other things did you get disciplined for?

Derek says this 1 evening came when we had no female staff at all. They either called in or were mistakenly scheduled off. So a female customer came into the store and she first went to the women's department to find some birth control pills and some panties. When she seen she couldn't find them and I was the first staff she seen from a distance. She came to the furniture department where I was and said since there's no women staff here today could I please help her in the women's department. I told her if it doesn't bother her for a man to help her with women things then I would be glad to help her. The customers name was Tonya. Tonya told me that even on the job at times a man has to work with women things. Just like a woman has to work with men things. So I helped her find some birth control pills and some panties. A few minutes later Don came over and seen me working in the women's department and asked me what am I doing working in the women's department? Then Tonya told Don that she went the furniture department where I was and asked me could I please help her. Don told Tonya it is against company rules for a male staff to work in the women's department. Tonya said she had no other choice. The women staff was not here that day. Then she asked Don what was she supposed to do? Don told her she just had to do the best she can to help herself. Or come back on a day when there is women staff here. Because he is not willing to lose his job for allowing men to work in the women's department. The items she did have she had to take to the men's department to pay for them. Then she left the store very ticked off. Later that day Don wrote me up for working in the women's department. The women cashiers Tina and Shirley work in the men's department. Earlier that day Tina helped a male customer get some bikini underwear and some Viagra and some condoms men personal items. And she did not get wrote up for it.

Angela says ok were you disciplined for any thing else?

Derek says yes. I had to go to the bathroom real bad. And the men's bathroom up stairs was not working right. The up stairs toilets were not flushing. Plus the bathroom down stairs was flooded. The housekeeper Joice told me I had to use the women's bathroom. Since I had to go real bad then I used the women's. Then later Don found out that I was in the women's bathroom and he suspended me for it. Earlier Katrisha was in the men's bathroom and she did not get suspended for going into a bathroom of the opposite sex. But I did.

Angela says Your Honor I have no further questions.

Angela walks back to her seat.

Bob stands up and says Your Honor may I please approach the witness?

Judge Sherri says yes.

Bob says I hope you do not talk crazy like your brother was talking. Now you knew the company law that men do not work in the women's department. You knew you would be in trouble. And did not care that your boss would be in trouble as well. Plus since you broke a company law your boss had to deal with a customer's rude attitude. Did it bother you at all to work with women's personal items?

Derek says no it did not.

Bob says it sounds to me like you wanted Don to get in trouble. First you break a company law. Then you sit here and complaint against the man.

Bob says Your Honor Don did nothing wrong. Don was just protecting the company's image and protecting his job. Then Derek sits here and complaints against Don for it. It would not be fair to discipline Don for that.

Bob says Derek you admitted to the court that you went into the women's bathroom. All because the men's bathroom was not working. You could have just waited until the maintenance men came and finished fixing 1 of the bathrooms. If a female customer had to go in there inconviently she would've had to wait for a man to come out. If she had to wait too long then she would've went to another store. And if she had planned to buy a lot then the store would've lost a lot of money and if the store looses too much money then a lot of employees including Don and Derek would have lost their jobs. So again Don was just protecting the company and every body's job. So when you came to court and complained about it you were doing wrong not Don. First you work with women's items. Second you go into the women's bathroom. Third you wear women's clothes. Let me ask you this. Are you gay?

Derek says yes I am.

Bob says Your Honor Derek just admitted that he is gay. I believe his brother Doug is in the closet about it. Derek is the one that should be disciplined for what Derek is doing not Don. It is not Don's fault that Derek is gay. Derek just admitted it about his self. So Your Honor please do not discipline Don or Vern. Your Honor I have no further questions.

Bob walks back to his seat.

Angela stands up and says Your Honor can Derek come back to his seat?

Judge Sherri says yes.

Derek walks back to his seat.

At the same time Angela says Your Honor may I call Greg Crave to the witness stand?

Judge Sherri says yes.

Greg walks to the witness stand and sit down.

At the same time Angela says Your Honor may I please approach the witness?

Judge Sherri says yes.

Angela walks up to the witness and picks up the bible and says will you please stand?

Greg stands up.

Angela says will you please raise your right hand and put your left hand on the bible?

Greg does just so.

Angela says do you swear to tell the truth and the whole truth and nothing but the truth?

Greg says I do.

Angela says thank you. You may be seated.

Greg sits down.

Angela says Greg on the day Doug was fired were you there?

Greg says yes I was.

Angela says who fired Doug?

Greg says the owner Vern Find.

Angela says ok why did Vern fire Doug?

Greg says because Vern and I seen Doug involved in a fight.

Angela says Doug says he was fired for wearing women's clothes.

Greg says that's a lie. Doug was involved in a fight. That is why he was fired.

Angela says when Doug was on the witness stand he said you gave him a verbal warning for calling men his boyfriend. Is that true?

Greg says yes I gave Doug a verbal warning but not for calling men his boyfriend. Doug got a verbal warning for calling other people bad names.

Angela says what kind of bad names did Doug call people?

Greg says Doug was calling people a dog and ugly cow and fat blimp.

Angela says who was he calling the bad names?

Greg says Doug was calling the customers and staff those names. I told Doug I don't tolerate my staff calling people out of their name. He kept on doing it so I gave him a verbal warning.

Angela says ok I hear what you said but if the verbal warning was for calling men his boyfriend. Did you ever hear female staff call other women their girlfriend?

Greg says no I did not.

Angela says ok Doug also said you gave him a written warning for saying men are cute.

Greg says saying men are cute had nothing to do with it. I gave Doug a written warning for calling people ugly dirty dogs. Just like I don't allow women to call people names I don't allow men to do it either. Plus that's 1 way problems with people get started. People start calling one another names then before you know it they start fighting. Trying to keep it from escalating to that point I don't allow name calling of any kind from either sex.

Angela says did you ever hear the women staff say other women are cute?

Greg says no I did not.

Angela says ok Doug also said he sat on another man's lap and later you pulled him into a private room and told him it is not proper for a man to sit on another man's lap.

Greg says first of all when he sat on another man's lap it was his brother Derek's lap he sat on. I would not suspect any thing wrong of Doug sitting on his brother's lap. Plus when I talked to Doug about where he was sitting. We were going to have a food day and Doug had the nerve to sit his behind right on the table that we were going to put the food on. That is very unsanitary.

Angela says well if sitting on another man's lap was the reason. Have you ever seen female staff sitting on another female's lap?

Greg says no I haven't.

Angela says if you seen a female sitting on another female's lap would you tell her don't sit on another women's lap?

Greg says yes I would. I am highly against discriminating.

Angela says ok Doug also said his neighbor came into the store and gave him a sympathy hug for his aunt passing away. And you told him it is not proper for a man to hug another man. So you suspended him for it.

Greg says well when I suspended him it had nothing to do with him hugging another man. It was because a female friend of his came into the store and she told him that she just graduated from a business administration course and now she is licensed to be an executive director. Doug told her congratulations. He is proud of her. Then he asked her can he give her a graduation hug. She said no. She don't like to hug. Doug said but you deserve a hug. His lady friend repeated herself and said she don't like to hug. And Doug forced a hug on her any way. When you force a hug on some one that is viewed as sexual harassment. And sexual harassment is illegal. And that is why I suspended him. It had nothing to do with him hugging the same sex.

Angela says have you ever seen female staff hugging customers?

Greg says no I have not. From all the questions you have just asked me I can see that Doug came to you and told some lies on me. He is trying to get me in trouble for no reason. I have not done any thing bad to him.

Angela says Your Honor I have no further questions for Greg at this time. May Greg go back to his seat?

Judge Sherri says yes.

Greg walks back to his seat. At the same time Angela says Your Honor may I please call Don Stream to the witness stand?

Judge Sherri says yes.

Don walks to the witness stand. Before his sits down Angela grabs the bible and says before you sit down will you please raise your right hand and put your left hand on the bible. Don does just so.

Angela says do you swear to tell the truth and the whole truth and nothing but the truth?

Do says I do.

Angela says thank you. You may be seated.

Don sits down.

Angela says Don on the day that Derek was fired was you there?

Don says yes I was.

Angela says who fired him?

Don says the owner of the business Vern Find.

Angela says why did Vern fire Derek?

Don says it is because Vern and I both seen Derek involved in a fight. You are not supposed to allow any thing violent on the job. You are supposed to keep the work place safe. Vern and I both seen it. So Vern fired Derek for violence on the job.

Angela says Don when I ask you a question please just answer the question. You don't need to add more statements. Now when Derek

Two Women Are Opposite Sex

was on the witness stand he said a day came when there was no female staff in the store AT ALL. They called in or were scheduled off. A female customer came into the store and asked Derek for help in the women's department and he did it. And you wrote him up for it is that true?

Don says the reason why I wrote him up is not true. Derek lied on me. When I wrote him up it was because I caught Derek in my office selling things for a private company. And since I was on duty that day he should not have been in my office without my permission. I don't care if the door was wide open. Second he was soliciting on the job. He knew the company's rule no soliciting. It is in the hand book. Plus he was selling competitor's products. With those 3 things. In my office without my permission. 2 soliciting on the job. And 3 soliciting a competitor's product. That is why I gave him a written warning.

Angela says ok if it was the case of Derek working in the women's department. Do you hire men to work in the women's department?

Don says I manage the furniture. Denise manages the women's department. Not me.

Angela walks over to Vern and says is it against your law for a man to work in the women's department?

Vern says no it is not.

Angela says ok.

Now she walks back to the witness stand.

Angela says Mr. Stream Derek also said he had to go to the bathroom real bad and the men's bathroom up stairs was not flushing at the same time the men's bathroom down stairs was flooded and Joice told him he would have to use the women's bathroom and so he did. And later when you found out about it you suspended him for it. Is that true?

Don says that is another lie. When I suspended Derek it was not for going into the women's bathroom. Derek had seen the door open to the security office and with no security staff in there he snuck in there and turned off the security camera. The security staff named Steve walked in there and caught Derek then told me. That's how I found out. And what other reason would a person would some one sneak into the security office and turn off the security cameras except to steal

145

some thing. Only security staff is supposed to be in the security office because there's money in there. And that's why Derek was suspended.

Angela says ok.

Angela says Your Honor I have noticed when I question Derek and Doug about what they were disciplined or fired for. Derek and Doug are saying they were disciplined for 1 thing but Vern and Don and Greg are saying that Derek and Doug were disciplined for some thing else. Doug and Derek both brought their employee file with them to show in writing what they were disciplined for.

Vern and Don and Greg immediately put a shocked look on their face.

Angela says may I show them to you?

Judge Sherri says yes you may.

Angela takes both files off Derek and Doug's table and gives them to Judge Sherri.

Judge Sherri says thank you.

Angela says you are welcome.

Judge Sherri opens Doug's file and first notices Doug's evaluation.

Judge Sherri says ok I see here Doug was evaluated it says Doug is a good worker and he never calls in. He is never late. Doug is good with the customers. Doug follows the dress code by always having a neat and dressy appearance. As a cashier he is always honest with the way he handles money. As his boss Greg Crave is happy to have Doug Styles as my employee. And would recommend Doug for a raise. Doug got a very good evaluation.

Then Judge Sherri puts the evaluation to the side and reads Doug's other papers and sees that he was given a written warning and he was suspended and later he was fired and why these things were done.

When Judge Sherri finished looking at all the forms she says Greg from what I see in Doug's file he was a very good worker and Greg according to what's on paper you did write him up for saying men are cute. And according to what's on paper you did suspend Doug for hugging other men. And Vern the paper here is showing you did fire Doug for wearing women's clothes.

Vern says Your Honor may I speak?

Judge Sherri says yes.

Vern says if there is a firing form for Doug then I did not do it.

Greg says Your Honor may I speak?

Judge Sherri says yes

Greg says Your Honor I didn't fill out the write up and suspension form.

Judge Sherri says are you 2 telling me I see a write up form and suspension form and a firing form here for Doug and you did not do it? Even though it has your signature on it.

Vern says that is correct. I did not write that form. My signature was forged.

Greg says mine too.

Judge Sherri says ok I will give you 2 a piece of paper and pen and I want you 2 to write your first and last name 10 times and when you finish I will compare signatures.

Judge Sherri takes 2 pieces of tablet paper off a tablet and says Alex will you please hand these papers to Vern and Greg?

Alex says sure.

Alex puts the papers and pens on the table in front of Vern and Greg.

Vern and Greg picks up the pen and start writing their first and last name 10 times each. Now when they finish writing they hand their paper and pen back to Alex and Alex gives the papers and pens back to Judge Sherri.

Judge Sherri looks at Vern's hand writing on the tablet and then looks at Vern's hand writing on the firing form. When she finish reading the form then Judge Sherri looks at Greg's hand writing on the tablet and compares it to his signature on the write up and suspension form.

When she finish reading she says Vern and Greg you 2 are saying that your signature was forged but as I look at your signature on both the tablet and on the form. The hand writing looks the same to me.

Vern says Your Honor my signature WAS forged.

Greg says Your Honor my signature WAS forged too.

Judge Sherri says ok I will get back with you 2 later. I will now look at Derek's folder.

Judge Sherri opens Derek's folder and starts reading and notices Derek was also evaluated.

Judge Sherri says I see Derek was also evaluated. It says here Derek is a good worker. He is good with all the customers. Derek is willing to be here when he is needed. Rather it is to open or close the store. Derek keeps the furniture polished and looking real pretty and always willing to help where he is needed. As a cashier he is always very honest with money. He gives the customers the right amount of change and keeps the right amount of money in his drawer. As his boss Don Stream is very happy to have Derek Styles as my employee. And would recommend Derek for a raise.

Judge Sherri says I see according to Derek's evaluation he was a very good worker.

Judge Sherri lays the evaluation to the side and says let me see what the other forms says.

Judge Sherri reads the write up form. When she finish reading she says I see Derek was wrote up for working in the women's department. Then she puts the write up form to the side and reads the suspension form.

When she finish reading the suspension form Judge Sherri says Don when Derek was on the witness stand he said you wrote him up for working in the women's department and later you said he lied. It was for selling things in your office. Well according to these forms you wrote him up for working in the women's department. And you suspended him for going into the women's bathroom. You said it was for sneaking into the security office.

Don says Your Honor may I speak?

Judge Sherri says yes

Don says Your Honor I did not write those forms.

Judge Sherri says are you saying your signature was forged too?

Don says yes it was Your Honor.

Judge Sherri says ok I want you to write your first and last name on a piece of paper 10 times.

Judge Sherri tears off a sheet of tablet paper and says Alex will you give this paper and pen to Don?

Alex says sure.

Judge Sherri says thank you.

Alex says you are welcome.

Alex puts the paper and pen on the table in front of Don. Alex stands by the table.

Don picks up the pen and starts writing his first and last name 10 times. When he finish writing Don picks up the paper and pen and hands it back to Alex. Alex hands them back to Judge Sherri.

Judge Sherri says thank you.

Alex says you are welcome.

Judge Sherri reads all the signatures on the tablet paper comparing them to the signature on the write up and suspension form.

When Judge Sherri finish reading she says Mr. Stream your signatures on the tablet paper looks just the same as the signature on the write up form and suspension form. And you 're telling me your signature was forged.

Don says yes it was.

Judge Sherri says ok Vern and Don and Greg all 3 of you. If you guys did not write up these forms then tell me who did?

Vern says Your Honor I do not know.

Greg says Your Honor I later started having a problem with Doug because he did not like the fact that I wasn't going to let him have his way. So now I see that he does a write up and suspension form and forges my signature on there trying to set me up for being unfair and reasonable.

Don says Your Honor I agree this is a set up. Because Derek is lying on paper trying to make it look like he's got proof.

Judge Sherri says ok I am hearing 1 thing from the plaintiff and another form the defendant and his witnesses. Plus the defendant and his witnesses are saying that their signature was forged. So what I will do to prove what actually happened. When I dismiss this court Mr. Find and Alex I want you 2 to come with me to my office. You 2 will be dismissed later on. Also I will continue with this case 1 week from today at the same time. That means you 3 Doug and Derek and Angela be back in here 1 week from today at the same time. Also Greg and Don and Bob be back in here 1 week from today at the same time. So now court is dismissed.

Every one leaves the courtroom.

Judge Sherri says Alex and Vern you 2 come with me to my office.

When they get to the office Judge Sherri says you guys have a seat while I fill out a form.

Judge Sherri sits behind her desk and opens a drawer and pulls out an approval form and fills it out. When she finish filling it out she says Vern I wrote an approval form. What this form says is that you are giving me permission to buy all of your surveillance cameras in your store. I will also pay you to buy new cameras. I am taking this money out of my own personal checking account. Will you please read this and sign it?

Judge Sherri hands the approval form to Vern and he reads it.

Judge Sherri sits quietly and waits for Vern to finish reading. When he finish Vern signs the form then hands it back to Judge Sherri

Judge Sherri says thank you.

Then she puts the form in her desk. Then she takes out a blank check.

Judge Sherri says Vern how much did the surveillance cameras cost?

Vern tells her how much the cameras cost. Then she writes the check to Vern's company. Then she hands the check to Vern.

Vern says thank you.

Judge Sherri you're welcome.

Judge Sherri takes the approval form out of her desk and puts it in her purse.

Judge Sherri says I need you to call your general manager and let him know I am coming. You may use my desk phone to call him.

Vern picks up the receiver and dials Good Quality's number and Larry's extension. Then Larry's office phone rings and he picks it up.

Larry says Larry speaking may I help you?

Vern says Larry this is Vern.

Larry says ok.

Vern says I really need you to stay at work long enough for me to come in and talk to you about some thing I just did with that store ok.

Larry says ok I'll stay.

Vern says thank you bye.

Larry says bye.

Then they both hang up their phone.

Judge Sherri says now all 3 of us will go to the store and talk to Larry.

Alex and Vern says ok.

While they are at the store they are in Larry's office.

Vern says Larry this is Judge Sherri and Alex her security staff Alex. Judge Sherri has a form she needs to show you.

Judge Sherri pulls out the form and hands it to Larry and he reads it.

Larry finishes reading the form and says ok you're the boss.

Vern says I will have maintenance men in here tonight when the store closes to take out all the surveillance cameras and put in new cameras. Just so you will know what is going on in your store.

Larry says ok.

Judge Sherri says Vern thank you for all of your help. You may go home now. I will see you next week.

Vern says ok and leaves the store.

Later that evening at Good Quality Alex and Larry and Judge Sherri are standing in the security office watching the maintenance men finish unscrewing the surveillance cameras off the wall.

The maintenance guy says Judge where do you want us to put the cameras?

Judge Sherri says you can roll it to my truck out side right at the front door.

Now Judge Sherri and Alex are at the courthouse conference room and Alex is helping Judge Sherri to roll the surveillance cameras into the conference room. They park the camera and plug it into an outlet.

Judge Sherri says Alex thank you for all of your help. You may go home now.

Alex says do you need me to watch the camera with you?

Judge Sherri says no thank you any way. I am going to be here for 8 hours every night of the week to watch every thing from start to finish. So you may go home now.

Alex says thanks Your Honor.

Judge Sherri says you are welcome.

ONE WEEK LATER

It is now 1 week later and Doug and Derek and Angela are back in the courthouse as the plaintiffs. And Vern and Greg and Don and Bob are back as the defendants. Alex and Sam are standing up front facing the audience. Judge Sherri walks from her office and opens the door to the courtroom.

Sam says ALL RISE.

Then every one stands up.

Judge Sherri walks into the courtroom straight to her bench then sits down.

Alex says you may be seated.

Judge Sherri says last week every one was sworn in and gave their witness on the witness stand. Now Derek and Doug you 2 said you were discriminated against because you were fired for an unfair reason because you were wearing women's clothes. And the women were wearing men's clothes and did not get fired. Now Vern you said Derek and Doug lied. They were fighting on the job. That is why I bought your surveillance camera from you. I wanted to see proof on camera as to what actually happened. That is 1 one thing I love about cameras. They don't take sides. Plus they don't lie to you nor for you nor on you. Cameras tell the truth all the time and all the way. Plus I noticed there are cameras ALL OVER that store. Plus the cameras have built in microphones. So you can see every thing and hear every thing being said and done all over that store. Cameras are on the sales floor and in the hallways right and in the break room and even in the manager's offices. ALL OVER that store. Vern according to the camera Derek and Doug were not fighting on the job. When you were in the conference room you fired them for wearing women's clothes. You also seen Tina and Katrisha wearing men's clothes in the conference and did not fire them. They just got away with it. Now Greg when you were on the witness stand you said that you gave Doug a verbal warning for calling other people bad names. Well according to the camera and microphone the verbal warning was for calling his men friends his boyfriends. Plus later you said you gave him a written warning for calling people ugly dirty dogs. On the camera the written warning was for saying men are cute. Then later you said you just talked to Doug for sitting on a table where you were going to put food on. On the camera and microphone you talked to Doug about sitting on another man's lap. Last of all with Doug. You said you suspended Doug for forcing a female customer to hug him. According to the camera Doug did not force a hug on any body. First a male customer gave Doug a sympathy hug then Doug hugged the customer in return. Now Don when you were on the witness stand you said you gave Derek a written warning for selling products for a private company in your office. On the camera the written warning was for working in the women's department. And last with Derek. You said you suspended Derek for sneaking in the security office with no security staff or any staff at all and turning off the surveillance cameras. What I seen on camera was after he came out of the women's bath room you got informed about it and called him into your office and suspended him for it.

Vern raises his hand.

Judge Sherri says you may speak.

Vern says Your Honor the only reason why I did it is because with that kind of appearance they were disgracing the store by wearing women's clothes.

Judge Sherri says according to the camera Tina wears men's clothes all the time even on the job. Were the women Tina and katrisha disgracing the store by wearing men's clothes?

Vern says no they weren't. I felt uncomfortable with it because of the way it looks to see a man wearing women's clothes.

Judge Sherri says it doesn't look any worse to see a man wear women's clothes than it does to see a woman wear men's clothes. Plus it looks just as bad to see a woman wear men's clothes as it does to see a man wear women's clothes. The whole point of my statement is. What ever way it looks for 1 sex. It looks the same way for the other sex. Society says men should look masculine and a woman should look feminine. Well society contradicts the statement that women should look feminine when society allows women to wear men's clothes because then a woman is looking masculine and not feminine. Some women say they wear men's clothes because men's clothes feel more comfortable. Well some men feel women's clothes are more comfortable. With the women people are judging by how do they feel about it? But with the men people are judging by a different view. How does it look? You should judge both sexes by the same view. Plus keep this in mind. When you fire some one it is supposed to be because they broke a company law or a government law. Not because they did some thing that society does not accept. Let me ask you this. When Tina and Katrisha cross dressed what company law or government law did they break?

Vern says none.

Judge Sherri says it was the same way when Doug and Derek cross dressed they weren't breaking any company laws nor government laws either. To be fair just like you didn't fire Tina and Katrisha you should not have fired Derek and Doug for that same reason.

Greg raises his hand.

Judge Sherri says you may speak.

Greg says Your Honor I think it sounds like 2 men are in a gay relationship when a man calls his men friends his boyfriends.

Judge Sherri says does it sound like 2 women are in a gay relationship when a woman calls her women friends her girlfriend?

Greg says no. But that is a girly thing.

Judge Sherri says it is a manly thing for a man to call his men friends his boyfriends.

Greg says Your Honor I feel that when a man says another man is cute it sounds like he is sexually attracted to other men or like he wants to have sex with another man.

Judge Sherri says when a woman says another woman is cute does it sound like she is sexually attracted to other women or that she wants to have sex with another woman?

Greg says no. But Your Honor I am just not use to men doing these thing with other men.

Judge Sherri says just because you're not use to it that does not make it wrong. I have noticed people would rather a man say an ANIMAL is cute. Or say another man is ugly. Rather than give a nice compliment about another man's attractive face and says he's cute. You didn't think any thing of it when Tina said Denise is cute. You did not think Tina was sexually attracted to Denise or wanted to have sex with her. And Tina made that comment to the same sex as well.

Greg says Your Honor even if you don't look at the things he actually said then look at the things he actually did. When he sat on another man's lap it looked like they were being romantic with each other.

Judge Sherri puts a firm look on her face and in a firm voice says like he said earlier it was his brother's lap he sat on.

Greg says Your Honor if a woman sits on a man's lap it is to be romantic with him. So 2 men who are not related to each other if they sit on one another's lap it looks like gay romance.

Judge Sherri says in a firm voice I disagree with you. In the break room you did not feel like it was gay romance when Tina sat on Katrisha's lap. And there was 9 empty chairs left. If it does not look like gay romance when a woman sits on another woman's lap then it does not look like gay romance when a man sits on another man's lap.

Greg says Your Honor what about when Doug hugged a customer on the job. Hugging on the job is considered as sexual harassment.

Judge Sherri says first of all sexual harassment is when it is unwanted and unwelcomed. That hug was wanted and welcomed. Second of all that hug was first done by the customer. Not by the employee. Then the customers wanted Doug to hug him in return for sympathy. Plus there is a difference between hugging and caressing. They were not caressing each other. They were just hugging. Plus earlier you did not think anything of it when Katrisha hugged Vernitta and even called her honny bun. You did not think that was sexual harassment or being sexual. Two women who are not related to each other If they hug each other with both arms each and even kiss each other on the cheeks. People think nothing of it. But 2 men who are not related to each other if they hug each other with both arms each and most definitely kiss each other on the cheeks people automatically judge the men as gay. Women get away with it but men get persecuted for it. On the job when a woman hugs some one she is not related to the only way she is judged as being sexual is if a complaint comes from the person she hugged. But if that person does not complain about it then she is not considered as being sexual. But if a man hugs some one he is not related to even if nobody complains about it. A man is still judged as being sexual and gets disciplined for it. You managers were discriminating. You were letting the women hug but not letting the men hug. Some people think it is a crime for a man to hug some one especially another man. But they don't think it is a crime for a woman to hug some one even another woman.

Don raises his hand.

Judge Sherri says you may speak.

Don says Your Honor for my opinion it does not look right to see a male staff working in the women's department selling women things.

Judge Sherri says it is the same for a woman. It does not look right to see a woman in the men's department selling men things.

Don says Your Honor it does not look right to see a man selling women panties and sanitary napkins and birth control pills.

Judge Sherri says a man's underwear and condoms and Viagra is just as personal. And women are still allowed to work in the men's department. If it does not make a woman look masculine to sell a man's suit and tie. Then it does not make a man look feminine to sell a woman's dress. Now Vern your law discriminates. You allow women to sell men things but don't allow men to sell women things. On the day when you had no women staff in the store you should have let the men staff work in the women's department as well. Because you forgot the customer is the reason why any business exist. Now if the female customer don't want a male staff to help them with women things then let the female customer choose for them selves to go to another store. But you don't just tell a female customer that a male staff can't help them in the women's department and that they have to go to another store because there's no female staff that day. Derek did the right thing by helping the woman customer even in the women's department with women things.

Don says Your Honor when Derek went into the women's bathroom he made his self and the store look bad.

Judge Sherri says when Katrisha went into the men's bathroom you did not think she made her self and the store look bad. People think nothing of it when a woman goes into a men's bathroom but when a man goes into a women's bathroom people discipline the man. If there is no woman in the women's bathroom and a man goes in there. There is a toilet for his 2 buttocks and anal. But if a woman goes into a man's bathroom she does not have a penis for the urinal. But people highly accept her going in there.

Don says Your Honor I am not trying to be rude but there are some men who would love to see a woman come into the men's bathroom.

Judge Sherri says you also have some women who would love to see a man come into the women's bathroom. Because you see when it comes to sex acts. It is both ways. Men do sex acts toward women. And women do sex acts toward men. Derek had to go to the bathroom real bad. Rather than making sure the women's bathroom is empty and allowing Derek to use the women's bathroom. You expected Derek to hold his bowels until the men's bathroom got fixed. That was VERY inhuman. Since he could not hold it and went into the women's bathroom you suspended him for it. Don and Greg you 2 came in here to be Vern's witnesses. But at the same time you also had to defend your self as well. Because just like Vern discriminated against Derek and Doug so did you 2. All 3 of you were allowing the women staff to do these things but when the men staff did them you disciplined the men for it. Plus from what I heard in the courtroom and from what I seen on camera all 3 of you lied about why you disciplined Derek and Doug. Plus you lied about you did not see the women staff do these things. Now by law I can have the business shut down for discriminating. But if I shut the business down then Derek and Doug would have to look for another job. And that would be disciplining them for what the managers and owner did. So to keep from making things hard on Derek and Doug Don and Greg since you discriminated against these 2 men then you 2 have to pay a fine of $6,000.00 each. Now Vern since you are the owner of the business. You have to pay Derek and Doug for lost time of employment. Plus since you discriminated as well you have to pay a $12,000.00 fine. When court is dismissed today all 3 of you Don and Greg and Vern have to write a check for your fines today. Now that is only your discipline for discriminating. All 3 of you lied under oath. This is a federal offense. For lying under oath each of you will serve 1 year in the state prison. When you finish paying your fines you will be taken to jail and held there until taken to prison. Plus Vern you also have to give Derek and Doug their job back.

Don raises his hand.

Judge Sherri says go ahead and speak.

Don says Your Honor the only reason why I lied under oath is because Vern threatened to fire me and Greg if we did not defend him.

Judge Sherri says that is still no excuse to lie under oath. Plus even if you had told the truth you still discriminated. So now you did both discriminated and lied under oath. So that is why all 3 of you have fines for discriminating and prison terms for lying under oath.

Don says isn't that too hard on a person?

Judge Sherri says you were being too hard on them so I am being too hard on you.

Doug raises his hand.

Judge Sherri says you may speak.

Doug says Your Honor there is some thing I forgot to say when I was on the witness stand. May I go ahead and add a statement to my testimony?

Judge Sherri says yes you may.

Doug says the day before our 1st court session Vern called my house and made a threat. Vern told me if I win this case he would make my life miserable. I recorded the phone conversation on cassette tape. Would you like to hear it?

Judge Sherri says thank you for telling me about that but I don't need to hear it on cassette tape because I already seen it on the surveillance camera in the conference room. And Doug I also know Vern called you and threatened you as well. Now Vern at 1st you had to serve a 1 year prison sentence for lying under oath. Now you have to serve an extra 2 years for making 2 threats. That will give you a total of 3 years in prison. Derek and Doug is there any thing else you would like to add to this case?

Doug and Derek both says no. Thank you Your Honor.

Judge Sherri says ok this case is over and court is dismissed.

Judge Sherri picks up her hammer and hits it on her block of wood and lays down her hammer and walks back to her office. Now every one leaves the courtroom. Sam and Alex escort Vern and Don and

Greg to the to the courthouse clerk. Then Vern and Don and Greg pull out their check book and pen and write a check for the fines they owe. When they finish writing the checks Sam and Alex escort them to the phone.

Sam says gentlemen you are allowed 1 phone call.

Vern says I need to call the corporate office. May I please go first?

Sam says yes you may.

Vern picks up the phone and dials Good Quality's corporate office then dials Corey's extension. Corey is in his office and the phone rings and he picks it up.

Corey says Corey Seek speaking may I help you?

Vern says Corey this is Vern.

Corey says ok.

Vern says I just got out of court. And the judge ordered me to give Derek and Doug their job back.

Corey says ok.

Vern says plus the judge ordered me to pay them for all their time lost from the job. From the day they got fired to their first day back to work.

Corey says ok I will take care of it.

Vern says unfortunately Greg and Don and I have to serve time in prison. Greg and Don have to serve for a year each. And I have to serve for 3 years. Since you have the highest seniority of all the district managers I want you to run the company for me until I get back.

Corey says ok.

Vern says plus since I am allowed only 1 phone call. I want you to call Larry Goods store since that is the store that Derek and Doug worked at and tell Larry that I had to go to court and the judge ordered me to give Derek and Doug their job back and he needs to write a check to Derek and Doug for all their time lost from the day they were fired to the day they came back.

Corey says ok I will take care of it.

Vern says thanks Corey bye.

Corey says bye.

They both hang up their phone.

Now Corey picks up his phone again and dials Good Quality at Larry's store.

Larry is in his office and his phone rings and Larry picks it up.

Larry says Larry Good speaking how may I help you?

Corey says Larry this is Corey Seek the district manager.

Larry says ok.

Corey says I just got a call from Vern and he said he had to go to court. And the judge ordered him to give Derek and Doug their job back.

Larry says ok.

Corey says Vern also said the judge ordered Vern to pay Derek and Doug for all their time lost from the job. From the day they got fired to the day they come back. Vern also wants you to write the check for them since they were at your store. Vern said Don and Greg will be in prison for 1 year and he will be in prison for 3 years. Until he gets back he wants me to run the company for him. Because I have the most seniority of all the district managers.

Larry says ok.

Corey says bye.

Larry says bye.

Then they both hang up their phone.

Now Angela and Doug and Derek are standing in the hallway at the courthouse.

Doug says Angela thank you for all of your help in court.

Angela says you are welcome.

Derek says I thank you too.

Angela says you are welcome too.

Then Derek gives Angela a hug.

Then Doug gives Angela a hug.

Angela says you guys I am inviting some of my high school friends to my house for a social meal. Would you like to come?

Derek and Doug both says yes. Thank you Angela.

Angela says you are welcome. I will see you tonight bye.

Doug and Derek say bye.

Angela and Doug and Derek get in their car and drive home.

Two Women Are Opposite Sex

Later that evening at Angela's house Tommy Cloud and his girlfriend Gloria is sitting next to him. Also Doug Styles and his girlfriend Pam is sitting next to him. And Derek Styles and his gay partner Mike Cloud is sitting next to him. And Angela Wing and her gay partner Tina Styles is sitting next to her. And Katrisha Cloud and her boyfriend Jake is sitting next to her. And Wendle Velet and his girlfriend Deana is sitting next to him. They all are at Angela's house sitting in her living room. And they all have just finished eating.

Tommy says may I have every one's attention?

Every one looks at Tommy.

Tommy says I have noticed we have a few new faces in here. I want to introduce every one to my girlfriend. This is Gloria we are engaged to get married.

Gloria says hi every one. It is good to meet you all.

Every one says it is good to meet you as well.

Doug says I want every one to meet my girlfriend. This is Pam we are engaged to get married.

Pam says hi every one. It is good to meet you all.

Every one says it is good to meet you as well.

Katrisha says I want every one to meet my boyfriend Jake. We are engaged to get married.

Jake says hi every one. It is good to meet you all.

Every one say it is good to meet you as well.

Now Wendle says I want every one to meet my girlfiend. This is Deana. This is an amazing surprise because we are engaged to get married as well.

Deana says I am please to meet you all.

Every one say I am please to meet you too.

Mike says hey every body the last time we had a social gathering we all just ate and played some games. This time how would every one like to go to the bar called The Fun Place? The driver of each car drinks no liquor but only soda. So we can all stay safe from any body drinking and driving.

Every one says fine.

Mike says I will call to reserve seats.

Mike get on the phone and dials the number to the bar when the phone rings the bar tender Ryan picks up the phone.

Ryan says thank you for calling The Fun Place this is Ryan may I help you?

Mike says yes we have 12 people coming into the bar and I was wondering if I could reserve 2 tables?

Ryan says what time are you coming?

Mike says we are on our way now.

Ryan says ok we will have 2 tables ready for you.

Mike says ok thank you bye.

Ryan says bye.

Then they both hang up their phone.

Mike says hey every one I just got 2 tables reserved for us at The Fun Place. So now we are ready to go.

Now every one is leaving Angela's house and gets in their car and drives to The Fun Place.

When they get to The Fun Place Mike speaks to the waiter.

Mike says mam we are the group of 12 that have 2 tables waiting for us.

The waiter says just follow me.

Every one follows the waiter to their table and sits down. The 2 tables are rectangle and connected to each other side by side. The 2 side chairs are left empty but still at the table. Katrisha sits on a chair at the end and Jake sits next to her. Next to Jake Mike sits down and Derek sits next to him. Next to Derek Deana sits down and Wendle sits next to her. Across from Katrisha Tommy sits down and Gloria sits next to him. Next to Gloria Angela sits down and Tina sits next to her. Next to Tina Doug sits down and Pam sits next to him.

After every one is seated Pam says it is amazing as to how many of us are getting married. I wanted a simple ceremony but Doug wants to give me a big fancy church wedding. So we are trying to think how are we going to get all of that money? Does any body know of a high paying job that is hiring?

Katrisha says we already have the money for our wedding. So I can't think of any high paying job that is hiring.

Tommy says I can't either.

Angela says Tina and I want to get a new car. Since we couldn't find a part time job we both decided to fill out an application and hopefully get accepted to do some acting for an xxx company.

Pam says that's a good idea. I never thought about that.

Doug says can you just imagine the money that actors make. Especially nude actors. Pam do you want to try to make some extra money in that way?

Pam says sure I will try it.

Tommy says will you have the courage to expose your body like that?

Angela says we will have the courage to collect the money that they make.

Tina says that's right.

Pam says when do you plan to fill out your application?

Tina says tomorrow.

Pam says call me and let me know when you are going and Doug and I will come with you.

Tina says ok.

Mike says Derek how would you feel if we went with them to make some extra money?

Derek says sounds fine with me. I would love to make the money that nude actors make.

Mike says ok Tina and Pam tomorrow Derek and I will come with you all.

Tina and Pam says ok.

Now the dj plays a fast song with a good beat that last for about 6 minutes. Katrisha and Wendle stay at their seat. Every body else from Angela's group likes the beat so much that they get on the floor and start dancing. Along with other customers from the bar.

A feminine customer lady named Marsha walks up to katrisha and she is wearing a dress and heels and jewelry and stands behind the empty chair on the side of the table.

Marsha says excuse me man is any body sitting here in this chair?

Katrisha says you are.

Marsha says thank you.

Marsha sits down.

Katrisha says you are welcome. What is your name?

Marsha says my name is Marsha. What is your name?

Katrisha says my name is Katrisha. Welcome to the table.

Marsha says thanks.

Katrisha holds out her hand to shake hands with Marsha and Marsha shakes her hand.

Marsha says do you like fast music?

Katrisha says I like fast music but I don't want to dance to this song. Do you like fast music or slow music?

Marsha says most of the time I only dance to fast music. Not slow music because with my husband being gone from home a lot I don't dance with other men. I don't want him to think I am cheating and get jealous and cause problems.

Katrisha says that makes sense to me. What makes him gone from home a lot?

Marsha says he is a full time truck driver. So most of the time I am home by my self.

Katrisha says do you and your husband have any kids?

Marsha says yes we have 2 kids but they are both grown now and got their own home out of town.

Katrisha says do you like to hang out with other people?

Marsha says yes I do but I don't have very many friends because of my home and marriage situation.

Katrisha says how do you feel about talking on the phone at times?

Marsha says I enjoy that at home at times.

Katrisha says well I understand you don't want your husband to be jealous with you hanging around a bunch of men friends. So to help you with your women friends association how would you feel about it if you and I exchange phone numbers so we can call one another from time to time.

Marsha says that sounds fine with me.

Katrisha and Marsha both open their purses and pull out a paper and pen and write down their name and phone number. When they finish writing they hand their paper to each other.

Marsha says thank you Katrisha. You seem like a very nice person.

Katrisha says I enjoy trying to be nice.

Two Women Are Opposite Sex

Now a masculine man walks up to Wendle. His name is Victer. Victer is standing behind the empty chair on the side of the table. Victer has a mustache and is wearing dark blue jeans and tennis shoes and an old pull over shirt.

Victer says excuse me sir is any body sitting here?

Wendle says you can sit there.

Victer says thank you.

Victer sits down.

Wendle says what is your name?

Victer says my name is Victer. What is your name?

Wendle says my name is Wendle. Good to meet you.

Victer says good to meet you too.

They both stretch out their arms and shake hands.

Windle says what kind of work do you do?

Victer says I do construction work.

Wendle says boy I can imagine your wife really appreciates the good money you make. So she don't have to work.

Victer says oh she works and most of the time a lot more hours than I do. Because of my construction job I am an hourly employee. On her job she is the head manager working for a salary of a fast food restaurant. So most of the time she deals with an extreme high turn over for managers. On the day shift and the evening shift some people feel the job is too stressful and they don't like the responsibility in it so they quit on her. So she has to be available to cover the shifts. So most of the time she works a lot more hours than I do. So a lot of times I am home by my self.

Wendle says do you have any kids?

Victer says yes we have 3 kids but they live out of town now.

Wendle says what kind of things do you like to do for fun?

Victer says I like to watch sports games on television plus build things in my shed plus work in my yard.

Wendle says well to give you some one to hang out with if you would like to I will invite you to my house to watch some sports games on my video.

Victer says thank you. You seem like a very nice person.

165

Wendle says thank you. I don't believe in treating any body like a stranger.

Victer says we need more people in the world like you.

Wendle says just so I can call you to make arrangements for a day and time. How would you feel about it if you and I exchange phone numbers?

Victer says that sounds fine with me. Wendle says let me go to the bartender and see does he have a paper and pen.

Wendle walks over to the bartender.

Wendle says excuse me Ryan do you have 2 pieces of scratch paper and pen I can borrow?

Ryan says yes.

Ryan looks around the counter and finds some note pad paper and hands 2 pieces to Wendle.

Wendle says thank you.

Ryan says you are welcome.

Wendle walks back to his table and hands Victer 1 piece of paper and they both write down their name and number. When they finish they exchange the papers.

Wendle says ok I will call you and let you know a day and time.

Victer says ok.

Now the dj plays another fast song with a good beat and Katrisha and Marsha and Wendle and Victer goes to the dance floor and join the others dancing. The song last about 5 and a half minutes.

Now the song is over.

The dj says ok the next song is for couples only. That's couples only. The dj plays a slow song. Then in front of the crowd where the audience can see them Tommy and Gloria slow dance together. Next to them Doug and Pam slow dance together. Next to them Angela and Tina slow dance together. Next to them Mike and Derek slow dance together. Next to them Katrisha and Jake slow dance together. Next to them Wendle and Deana slow dance together.

After the music plays for 2 minutes then a male staff named Danny looks at every one slow dancing together. Then he notices Doug and Pam dancing together. Then he notices Angela and Tina slow dancing together. Then right next to them he notices Mike and Derek are slow dancing together. Danny puts a shocked look on his face and walks up to them.

Danny says excuse me gentlemen but you 2 are going to have to sit down.

Mike says why?

Danny says this is not appropriate for 2 men slow dancing together.

Tommy and Angela and Katrisha and Wendle see Danny talking to Mike and wondering what is he saying?

Mike says what is wrong with 2 men dancing together?

Danny says this is a straight bar. We don't want 2 men dancing together.

Mike points at Angela and Tina and says well look at those 2 women they are dancing together.

Danny says sorry guys we don't allow 2 men dancing together. You can dance at the same time but not together. You'll have to sit down when we say couples only.

Mike and Derek sit down and go back to their seat. Katrisha and Angela see them going back to their seat. Danny goes to the bathroom. When the music is over with every one in Angela's group come back to their seat.

Katrisha says Derek what did the staff guy say?

Derek says he told us when they say couples only we can't dance together because this is a straight bar. They don't allow 2 men dancing together.

Katrisha says that's not fair Angela and Tina were dancing together right next to you and Mike and he did not say a word to Angela and Tina.

Derek says I know.

Now the dj gets on the microphone and says ok ladies now it is time for you to get on top of the bar and dance real sexy with another woman.

The dj starts playing another fast song and all the lesbian women including Angela and Tina get on top of the bar and keep their clothes on and dance in a real sexy way.

Mike says Derek lets go up there.

Derek says are you sure?

Mike says yes I am sure. I want to go up there.

Mike and Derek go up to the bar and climb on top and keep their clothes on and dance in a sexy way. Next to them is Angela and Tina. Women customers walk over to the bar to see Derek and Mike dancing together.

The women in front of them are saying we love what we see. Keep on doing it. We love to see 2 men being sexy together.

Danny comes out of the men's bathroom and hears the crowd cheering the bar dancers. So Danny walks over to the crowd and looks on top of the bar and watches the lesbian dancers. First he notices how sexy the lesbians are dancing with each other. Then he notices how sexy Tina and Angela are dancing together and right next to them he also notices how sexy Derek and Mike are dancing together and he puts a real shocked look on his face. Danny also notices the women audience standing in front of the bar watching them and telling them that they like what they see and keep doing it and they love it. Danny walks through the crowd of women up to the bar and gets Mike's attention by pointing his finger at Mike telling Mike to come here. Derek and Angela see Mike bend over to talk to Danny.

Danny says I told you earlier that you can't do this. Two men can't dance together sexually in a straight bar.

Mike says what do you mean we can't dance like this? All these women up here dancing with other women sexually.

Danny says sir I am not going to argue with you this is not acceptable. You 2 have to leave right now.

Mike puts a firm look on his face and says I want to see your manager.

Danny says ok and walks to Brian's office the manager.

Danny says Brian I am having a problem with 2 gay men customers.

Brian says what is the problem?

Danny says 1st they were on the floor slow dancing together and I told them they couldn't slow dance together because this is a straight bar. Then later they get on top of the bar with the ladies and start sexual dancing. I told them we can't allow that in here. Since this is my 2nd time talking to them about the same thing I told them they have to leave right now. They are refusing to leave and he told me he wants to see my manager. So that's why I came to you.

Brian says ok I am coming out there with you.

Brian and Danny walk to the bar area where Mike and Derek are dancing on the bar. Danny is standing with Brian in front of the bar in the crowd of women while the women are telling them to continue. Angela sees Brian pointing his 2 fingers at Mike and Derek. And she sees Mike bend over to talk to Brian and she wonders what is Brian saying to Mike?

Brian says you and your partner have to get off the bar. Danny here told me that he told you this is a straight bar so we don't allow 2 men dancing together. He also said you wanted to see the manager. I am the manager.

Mike says I did say that because this is supposed to be a straight bar but still they allow 2 women dancing together. But don't want 2 men dancing that is not fair.

Derek says sir you have some women here that love to see 2 men.

Brian says I am not going to argue with either 1 of you. My staff told you to get off the bar and leave now so that is what you have to do. Or I will have you thrown out of here or even call the police.

Angela and Tina see Mike and Derek climbing off the bar and leave so Angela and Tina climb down and walk over to Brian.

Angela says sir what is wrong?

Brian says mam we can't allow that in here 2 men dancing together. This is a straight bar.

Angela says sir I don't mean to be rude but if it is supposed to be straight then why are they allowing 2 women to dance together?

Brian says mam I am not going to argue about it. I am not willing to loose my job because I am allowing 2 men to dance together.

Angela and Tina walk over to the table where their group is sitting.

Angela says excuse me every one.

Every one looks at Angela.

Angela says Derek and Mike just got kicked out of the bar for dancing together. I talked to the manager about it and he agrees to them being kicked out. So I am leaving too.

Every one in Angela's group says I am too.

Angela's group gets out of their chair and walks out of the bar to the out side were they see Mike and Derek sitting in their car. Derek and Mike see Angela's group walking toward them so they get out of the car.

Derek says Katrisha where are you guys all going?

Katrisha says since they are not being fair and choose to discriminate against you guys then we all choose to leave.

Derek says you all didn't have to leave.

Katrisha says we are all hanging out together. I like it better that way.

Pam says Angela wich adult movie company are you going to tomorrow?

Angela says Hot and Fabulous. At 10 am. So what are we going to do for the rest of the night?

Jake says after getting on a full stomach at your house plus all the dancing I am ready to go home and go to bed.

Angela says is that what every one else wants to do for the rest of the night?

Every one says yes.

Angela says ok.

Now they all get in their cars and drive home.

THE NEXT MORNING

It is now the next morning and Angela and Tina pull up in the parking lot and park their cars at the Hot and Fabulous adult movie company. Right behind them Pam and Doug pull into the parking lot. Right behind them Derek and Mike pull into the parking lot. They all get out of their cars.

Angela says Derek you guys need the money too huh?

Derek says yes.

They all go inside and stand at the receptionist desk.

Derek says excuse me mam is this company looking for actors?

Jane says yes we are. Would you like an application?

Derek says all six of us would.

Jane says welcome to Hot and Fabulous. You all came at the perfect time because the casting director is doing auditions this week. You might get an audition. So keep your fingers crossed. You never know.

Jane picks up 6 applications and passes them out and then every one takes a seat and pulls out their pens and starts filling out their application. When every one finish their application they take it back to Jane and she puts them in the casting director's incoming mail box. Then Jane gets on the phone and dials Troy's extension.

Troy is in his office and his phone rings and he picks it up.

Troy says Troy speaking may I help you?

Jane says Troy I have 6 applicants here in the lobby and they all have just finished filling out their application.

Troy says ok I am on my way out there.

Jane says ok bye.

Troy says bye.

Then they both hang up.

Troy comes out to the receptionist desk and looks at the incoming mail and grabs all 6 applications then looks at the names on the applications then looks at the 6 people sitting down.

Troy says I want to make sure these are you alls application.

Troy looks at Angela's application and says who's Angela Wing?

Angela raises her hand and says right here.

Troy says ok.

Troy looks at Derek's application and says who's Derek Style?

Derek raises his hand and says right here.

Troy says ok.

Troy looks at Pam's application and says who's Pam Smart?

Pam raises her hand and says right here.

Troy says ok.

Troy looks at Mike's application and says who's Mike Cloud?

Mike raises his hand and says right here.

Troy says ok.

Troy looks at Tina's application and says who's Tina Style?

Tina raises her hand and says right here.

Troy says ok.

Then Troy looks at Doug's name and says well since this is the last application and you are the last person to call then you must be Doug Style.

Doug smiles and says yes.

Troy says ok my name is Troy I am the casting director. You six came at the right time because like Jane probably told you I am hiring plus today and right now I have time to do more interviews for audition. So you 6 want to come with me. I am going to interview you all in the conference room.

In the conference room Troy sits on the chair on the side of the table so he can see every one. And the others take their seats.

Troy says this is an actual interview. The company doesn't allow managers to give private or 1 on 1 interviews because knowing this is a company where actors are actually getting naked and having sex. In the interview we don't want people to think that employees and employers can get naked with each other and have sex because that is not allowed. Plus we show respect between employee and employer. Plus if you are married we don't want your marriage mate getting the wrong idea about us and you. At times when we have only 1 person to come in and fill out an application the manager is required to get at least 1 other staff in on the interview. I don't care if the applicant is the same sex or the opposite sex the managers is still required to have a 3rd person present. Now in the past at times we have had married applicants who apply for the job and their marriage mate doesn't like them getting nude on camera. And so at times this kind of work has led to employees getting divorced. So I have to ask you this question.

Troy says Angela are you married?

Angela says I am not married.

Troy says ok. Tina are you married?

Tina says I am not married.

Troy says ok. Doug are you married?

Doug points at Pam and says Pam and I are getting married to each other.

Troy says congratulations.

Doug and Pam says thank you.

Two Women Are Opposite Sex

Troy says Doug how do you feel about Pam getting naked on camera with you?

Doug says as long as it is with me I don't care.

Troy says Pam how do you feel about Doug getting naked on camera with you?

Pam says as long as it is with me I have no problem with it.

Troy says Derek are you married?

Derek says I am not married.

Troy says ok. Mike are you married?

Mike says I am not married.

Troy says ok. Now that I see nobody has a marriage mate who don't want them to do this kind of work. I have to ask you another question because some people think they can do this kind of work but when they are on the scene before you turn on the camera they back out and automatically quit the job. Because they are not as brave as they thought they were. Now Pam I have asked you about Doug but now how do you feel about your self getting naked on television?

Pam says it doesn't bother me.

Troy says ok. Now Doug I have asked you about Pam but now how do you feel about your self getting naked on television?

Doug says it won't bother me to collect the money so it won't bother me to do the work.

Troy says ok. Now Angela how do you feel about your self getting naked on television?

Angela says I doesn't bother me.

Troy says ok. Derek how do you feel about your self getting naked on television?

Derek says I am willing.

Troy says ok. Mike how do you feel about your self getting naked on television?

Mike says if the price is right I am willing.

Troy says ok. Tina how do you feel about your self getting naked on camera?

Tina says I am willing.

Troy says ok. Now that no one has a problem with them selves doing this kind of work plus their mate has no problem with them

173

doing this kind of work. Before I hire you or you agree to take the job. I will tell you how much you will get paid. First of all you are not paid by the hour. You will be paid $2,000.00 per movie. Plus you will be paid 20% on royalties. In other words you are paid .20 cents out of every dollar in the retail price of the dvd. Now does every one here still want the job?

Every one says yes.

Troy says ok every one is hired. You all will be starting tomorrow for orientation and shooting your 1st scene. Welcome to Hot and Fabulous. Every one says thank you.

Tina says Troy I noticed earlier you asked how do marriage mates feel about us doing this kind of work. I am a woman who is sexually attracted to other women. So I only have sex with other women. And not men.

Can you do movies with 2 women having sex?

Troy says yes we do.

Tina says is this company a straight sex movie company or a gay sex movie company?

Troy says it is straight but we do a tiny bit of 2 women. Is your gay partner in here?

Tina says yes she is Angela.

Troy says that is fine. You 2 won't be able to get as many scenes. But you will get 1 scene in the whole movie.

Tina says ok.

Mike says Troy you just said this company is straight but you do a tiny bit of 2 women having sex together. How does the company feel about 2 men on camera having sex together?

Troy says I am sorry but we don't allow 2 men having sex together.

Mike says what is the difference?

Troy takes a deep breath and says I will tell you what I will do. I will ask the administrator can we film 2 men. Then I will tell you what the administrator said.

Mike says when will you get back with me?

Troy says wait here I'll go ask now.

Mike says ok.

Troy walks to the administrator's office and says Todd listen real close.

Todd says ok.

Troy says I just hired 6 new actors.

Todd says ok.

Troy says 2 of them are a straight man and woman. And 2 more are gay women. And I just told them this is a straight adult movie company. But we will film 2 women having sex together for only 1 scene through the whole movie. Now the last 2 actors are gay men. I just told them we don't film 2 men having sex together. He asked me what is the difference? I told him I am very sorry but that is a thing that the company just doesn't allow is 2 men. Then I told him I would come and ask you can we film 2 men.

Todd says ok I will come out there with you.

Todd and Troy both walk to the conference room. Troy points to Mike and says this is Mike he is the 1 who was talking about filming 2 men.

Mike says excuse me administrator what is your name?

Todd says Todd.

Mike says that is not fair you call it straight but you show 2 women but not 2 men. What is the difference?

Todd says the difference is that the owner of the company allows 2 women but not 2 men. And the reason why he does it that way is because you have a lot of men that request for sex movies. You even have a lot of straight men that request for 2 women. But with them being straight they don't want to see 2 men. And since I am trying to keep my job I am going to do it in the way that the owner tells me. Let me ask you this. Are you gay?

Mike says yes.

Mike points to Derek and says my gay partner is right here.

Todd says I am sorry to disappoint you 2 but the only way I can let you 2 work for me. You would only be allowed to have sex with a woman and not another. Do you understand the rule here?

Mike puts a ticked off look on his face and says yes I understand.

Todd says thank you. I will let Troy continue with you all.

Todd walks back to his office.

Troy says if there are no further questions then you all are dismissed.

Now all six go out side to their cars.

Mike says now that's 2 days in a row we got discriminated against. It is not fair people allow women to do these things with other women but don't let men do them with other men.

Angela says so what are you going to do about it? Are you just going to take being discriminated against? Or what?

Derek says I know what I am going to do.

Angela says what?

Derek says first I am not going to be an actor for Hot and Fabulous because they are discriminating. Second of all this is a similar thing Doug and I dealt with in the past. We were discriminated against by our employer. This time it was by some one providing entertainment. And later by some one who was going to be our employer. They don't treat every one the same. Plus I am going back to the court house and file another complaint. But this time I am going to file 4 complaints. One against the bar staff and another against the manager and another against the manager at Hot and Fabulous and another against the administrator.

Mike says that sounds like a good idea to me because what they did was not fair.

Angela says if I were dealing with the same things you guys are dealing with. I would do the same thing.

Mike says Angela would you defend Derek and I in court again?

Angela says I sure will. I love being a lawyer.

Now except Derek and Mike every one else leaves and goes home. Derek and Mike drive to the court house and talk to the same court house clerk Peter.

Derek says we want to file charges of discrimination. We both need 4 forms. Because we both were discriminated by 2 entertainers and by 2 employers.

Peter says ok and walks over to the file cabinet and opens the drawer and pulls out 8 discrimination forms and closes the door and walks back over to Mike and Dereka and hands them the 4 forms each. Derek and Mike sits down and fills out their forms. When they are almost done Derek walks back to the counter.

Derek says excuse me sir. May I please have a phone book?

Peter says sure and gives Derek a phone book.

Derek takes the book and says thank you.

Peter says you are welcome.

Derek sits back down in his chair and looks in the phone book for the Fun Place. When he finds it he reaches into his front pocket and pulls out his cell phone and dials the number. When the phone rings the bartender Ryan picks it up.

Ryan says thank you for calling the Fun Place this is Ryan may I help you?

Derek says Ryan may I please speak to your manager?

Ryan says sure let me transfer you to his office.

Derek says ok.

Ryan transfers the call to Brains office. Brian is in his office and the phone rings and he picks it up.

Brian says thank you for calling the Fun Place this is Brian may I help you?

Derek says yes. Brian what is your last name?

Brian says wrong.

Derek says ok. Your staff Danny what is Danny's last name?

Brian says wom. It is spelled w-o-m. You called me just in time I am on my way home. Do you need any thing else?

Derek says no thank you.

Brian says you are very welcome. Come by the bar and enjoy your self some times.

Derek says ok I will thank you bye.

Brian says bye.

And they both hang up the phone.

Derek puts his cell phone back in his front pocket and on his complaint form he writes down Brian's first and last name and Danny's first and last name. Then looks in the black and white pages for Brian and Danny's name. When Derek finds the names then he writes down the address for Brian and Danny on the complaint form. Then Danny looks in the phone book for the number to Hot an Fabulous. When he finds the number then he pulls out his cell phone again and dials the number. When the phone rings at the receptionist desk Jane picks it up.

Jane says thank you for calling Hot and Fabulous this is Jane how may I help you?

Derek says what is the name of the manager that hires the actors?

Jane says Troy Caught.

Derek says ok.

Derek writes the name.

Derek says what is the name of the administrator?

Jane says Todd Mine.

Derek says ok thank you bye.

Jane says bye.

Then they both hang up their phone. Derek puts his cell phone back in his front pocket. Then he looks in the black and white pages for Troy's name. When he finds Troy's name then he writes down the address. Then Derek looks for Todd's name. When he finds Todd's name he writes down the address. When he finish writing he hands his forms to Mike.

Derek says here you are going to need to write these names on your forms.

Mike writes the names and addresses of the defendants on his forms.

Then they both take the forms back to the clerk.

Mike hands all 8 of the complaint forms to the clerk and says here are our complaint forms. Thank you for all of your help.

Peter says you are welcome. I will take this to the sheriff.

Derek and Mike says ok bye.

Peter says bye.

Derek and Mike both leave the court house.

Peter walks to Sam's office and says I just had 2 people fill out 4 complaints each.

Peter hands the complaints to Sam.

Peter says unfortunately it looks like you have to drive to 4 different addresses.

Sam says that's my job. And plus it's the city's police car I am using. Not my own. So it's not costing me any more money in gas. So I don't mind. The city pays for the gas not me.

Peter leaves Sam's office.

Sam walks to his police car and drives to Brian's house. When he gets there he knocks on the door. Brian opens the door and puts a shocked look on his face.

Brian says what is the matter? I did not call a police.

Sam says sir I am sorry to bother you but may I please speak to Brian Wrong?

Brian says I am Brian Wrong.

Sam says Mr. Wrong you have 2 notices to appear in court. Would you please sign the carbon copy? Here's a pen.

Sam hands Brian a pen and Brian signs the notices and gives Sam back the original forms and pen.

Sam says thank you sir.

Brian says you are welcome.

Brian closes the door.

Sam leaves the door and goes back to his car and drives to Danny's house. When he gets there he rings the door bell. Danny comes and opens the door and puts a shocked look on his face.

Danny says what's going on?

Sam says sir I am sorry to bother you but may I please speak to Danny Wom?

Danny says I am Danny Wom.

Sam says sir you have 2 notices to appear in court. Would you please sign them and give me back the original copies?

Danny says sure.

Sam hands Danny a pen and the notices. Danny signs the notices and gives Sam back the original forms and the pen.

Sam says thank you sir.

Danny says you are welcome.

Danny closes the door.

Sam now gets back in his police car and drives to Troy's house. When he gets there he rings the door bell. Troy comes and opens the door and puts a shocked look on his face.

Troy says may I help you?

Sam says yes may I please speak to Troy Caught?

Troy says I am Troy Caught.

Sam says Troy I am sorry to bother you but you have 2 notices to appear in court.

Sam hands the notices and a pen to Troy and says will you please sign the forms and give me back the original forms.

Troy says sure and signs the forms and hands the pen and original forms back to Sam.

Sam says thank you.

Troy says bye.

Troy closes the door.

Sam gets back into his police car and drives to Todd's house. When he gets there he rings the door bell. Todd's wife Mrs. Mine opens the door and puts a shocked look on her face.

Mrs. Mine says what in the world is going on?

Sam says mam I am sorry to bother you but may I please speak to Todd Mine?

Mrs. Mine says sure I will go get him.

Mrs. Mine opens the door all the way and says please come on in.

Sam walks in and stands next to the door. Mrs. Mine walks to the kitchen where Todd is.

Mrs. Mine says honny there is some one here to see you.

Todd says who is it?

Mrs. Mine says it is a police.

Todd puts a shocked look on his face and says a police for what?

Mrs. Mine says I don't know go see.

Todd and Mrs. Mine walk to the door where Sam is.

Todd says may I help you?

Sam says yes are you Todd Mine?

Todd says I am.

Sam says sir I am sorry to bother you but you have 2 notices to appear in court.

Todd says appear in court for what?

Sam says sir I am not allowed to discuss it. I am only allowed to get signatures and turn the papers in to the judge.

Todd says some thing is not right. I did not do any thing illegal. Sam says sir would you please sign the notices?

Todd says I'll go ahead and sign.

Sam hands the papers and pen to Todd and Todd signs both forms and hands the papers and the pen back to Sam. Sam hands the carbon copy back to Todd.

Sam says thank you sir.

Todd says you are welcome.

Sam says bye Mr. Mine and walks back to his car.

Todd says bye.

Todd closes his door.

Now back at Danny's house. Danny gets on his phone and dials Brian's home phone number. Brian is looking at his 2 notices and his phone rings and he picks it up.

Brian says hello.

Danny says hello may I please speak to Brian Wrong?

Brian says this is Brian speaking.

Danny says Brian this Danny from the Fun Place.

Brian says ok.

Danny says I am at home and I was wondering have you started doing the very next schedule yet?

Brian says not yet.

Danny says good because I need to request a day off work because a sheriff just came to my door today and now I have 2 notices to go to court.

Brian puts another shocked look on his face and says I can't believe this a sheriff just came to my door today too. He gave me 2 notices to go to court. Tell me the name of the people who are complaining about you.

Danny reads the names and says Mike Cloud and Derek Styles.

Brian says I have the same 2 people on my forms. Tell me what are they complaining about?

Danny reads both forms and says they are complaining that they were told to leave the bar for doing the same things that the women were doing.

Brian says those 2 people are complaining about the same thing on my forms. Yes I will give you the day off. Sounds like we both have to go to court about this.

Danny says ok thanks Brian.

Brian says you are welcome.

Danny says can I have off Tuesday of next week?

Brian says sure.

Danny says ok bye.

Brian says bye.

Then they both hang up their phone.

Now Danny picks his phone back up and calls his lawyer Kenny Church. The phone rings and Kenny is in his office and the phone rings an he picks it up.

Kenny says Kenny Church speaking how may I help you?

Danny says Kenny this is Danny Wom. Today I just got a notice to go to court. I work in a straight bar and 2 gay guys came in and wanted to dance together. I told them this is a straight bar we can't allow 2 men dancing together. They refused to listen to me so I kicked them out of the bar. Now they are accusing me of discriminating against them. Would you defend me in court?

Kenny says I don't understand why gay men will come into a straight bar. Yes I will defend you. It sounds to me like you have a good case. When is the court date?

Danny says Tuesday of next week.

Kenny says ok I will get with you some time today to fill out the paper work then I'll see you in court on Tuesday of next week.

Danny says ok thank you Kenny.

Kenny says you are welcome.

Danny says bye.

Kenny says bye.

Then they both hang up their phone.

Now at Brian's house. Brian is in his living room and has just finished eating and walks to his kitchen and washes his plate and puts the plate in dish drainer then Brian walks to his home phone and picks up the receiver and dial Kenny's number. When Kenny's phone rings he picks it up.

Two Women Are Opposite Sex

Kenny says Kenny speaking how may I help you?

Brian says Kenny this is Brian. I am 1 of your clients. Today I received a noticed to appear in court.

Kenny says what is the complaint?

Brian says I am a manager of a straight bar. And 2 gay men came in wanting to dance together. And I told them it is a straight bar. We can't allow 2 men dancing together. They refused to listen to us so we told them they had to leave. So they filed a law suit against me.

Kenny says well since it is a straight bar then 2 men is not right. They should have went to a gay bar. It sounds like you have a good case. What day is your court day?

Brian says Tuesday of next week.

Kenny says it sounds good to me. Yes I will defend you in court.

Brian says ok thank you Kenny.

Kenny says you are welcome.

Brian says bye.

Kenny says bye.

They both hang up their phone.

Now at Troy's house. Troy is in his home office and gets on his home phone and dials Todd's number. Todd is home and when the phone rings he picks it up.

Todd says hello.

Troy says may I please speak to Todd Mine?

Todd says this is Todd Mine.

Troy says this is Troy I am calling from home. I need to request a day off work because today I just got 2 notices to appear in court.

Todd says hmm that is strange today I just got 2 notices to appear in court too. Let me ask you this. What are the people complaining about?

Troy reads both of the notices and says 2 men are complaining that they came to our movie company and were not allowed to make a movie together because they are 2 men.

Todd says that is the same kind of complaint on my form. Tell me what is the name of the people who are complaining?

Troy reads the name on both forms and says Mike Cloud and Derek Styles.

Todd says those 2 names are on my notice too. What day do you have to go to court?

Troy says Tuesday of next week.

Todd says we have to go on the same day. So yes I will give you the day off.

Troy says thank Todd.

Todd says you are welcome.

Troy says bye.

Todd says bye.

They both hang up their phone.

Todd picks his phone up again and dials Kenny's number. When Kenny's phone rings he picks it up.

Kenny says hello.

Todd says may I please speak to Kenny Church?

Kenny says this is Kenny.

Todd says this is Todd Mine. I'm 1 of your clients.

Kenny says yes I know.

Todd says today I received 2 notices to go to court.

Kenny says what happened?

Todd says on my job I am an administrator for a straight adult movie company. And we had 2 gay men come in there and we told them it was a straight adult movie company. So we couldn't film 2 men together. I also told him the owner doesn't approve of 2 men together so they charged me with discriminating against them.

Kenny says it sounds like you have a good case. When do you go to court?

Todd says Tuesday of next week.

Kenny says ok I will defend you.

Todd says thanks Kenny.

Kenny says you are welcome.

Todd say bye.

Kenny says bye.

They both hang up their phone.

Now at Troy's house Troy picks up his phone and calls Kenny. Kenny phone rings and he picks it up.

Kenny says Kenny Church speaking how may I help you?

Troy says Kenny this is Troy Caught I am 1 of your clients. Today I just received a notice to go to court.

Kenny says what happened?

Troy says I am a department manager for a straight adult movie company. We had 2 gay men come in and filled out an application and while I was interviewing them I told them this is for straight adults. We don't film 2 men together. So they filed a complaint against me and accused me of discriminating against them. Could you defend me in court?

Kenny says when do you go to court?

Troy says Tuesday of next week.

Kenny says yes I will defend you.

Troy says thanks Kenny. I will see you Tuesday of next week.

Kenny says ok.

Troy says bye.

Kenny says bye.

They both hang up their phone.

IT IS NOW COURT DAY

It is now court day. At the court house in the court room Angela and Mike and Derek are standing at 1 table as the plaintiffs. At the other table Kenny and Todd and Troy and Brian and Danny are standing as the defendants. Alex and Sam are standing in front of the judges table waiting for Judge Sherri to come.

Now Judge Sherri is leaving her chambers. She opens her chambers door and walks out and closes the door behind her. Judge Sherri opens the courtroom door.

Sam speaks loud enough so every one hears him and says ALL RISE.

Every one stands up.

Judge Sherri walks to her bench and sits down.

Alex speaks loud enough so every one hears him and says YOU MAY BE SEATED.

Every one sits down.

Judge Sherri says ok we will go ahead and get started. This is a case where 2 plaintiffs Derek Styles and Mike Cloud they both said they went to a straight bar and started dancing together and they were told to get off the dance floor. And later you were told to leave because the bar doesn't accept 2 men dancing together. Later Derek and Mike went to an adult movie company and you were told they could not accept 2 men. So you are charging the bar and the adult movie company with discriminating against gay men. Ok I'll let the plaintiff's lawyer speak first.

Angela says Your Honor may I please call Mike Cloud to the witness stand and may I please question him?

Judge Sherri says yes.

Mike Cloud and Angela walk to the witness stand. Mike continues standing and Angela picks up the bible and holds it in front of him.

Angela says will you please raise your right hand and put your left hand on the bible?

Mike does just so.

Angela says do you swear to tell the truth and the whole truth and nothing but the truth.

Mike says I do.

Angela says thank you. You may be seated.

Mike sits down.

Angela says last week where did you go for entertainment?

Mike says I went to a bar called The Fun Place.

Angela says did any one go with you?

Mike says yes.

Angela says who all went with you?

Mike says a group of my friends Angela and Tina and Derek and myself and Doug and Pam and Tommy and Gloria and Katrisha and Jake and Wendle and Deana.

Angela says what happened while you were there?

Mike says 1st of all the dj said we will have couples only. He started playing a slow song and all the couples got on the dance floor and started slow dancing. Including the gay women couples they started slow dancing together too. So me and Derek got on the dance floor and started slow dancing together. Then shortly after that the bar staff Danny came up to me and Derek and says excuse me I am sorry but you 2 can't dance together. I said why? Danny told me the staff can't allow 2 men dancing together. I said why can't 2 men dance together? Danny said this is a straight bar 2 men aren't allowed to do that. I asked him what is the difference? Right next to us Angela and Tina were slow dancing together and Danny did not says a word to them. So me and Derek stopped slow dancing and got off the dance floor and went back to our seats. Then later the dj announced for all the lesbian ladies to get on top of the bar and start dancing in a sexy way. I looked at Derek and said lets go up there. So Derek and I got on top of the bar and started dancing in a sexy way. Some of the women came to watch us and enjoyed what they were seeing. Then later Danny came up to the bar where we were dancing and says sir I told you 2 earlier that 2 men can't dance together. Since we were ignoring him and now dancing in a sexual way then we have to leave now. I told Danny I want to see his manager. So Danny went to get the bar manager Brian. And a couple of minutes later Danny came back with Brian. Brian said you want to talk to the manager. I am the manager. Then I told Brian that is not fair they call this a straight bar but still they allow 2 women to dance together but they don't allow 2 men dancing together. Brian said he is not willing to loose his job because of it. Then he said since Danny told us to leave then that is what we have to do. Or he will have us thrown out or even call the police. So Derek and I got off the bar and went outside and waited for the rest of the group.

Angela says did any thing else happen?

Mike says no. After that me and Derek went out side and stood by our cars until the rest of the group came out side and we all decided to go home.

Angela says I have no further questions Your Honor.

Angela went back to her seat.

Kenny says Your Honor may I please approach the witness?

Judge Sherri says yes.

Kenny walks to the witness stand and says Mike are you gay?

Mike says yes I am.

Kenny says ok since you are gay how come you did not go to a gay bar?

Mike says the group I was with decided to go to The Fun Place.

Kenny says why didn't you remind the group that The Fun Place is a straight bar?

Mike says I wanted to stay with the group.

Kenny says ok you knew The Fun Place is a straight bar but only because of a selfish reason which is you wanted to stay with your group of friends then you chose to go to a straight bar and expect them to break the rules and let you dance with another man. Plus the bar staff Danny was trying to be nice the 1st time when he just told you and Derek to sit down. The 1st time he did not throw you out he just told you to sit down. Then later you went behind his back and ignored him and broke the rule again but to a worse extent. The 2nd time he said some thing to you. You 2 were dancing in a sexual way. Really disgracing the bar. If you went to a gay bar you would not be breaking any rules because gay bars are for gay people to express their sexual preference. But since I am straight I am proud to remind you that straight bars are strictly for people to express their straight sexual feelings. Next time remind your friends that you need to go to a gay bar so you can dance with another man. Your Honor I have not further questions.

Kenny walks back to his seat.

Judge Sherri says Mike you may go back to your seat.

Mike walks back to his seat.

Angela says Your Honor may I please call Danny Wom to the witness stand? And may I please come to question him?

Judge Sherri says yes.

Angela and Danny walks to the witness stand and Danny continues standing. Angela picks up the bible and holds it in front of Danny.

Angela says will you please raise your right hand and put your left hand on the bible?

Danny does just so.

Angela says do you swear to tell the truth and the whole truth and nothing but the truth?

Danny says I do.

Angela says thank you. You may be seated.

Danny sits down.

Angela says where is your place of employment?

Danny says I work at a straight bar called The Fun Place.

Angela says what is your position?

Danny says I have to rotate positions. Some times I have to bartender and other times I have to walk around the floor to make sure nobody is doing any thing wrong.

Angela says were you there the night Mike Cloud and Derek Styles got verbally kicked out of the bar?

Danny says yes I was.

Angela says who kicked them out?

Danny says I was the 1st person who told them they had to leave.

Angela says why did you tell the 2 guys to leave?

Danny says well I know it's a straight bar plus at first I seen them slow dancing together on the dance floor and I told them 2 men aren't allowed to dance together so they'll have to sit back down. Then later I seen them on top of the bar dancing together in a sexual way. I told them this is the 2nd time I have had to say some thing to them about dancing together and this time it is to a worse extent in a sexual way. So they have to leave now. They wanted to argue with me and refuse to leave. So Mike said he wanted to see the manager. So I went to get the bar manager Brian and Brian came back with me and made them leave.

Angela says Your Honor I have no further questions for Danny. Can he go back to his seat? And call Brian Wrong to the witness stand?

Judge Sherri says yes.

Danny walks back to his seat and at the same time Brian walks to the witness stand and continues standing.

Angela holds the bible in front of Brian and says will you please raise your right hand and put your left hand on the bible?

Brian does just so.

Angela says do you swear to tell the truth and the whole truth and nothing but the truth?

Brian says I do.

Angela says thank you. You may be seated.

Brian sits down.

Angela says Brian where is your place of employment and your position?

Brian says I work at a bar called The Fun Place. And my position is bar manager.

Angela says ok were you there the night Derek and Mike got verbally kicked out?

Brian says yes I was.

Angela says who kicked them out?

Brian says I am the 2nd person who kicked them out.

Angela says tell me why did you kick them out?

Brian says I was sitting in my office and Danny came in and told me he is having a problem with 2 gay guys. He told me they were slow dancing on the floor and he told them 2 men can't dance together so they have to sit down. And later behind his back they got up on top of the bar and started a sexual dance and he told them since this is the 2nd time he's had to say some thing to them they have to leave the bar right now. Mike told Danny that Mike wants to see the manager so Danny came and got me. Then we both went out there to Mike and Derek. Then Mike told me it is not fair that 2 women can dance together but not 2 men. I told Mike since Danny told him and Derek to leave then they have to leave. That's just the way it is I am not going to argue about it. Then they both left. And that is the end of the story.

Angela says Your Honor I have no further questions for Brian can he go back to his and can I call Derek Styles to the witness stand?

Judge Sherri says yes.

Brian walks back to his seat at the same time Derek walks to the witness stand and continues standing and Angela picks up the bible and holds it in front of him.

Angela says will you please raise your right hand and put your left hand on the bible?

Derek does just so.

Angela says do you swear to tell the truth and the whole truth and nothing but the truth?

Derek says I do.

Angela says thank you. You may be seated.

Derek sits down.

Angela says last week did you go to an adult movie company?

Derek says yes I did.

Angela says what was the name of it?

Derek says Hot And Fabulous.

Angela says what did you do there?

Derek says I applied for an acting career.

Angela says did they hire you?

Derek says Mike and I were told the only way we could work for them we would have to have sex with a woman. Not another man.

Angela says are you gay?

Derek says yes I am.

Angela says why were you told you have to have sex with a woman?

Derek says the department manager Troy asked us how do our marriage mates feel about us being naked on camera. Then Tina spoke up and asked is this a straight adult movie company or a gay adult movie company? Troy said it is straight. Tina said she asked because her and Angela are gay partners. So they only have sex with other women. Troy told her they accept 2 women. But they would have only 1 scene in the entire movie. Then Mike spoke up and asked what about 2 men. Do 2 men get a scene in a straight sex movie? Troy said no. He is sorry but they don't film 2 men. Mike asked Troy what is the difference? Troy said it is a rule we have to follow. Then he said let me go and ask the administrator and see. When they both came back into the conference room the administrator who is Todd told Mike this is a straight adult movie company. But still we accept 2 women but not 2 men. And the reason is because that's the way the owner wants it. And the owner wants it that way because not only is he straight but also you have a lot of straight men that request for 2 women. So you have to have sex with a woman. Then Todd went back to his office and Troy told us he would see us tomorrow and dismissed us. And that was it.

Angela says Your Honor I have no further questions for Derek. Can he go back to his seat?

Judge Sherri says yes.

Derek walks back to his seat.

Angela says Your Honor may I please call Troy Caught to the witness stand?

Judge Sherri says yes.

Troy walks to the witness stand and continues standing.

Angela holds the bible in front of him and says will you please raise your right hand and put your left hand on the bible?

Troy does just so.

Angela says do you swear to tell the truth and the whole truth and nothing but the truth.

Troy says I do.

Angela says thank you. You may be seated.

Troy sits down.

Angela says will you please tell the court where you work at and the kind of business it is and your position?

Troy says I work for Hot And Fabulous. It is a straight adult movie company. I am a department manager. I hire all the new actors that come in.

Angela says last week did Mike and Derek and Tina and myself and Doug and Pam come in and apply for a job?

Troy says yes you all did.

Angela says did you hire them all?

Troy says yes I did.

Angela says did Tina tell you that her and Angela were gay partners?

Troy says yes she did.

Angela says did you tell every one it is a straight company?

Troy says yes I did.

Angela says ok if you told every one the company is for straight adults. When Tina told you her and Angela are gay partners. What did you say to Tina?

Troy says I told Tina her and Angela would get only 1 scene in the entire movie.

Angela says ok did Mike speak up and tell you him and Derek are gay partners?

Troy says yes he did.

Angela says ok what did you tell Mike?

Troy says I told Mike I am sorry but we just don't film 2 men. Then I told him I would check with my boss the administrator but when I did that the administrator said no. And that is the end of what I said.

Angela says Your Honor I have no further questions for Troy. Can he go back to his seat?

Judge Sherri says yes.

Troy walks back to his seat.

At the same time Angela says Your Honor may I please call Todd Mine to the witness stand?

Judge Sherri says yes.

Todd walks to the witness stand and continues standing.

Angela holds the bible in front of him and says will you please raise your right hand and put your left hand on the bible?

Todd does just so.

Angela says do you swear to tell the truth and the whole truth and nothing but the truth?

Todd says yes I do.

Angela says thank you. You may be seated.

Todd sits down.

Angela says will you please say your place of employment and your position?

Todd says I work for a straight adult movie company and I am the administrator.

Angela says ok last week did you have people apply for acting jobs?

Todd says yes we did.

Angela says who were the people that applied?

Todd says Doug and Pam and Angela and Tina and Mike and Derek.

Angela says did you tell the applicants that the company is for straight adults?

Todd says yes I did.

Angela says ok when you came into the conference room and Mike told you it is not fair you call this a straight company but still you accept gay women but reject gay men. He also said what is the difference? What did you say to Mike?

Todd says I told Mike the difference is that is the way the owner of the company wants it. Because the owner of the company is straight and lots of straight men request to see 2 women. But they don't want to see 2 men. And I also told Mike since I don't want to lose my job I am going to manage this building the way the owner tells me to. Because of that he would have to have sex with a woman to work for us. Then I asked him does he understand and he said yes. Then I went back to my office.

Angela says Your Honor I have no further questions for Todd. Can he go back to his seat?

Judge Sherri says yes.

Angela and Todd walk back to their seat.

At the same time Kenny Church says Your Honor may I please call Derek Styles to the witness stand? And may I please question him?

Judge Sherri says yes.

Kenny and Derek walk to the witness stand and Derek continues standing.

Kenny says you have already been sworn in and you are still under oath so you may be seated.

Derek sits down.

Kenny says Derek are you gay?

Derek says yes I am.

Kenny says are you and Mike a gay couple?

Derek says yes we are.

Kenny says while you were at the adult movie company once you found out it was for straight people why didn't you go to a adult movie company for gay people?

Derek says because I knew that wasn't fair they could accept 2 women but not 2 men.

Kenny says so you are expecting the staff to just break the owners rules and accept gay men and take a chance on losing their job. Is that what you are saying?

Derek says no.

Kenny says if they get fired from their job and can't pay rent or buy food are you going to financially support them?

Derek says no. I wasn't trying to get them fired. I was just trying to get fair treatment from them.

Kenny says I am not saying this because I am straight but in the future if you want to go to a bar and dance with other men I would advice you to go to a gay bar. If you want to have sex with other men on television I would advice you to go to a gay adult movie company for men. That way you are not breaking any rules and the staff is not taking any chances on losing their job. Your Honor I have no further questions for Derek.

Kenny walks back to his seat.

Judge Sherri says Brian and Todd before I tell you my decision I am 1st going to have you 2 to write down the owner's name and corporate phone number for me on a piece of note pad paper.

Judge Sherri pulls out 2 pieces of note pad paper.

Judge Sherri says Alex will you please give 1 piece to Brian and the other to Todd? Thank you.

Alex takes the paper and says you are welcome.

Alex gives the papers to Brian and Todd and they both start writing the name of the owner of the business and the corporate phone numbers. When they finish Alex takes both papers back to Judge Sherri.

Alex says here you go.

Judge Sherri says thank you.

Alex says you are welcome.

Judge Sherri says Mr. Wrong and Mr. Mine I was listening to what all of you were saying. Rather things happened at the straight bar or at the straight adult movie company. You did what you did because of what the owner of the business required of you. I am going to give this court a recess for 2 hours. In the mean time I am going to call the owner of the businesses and have them to come in here because since they own the business I want them to hear my decision. So now this court is in recess.

Judge Sherri hits her hammer on the block of wood then walks back to her office. In her office she sits down and looks at the note pad papers to see the numbers.

Judge Sherri says hmmmm both numbers are the same. Both corporate names are the same and both owner names are the same.

Judge Sherri picks up the phone and dials the number to the corporate office. When the phone rings the receptionist picks it up.

Yavonne says thank you for calling Hold Production this is Yavonne speaking how may I help you?

Judge Sherri says my name is Judge Sherri Fair. I am calling from the local courthouse and there is some thing I need to tell the owner. May I please speak to Phillip Hold?

Yavonne says yes let me transfer you to his office.

Judge Sherri says thank you.

Yavonne says you are welcome.

Phillip is in his office and the phone rings and he pick it up.

Phillip says Phillip Hold speaking how may I help you?

Judge Sherri says this is Judge Sherri calling from the local courthouse. Mr. Hold I am very sorry to bother you. Unfortunately I have 2 of your building managers at the courthouse. They both were charged with discriminating. And since you are the owner of the business I want you to hear the decision I have to make. So I was wondering could you please be in my courtroom in 2 hours.

Phillip says ok.

Judge Sherri says ok thank you bye.

Phillip says bye.

They both hang up the phone.

It is now 2 hours later and every one is back in Judge Sherri's courtroom including the owner Phillip Hold as 1 of the defendants to defend his managers and business. Judge Sherri opens the door to the courtroom.

Sam speaks loud enough so every one in the courtroom can hear him and says ALL RISE.

Every one sits stands up.

Judge Sherri walks to her chair and sits down.

Alex says YOU MAY BE SEATED.

Every one sits down.

Judge Sherri says this court is now back in session. Since the owner of the business is here we will get started.

Angela says Your Honor before you tell your decision, since the owner's managers have testified about it may we hear from the owner as to what his laws are for his business. May I call Phillip Hold to the witness stand and for me to question him?

Judge Sherri says yes you may.

Now Angela and Phillip walk to the witness stand and Phillip continues standing.

Angela holds the bible in front of him and says will you please raise your right hand and put your left hand on the bible?

Phillip does just so.

Angela says do you swear to tell the truth and the whole truth and nothing but the truth?

Phillip says I do.

Angela says thank you. You may be seated.

Phillip sits down.

Angela says Phillip how do you earn money?

Phillip says I own 2 kinds of businesses.

Angela says what kind of businesses do you own? And the name of them.

Phillip says I own a bar called The Fun Place and I also own an adult movie company called Hot And Fabulous.

Angela says your bar and adult movie company are they for straight people or gay people?

Phillip says they are for straight people.

Angela says in your bar would you allow 2 women dancing together in a sexual way?

Phillip says yes I would.

Angela says in your bar would you allow 2 men dancing together in a sexual way?

Phillip says no I don't.

Angela says in your adult movie company do you film 2 women having sex together?

Phillip says yes I do.

Angela says in your adult movie company do you film 2 men having sex together?

Phillip says no I don't.

Angela says rather it is your bar or your adult movie company why do you allow 2 women but not 2 men?

Phillip says because I am straight and my business is for straight people.

Angela says Phillip listen to your self. You call your business straight that's why you do not allow 2 men but still you allow 2 women. Your laws are discriminating. Causing your employees to discriminate.

Phillip says I don't understand how could I be discriminating when I own the business and being the owner I have a legal right to make what ever laws I want for my business.

Angela says your are discriminating because you are not treating every body the same. You allow 2 women to dance together even in a sexual way but don't allow 2 men to dance together rather slow dancing or definitely not in a sexual way. Your Honor I have no further questions for Phillip.

Angela walks back to her seat.

Judge Sherri says Phillip you may go back to your seat. Phillip walks back to his seat.

Judge Sherri says I understand the staff was just doing what the owner wants them to do. I also understand that the staff has to do what the owner says because he is paying them. It is reasonable to think that when a man is gay and he wants to go to a bar then he needs to go to a gay bar. Or if he wants to have sex with another man on television then he needs to contact a gay men's movie company. But if a gay woman doesn't have to go to a gay bar then neither does a gay man. If a gay woman can come into a straight bar so can a gay man. In a straight sex movie company if gay women can have a sex scene then gay men can have a sex scene. You treat EVERY BODY THE SAME regardless. People act like 2 women are opposite sex. Because most ways that a woman talks ABOUT or TO another woman. Plus most ways that a woman physically touches another woman to society it's all highly acceptable. Two women who are not related to each other they are allowed to dance together. But if 2 men dance together they get persecuted for it. Two women who are not related to each other they are allowed to sit on each other's lap. But 2 men who are not related to each other if they sit on each other's lap then they get persecuted for it. In a straight sex movie 2 women are allowed to have sex together but if

2 men have sex together they get persecuted for it. And 2 women have a vagina just like 2 men have a penis.

Phillip Hold raises his hand.

Judge Sherri says you may speak.

Phillip says Your Honor in straight bars and straight sex movies I have 2 women because I have lots of straight men requesting to see gay women together.

Judge Sherri says you also have lots of straight women requesting to see gay men together. But the bar and the movie. doesn't want to show it. You call it a straight bar and straight adult movie company but when the straight men request for 2 women you show it but when the straight women request for 2 men you don't want to show it. You are discriminating women Two women who are not related to each other are allowed to kiss each other on the cheeks and some times on the lips. But if 2 men kiss on the cheeks they get persecuted for it. If you go to a skating ring and 2 women who are not related to each other if they hold each others hand in the skating ring then people think nothing of it. But 2 men who are not related to each other if they hold each others hand then people they are gay. They get persecuted for it. If a woman says to another woman I love you. People automatically take it as agape love. Or what you call Christ like love but when a man says to another man I love you people automatically take it as sexual or gay love. And sexual or gay love is not the only kind of love there is even coming from a man to another man. A woman is allowed to talk about another woman's attractive face and says she is cute or she is beautiful or she is gorgeous and nobody thinks she is gay. But if a man says another man he is cute or he is beautiful or he is gorgeous people automatically judge the man as gay. Most straight women call their women friends their girlfriend. They don't just say their friend. They say their girlfriend and nobody thinks any thing of it. Nobody thinks she is in a gay relationship with another woman. But if a man calls his men friends his boyfriends then the 1st thing people think is. Is he in a gay relationship with another man? Two women who are not related to each other if they hug each other with BOTH ARMS EACH people think nothing of it. But 2 men who are not related to each other if they hug each other with BOTH ARMS EACH people judge the 2 men as gay. When women do these things with other women they get away with it. But when men do these things with other men then the men get persecuted for it and judged as gay. Also on the job it is HIGHLY acceptable for a woman staff to wear men's clothes. A man's shirt and a man's pants and a man's shoes and a man's tie and a man's hat. But if a man wears a woman's skirt and a woman's shirt and a woman's shoes and a woman's hat then he gets disciplined for it. When a woman staff goes into a man's bathroom people think nothing of it she is not automatically judged as gay and isn't disciplined. But if a man staff goes into a woman's bathroom he is automatically judged as gay and is disciplined for it.

Kenny raises his hand.

Judge Sherri says you may speak.

Kenny says Your Honor you have some women that don't feel comfortable going into a man's bathroom.

Judge Sherri says that's true but when they do society thinks nothing of it but when a man goes into a women bathroom he gets disciplined for it. On the job it is highly acceptable for a woman staff to work with men personal items such as his underwear and condoms and Viagra. But if a man staff work with women's panties and bras and sanitary napkins then he gets disciplined for it. As little kids it is highly acceptable for little girls to play with boy dolls but little boys are not allowed to play with girl dolls. As adults rather on the job or off the job when it comes to sex crimes people act like only men commit sex crimes. Rather it is toward the same sex or the opposite sex or both sexes. Just like men commit sex crimes women commit sex crimes too. People say according to surveys men commit sex crimes more. That is not true. Both sexes commit sex crimes in equal amounts. People will write it on paper more times about a man than they will write it about a woman. People are quick to tell a man don't take a little girl to the bathroom because he might sneak and have sex with her. But they don't tell a woman don't take a little boy to the bathroom because she might sneak and have sex with him as well. Just like men see sexual attraction and have sexual feelings toward the opposite sex and the same sex and both sexes. Women also see sexual attraction and have sexual feelings toward the opposite sex and the same sex and both sexes. Just like men like pornographic movies. Women like pornographic movies too. And just like men like to look at 2 women. Women like to look at 2 men.

Even though I am a woman and a very straight woman and I love being straight and I love my husband's penis. But still when I deal with gay men I don't treat them any different than gay women. You have some straight people that say they are against gay people but still they like to see 2 women. If you are against it then you don't want to see 2 men NOR 2 women. I am treating gay people the same as I am treating straight people. And I am treating gay men the same as I am treating gay women. If I reject a gay man then I will reject a gay woman. If I accept a gay woman then I will accept a gay man.

It is a federal law. You can not discriminate. You have to treat every body the same regardless. Rather on the job or off the job. People can see nationalistic discrimination. And race discrimination. And religious discrimination. And age discrimination. And even discrimination against women. But they can not see discrimination against straight men and especially gay men.

This case is real similar to a case I had before this one. Just like it is illegal to buy cigarettes if you are not 18 and it is illegal to buy liquor if you are not 21 and it is illegal to drive without a driver license or permit. It is also illegal to discriminate. The law says you must treat every body the same regardless.

Phillip raises his hand.

Judge Sherri says you may speak.

Phillip says Your Honor in straight bars you have a lot more men than women and the straight men are requesting to see 2 women. Judge Sherri says that is not true. You have just as many women in straight bars as you do men. And the straight women are requesting to see 2 men. Even if you did have more men than women you STILL serve ALL of your customers what they want and not just a certain kind because they are the majority group. It is the same as saying if it is a lot more men than women then you serve drinks only to the men and not the women. Because the majority of customers are men. I don't care if you have 199 men customers and only 4 women customers. You serve drinks to the 199 men customers AND serve drinks to the 4 women customers. At the same time if you let gay women dance for

199 straight men. Then you let gay men dance for 4 straight women. That is only fair and treating every body the same. Since you own the bar and the movie company and your laws are discriminating I am going to give you a fine. Television is a billion dollar industry so I am fining you 8 million dollars. You must write a check for it today.

Phillip says but Your Honor I am not the 1 who actually did the discriminating. It was my staff.

Judge Sherri says first of all your laws discriminate. Second of all even though you are not the one who did it verbally or physically but still as the owner you are responsible for every thing your staff does. It is just like being a department manager or building manager. You are responsible for all employees under your authority. Or just like parents with minor kids. Since parents have authority over their minor kids then parents are responsible for their minor kids actions. Business owners are the very same way. They are responsible for every employee working under their authority. Especially since the discrimination was done by the manager of the whole building. That causes the owner of the whole business to be disciplined. Since you own the bar and the adult movie company my judgment is to fine the owner 8 million dollars. So this case is done.

Judge Sherri picks up her hammer and hits it on her block of wood and walks back to her office.

At the same time Derek and Mike and Angela walk out of the courtroom to their cars.

Derek says Angela thank you for all of your help again. I highly appreciate it.

Mike says I thank you too. And I highly appreciate it.

Angela says you both are very welcome. I love being a lawyer. So if you ever need me again just let me know and I will be glad to help you out.

Then they get in their cars and drive home.

Now back at the courthouse in the hallway Kenny is talking to all of his staff.

Kenny says rather you work at the bar or the movie company I want all of my staff to meet me at The Fun Place. Todd when you get to The Fun Place I want you to call Hot an Fabulous and tell all the staff to meet me at The Fun Place in 1 hour.

Todd says ok.

Kenny says that's all of my staff meet me at The Fun Place in 1 hour.

Every body says ok.

Now Kenny goes to pay his fine and all his staff leaves the courthouse.

It is now 1 hour later and Kenny and all his staff are at The Fun Place and Kenny is having a meeting.

Kenny says I had every one to meet here because I know with the amount of seats there's enough room for every one to sit down. Second of all I apologize about my law about men not dancing with other men. I did not realize my law was discriminating. Since it did cause me to be fined, with the amount of money left in the company's bank account after paying the fine there is only enough money left to pay you all for 1 more month. You will be paid for all the hours you worked. But unfortunately your next check will be your last check. Besides your paid time off check. Unfortunately I have to lay off all of you. I am very sorry. So now you all are dismissed. Every one gets up and leaves.

Now Derek is standing in front of Mike's house and rings the doorbell. Mike comes and opens the door.

Mike says hi Derek.

Derek says hi Mike.

Mike says come on in and have a seat.

Derek comes in and they both walk to the couch and sits down.

Mike says it is good to see you again.

Derek says it is good to see you again too. But there is something I need to tell you.

Mike says what is it?

Derek says Mike I have reached a point in my life where I am tired of all the discrimination that gay men deal with. I am absolutely sick of it. I have been through 2 court cases because we're so discriminated against. And now I am tired of it. Like Judge Sherri said people act like 2 women are opposite sex. Because gay women get away with all of this stuff at the same time gay men get persecuted for it. So Mike I have decided to have a sex change. I have decided to become a woman. And since I have decided to become a woman, unfortunately I have to end our relationship. I don't want to but I have to.

Mike says Derek are you sure this is what you want to do?

Derek says I have been thinking about it for a long time. And I am just tired now.

Mike says well Derek I deal with discrimination too. But I don't want a sex change.

In a sad voice Derek says Mike even though we both are gay men but still you are a different kind of gay man than I am. You are a masculine gay man so you like to wear pants. I am a feminine gay man so I want to wear skirts and heels. You like men who are feminine and I like men who are masculine. I like every thing I see about you. I'm just tired of what we deal with. Mike I promise you. It's not you I'm tried of. I'm tired of the way society treats us.

Mike says I understand what you are talking about. At the same time I am still in love with you.

Derek says Mike I am still in love with you too. And that's why it is so hard for me to end the relationship. Because I know we both still love each other. At the same time since we both like men. That's why as much as I hate to do it I'm ending the relationship and going to have a sex change.

Mike says well I am going to miss our relationship.

Derek stands up and says I am too. Bye Mike.

Mike says before you leave let me ask you just 1 question.

Derek says ok.

Mike says can we just be friends?

Derek says sure I will be glad to be your friend.

Mike says ok thanks.

Derek says I will see you later bye.

Mike says bye.

Then Derek leaves.

Now at Derek's house Derek has invited all his family and friends to his house in his living room to let them know what he has decided to do. Every one is sitting down Jeff Styles and Grace Styles and Pam and

Doug Tommy and Gloria and Mike and Angela and Tina and Katrisha and Jake and Wendle and Deana.

Derek says I have something very serious and important I would like to tell every one. I feel like I am at a point in my life where I am just tired of all the discrimination that gay men deal with. I am not tired of Mike, we still love each other. I am just tired of the discrimination. So I have decided to have a sex change. I am going to become a woman.

Jeff says Mike since you and Derek were in a relationship how do you feel about this?

Mike says Derek and I have already talked about it and he told me that since he and I still love each other, plus he's tired of what he's dealing with. That it was a very hard decision for him to make. And I told him that I do understand. So we decided to end our romantic relationship and just be male friend boyfriends.

Jeff says Derek don't think because you told us this that we are going to love you any less. Because we're not. Rather you are straight or gay. Man or woman you are still our child and we still love you just the way you are. When you have your sex change and are a woman. You will still be the human being from my sperm.

Grace says I feel the same way gay or straight man or woman. You are still the human being I gave birth to. And I still love you just the way you are.

Tommy says Derek my only concern about any person is how that person as an individual treats me as an individual. You've always treated me with kindness and respect and willing to be my friend. So I will treat you with kindness and respect and be your friend regardless.

Doug says you are still my brother and I still love you regardless of gay or straight man or woman.

Tina says even though I am not having a sex change because gay women don't deal with discrimination like gay men do. But still since I am gay too. Brother I do understand. So of course I still love you regardless.

Pam says I'll support your decision because I'll still love you too.

Gloria says I'll support you. Because I'll still love you too.

Mike says though I still love you intimately because my feelings for you have not vanished yet. But like I said I do understand what you are going through and you're tired of it. And so in an agape way I still love you and support you.

Angela says I will support you legally in court again if I have to because I still love you regardless.

Katrisha says I still love you too. I'll support you Derek.

Jake says I still love you. I will support you Derek.

Wendle says I still love you too Derek. I'll support you.

Deana says same here. I love you and will support you.

Derek says boy. I love all of you. Thank you all for the love and support.

Jeff says Derek my child please stand up.

Derek stands up. At the same time Jeff and Grace walk over to Derek and Jeff puts both of his arms around Derek and Derek puts both of his arms around Jeff.

Jeff says I love you son.

Derek says I love you too dad.

Then Grace and Derek hug each other.

Grace says I love you son.

Derek says I love you too mom.

Now every one else stands up and walks over to Derek.

Doug gives Derek a hug.

Doug says I love you brother.

Derek says I love you too brother.

Pam gives Derek a hug.

Pam says I love you.

Derek says I love you too.

Tommy gives Derek a hug.

Tommy says I love you.

Derek says I love you too.

Gloria gives Derek a hug.

Gloria says I love you.

Derek says I love you too.

Mike gives Derek a hug.

Mike says I love you.

Derek says I love you too.

Angela gives Derek a hug.

Two Women Are Opposite Sex

Angela says I love you.
Derek says I love you too.
Tina gives Derek a hug.
Tina says I love you brother.
Derek says I love you too sister.
Katrisha gives Derek a hug.
Katrisha says I love you.
Derek says I love you too.
Jake gives Derek a hug.
Jake says I love you.
Derek says I love you too.
Wendle gives Derek a hug.
Wendle says I love you.
Derek says I love you too.
Deana gives Derek a hug.
Deana says I love you.
Derek says I love you too.
After every one has given Derek a hug they all sit back down.
Jeff says Derek where are you going to get that kind of money?
A sex change is expensive.
Derek says I have the money in my bank account.
Jake says you do?
Derek says Jake do you remember when you invited me to come with you and Katrisha to the casino to try to win some money?
Jake says oh yes I remember.
Derek says remember I won $200,000.00?
Jake says yes I remember.
Derek says I am going to use that money there to pay for the sex change.
Grace says when do you plan to talk to a surgeon about this?
Derek says I am going tomorrow to talk to a surgeon about it.

THE NEXT DAY

It's now the next day and Derek is at the hospital in Dr. Hapchan's office with the door closed talking to the dr. about Derek having a sex change operation.

Dr. Hapchan says Derek before I give you a sex change operation or even before starting hormone therapy I need to 1st ask you some questions to make sure a sex change is best for you.

Derek says ok.

Dr. Hapchan says some people will ask a doctor about surgery to be the opposite sex because of their desire to do things the opposite sex likes to do. But that is not a reason for a sex change. So to make sure this will be the right thing for you let me 1st ask you some questions. First of all why do you want a sex change?

Derek says well since I was a little boy I have always loved women's clothes. Plus I have noticed back in the 1700's and 1800's women were only allowed to wear skirts and men only allowed to wear pants but years later women are now allowed more variety women are now allowed to wear skirts and pants. But still men only allowed to wear pants. Men are not allowed to wear skirts. Men are not allowed the variety that women are allowed. I've allays loved women's clothes.

Dr. Hapchan says what do you love about women's clothes?

Derek says I love how fancy their skirts and tops are structured. At times even women's pants are structured in a fancy way but especially their skirts and tops. Women are allowed more variety than men with different fancy structures. The only variety men get with suits and ties is just different colors and different materials but for the most part they are all structured the very same way. With women's skirts and tops women get to chose more variety than just different colors and different materials. Women also get the variety of different fancy structures to choose from.

Dr. Hapchan says do you carry yourself in a feminine way or in a masculine way?

Derek says my natural ways of being my self. I have always been naturally feminine. I have tried to be what society says a man should be

Two Women Are Opposite Sex

which is masculine, but I've always had a hard time being masculine. It's just not in me to be masculine. Like I said I have always been naturally feminine.

Dr. Hapchan says Derek in your life time have you always been around men or women or both?

Derek says I've mostly been around men.

Dr. Hapchan says this next question may sound strange and you may not see how it could relate to you but, your dad is he feminine or masculine?

Derek says my dad is very masculine.

Dr. Hapchan says is your mother feminine or masculine?

Derek says my mother is very feminine.

Dr. Hapchan says do you have brothers and sisters?

Derek says yes I do.

Dr. Hapchan says are they feminine or masculine?

Derek says my sister is masculine and my brother is masculine.

Dr. Hapchan says even though your body is physically structured as a man but in your mind do you think of yourself as a woman or man?

Derek says in my mind I think of myself as a woman.

Dr. Hapchan says are you sexually attracted to women or men?

Derek says I am sexually attracted to men.

Dr. Hapchan says what age did you 1st start seeing attraction in men?

Derek says when I was around the age of 7 years old.

Dr. Hapchan says have you had sex with men or women?

Derek says I have had sex with both.

Dr. Hapchan says which did you like better?

Derek says I like the man better.

Dr. Hapchan says ok if you're sexually attracted to men and like sex better with a man then why did you have sex with a woman?

Derek says because I had a lot of straight people telling me since I have a penis I would like a woman better. So just to learn from my own experience I tried sex with a woman. But to me the feeling was not satisfying me as much as it did when I had sex with a man. To me it was a lot more satisfying with a man. Physically and mentally and emotionally. Because not only was he satisfying me on the out side but he also satisfied me on the inside as well.

Dr. Hapchan says what made your inside like the man better?

Derek says I loved the feeling of his manly body.

Dr. Hapchan says when you had sex with a man what was the sexual position?

Derek says I laid on my back and spread my legs and he laid on top of me on his stomach.

Dr. Hapchan says what did you like about the postion?

Derek says the inside of me the emotional part of me loved feeling his manly body lying on top of mine. I want a sex change because I want to enjoy sex in the exact same way that a woman does and to the fullest extent. My insides won't be fully satisfied until I have a vagina and can enjoy feeling a manly man's penis going inside of me. Just exactly like a woman enjoys it.

Dr. Hapchan says the reason why I asked these kind of questions is because some men who only had sex with the same sex think they like it better and they'll ask for a sex change and have never tried sex with the opposite sex. I have had some gay women come to me in the same situation.

Derek says when I was a teenager if I would sneak and watch a sex movie I couldn't understand why I would get an erection if they showed a man's penis knowing that I have one too. I am tired of having feelings in me that I can't physically satisfy all the way. Even though it is an expensive operation but still I want to do it.

Dr. Hapchan says well from what you've just told me. Inside your body you do have mostly a woman's hormones. Because you see sexual attraction toward men plus you like a man's manly body plus erecting just from looking at the penis. I'm also saying this to you because I've had other gay men to say the same thing to me. Even gay women have said the same thing about other w omen. Because a lot of gay women have mostly men hormones so they will ask a dr. for a sex change as well. And as for sexual attraction some people fail to realize what causes sexual attraction. Sexual attraction is caused by the hormones. Some people think sexual attraction is caused by the sex organ but it's not. The only thing the sex organ does is give and receive sexual pleasure while having sex. But sexual attraction is caused by the hormones. A good example of what I am saying look at a virgin. A virgin has never had sex not 1 time and so doesn't know what it feels like but still sees sexual attraction, why because of hormones. That's how a gay person can look at the same sex and see that person as cute or beautiful or gorgeous. Now since you do have mostly female hormones I will give you the sex change operation. But before the operation I have to 1st give you hormone therapy.

Dr. Hapchan hands a prescription to Derek and says take these prescriptions and come back exactly 1 week from today ok.

Derek says ok.

Dr. Hapchan says now do you have any questions for me?

Derek says yes. If a patient comes to you about a sex change operation do they always get psychiatric and hormone treatment before the operation?

Dr. Hapchan says yes. Before a patient is taken in for surgery he or she is evaluated very carefully by a psychiatrist and experts. We have to see whether he or she fulfills the criteria to be the new gender. And make sure the patient is not suffering from other mental disorders and the patient can be the new sex socially. After the evaluation the psychiatrist certifies that the patient will be given the surgery.

Derek says after a sex change can people still have sexual intercourse?

Dr. Hapchan says yes and in both situations rather you become a man or a woman. You can definitely have sexual intercourse.

Derek says after having a sex change can a new woman get pregnant and can a new father give sperm?

Dr. Hapchan says no. Biological sex remains the same whether you have a male to female transformation or a female to male transformation. Biological sex means your xy and xx chromosomes will remain the same. You will not be able to reproduce in your new sex. And this is an irreversible operation.

Derek says what do you actually do to change a man into a woman?

Dr. Hapchan says basically we have to create a vagina and that is created under the scrotum. We fillet out and preserver the penile skin and the scrotum skin. Then we create an opening behind the prostate and the urtethra and a vagina is created in front of the rectum. But we don't give them a new uterus or an ovary. We line the vagina with the penile skin that we have left. The scrotal skin is used to make the labia and the lips of a vagina.

Derek says how many successful sex changes have you done?

Dr. Hapchan says in my 21 years of being a plastic surgeon I have done around 242. I have done other surgeries but that's how many sex changes I've done. Most of the time my patients are asking me for a sex change.

Derek says were your patients happy with the surgery?

Dr. Hapchan says what I have experienced is most of the time if they're not happy with the change then they'll come back with questions. If they are happy with the change then they don't come back for a follow up. Plus you need to know that the doctor is experienced and has done the surgery in the past. This should not be taken lightly because these are permanent operations.

Derek says ok I understand now.

Dr. Hapchan says do you have any more questions? I will be happy to answer them.

Derek says that's all the questions I can think of.

Dr. Hapchan says ok.

Dr. Hapchan reaches for hormone pills and gives them to Derek.

Dr. Hapchan says start taking these hormone pills and come back to me 1 week from today.

Derek says ok. Thank you Dr. Hapchan.

Dr. Hapchan says you are welcome.

They both shake each others hand and Derek leaves the office and goes back home.

ONE WEEK LATER

It is now 1 week later at Derek's house and he is in bed sleeping and he wakes up and climbs out of bed and goes to the bathroom and looks in the mirror and he notices he's growing breast. They are the size of a 13 year olds breast. Plus the muscles on his chest and arms and legs have shrunk to the size of a 13 year olds female's muscles. Derek goes back to his bedroom and gets on the phone and dials Dr. Hapchan's office. Dr. Hapchan is in his office sitting at his desk and his phone rings and he picks it up.

Dr. Hapchan says this is Dr. Hapchan may I help you?

Derek says Dr. Hapchan this is Derek Styles. I am the patient that was talking to you last week about the sex change operation.

Dr. Hapchan says yes I remember. How are you doing?

Derek says I am fine especially since I woke up this morning and went to the bathroom and looked at my body in the mirror.

Dr. Hapchan says how are the hormone pills working for you?

Derek says I have noticed that I have started to grow breast plus on my chest and arms and legs my muscles have started to shrink. It looks like the pills are working.

Dr. Hapchan says do you have anything you have to do today?

Derek says no I don't.

Dr. Hapchan says can you be in my exam room in 2 hours from now? I would like to see how the pills are working.

Derek says I sure can.

Dr. Hapchan says ok I will see you in 2 hours.

Derek says ok bye.

Dr. Hapchan says bye.

Then they both hang up their phone.

It is now 2 hours later and Derek is at the hospital in Dr. Hapchan's exam room. Derek is wearing his hospital gown and underwear and t-shirt. Dr. Hapchan opens up Derek's gown and lifts up the top part of his t-shirt and looks inside at his growing breast then lifts the bottom part of Derek's gown and looks at Derek's muscle tone on his legs and thighs and then buttons the gown back up and then looks at both of Derek's arms.

Dr. Hapchan says I see the hormone pills are working for you. In 3 more days I want to bring you in for the sex change surgery. I can't do it before then because I have other patients I am going to do surgery on. But I have nobody scheduled for 3 days from now. Can you come back 3 days from now?

Dereks says yes I can.

Dr. Hapchan says ok I am going to go take care of some other patience and you can get back into your street clothes.

Derek says ok thank you Dr. Hapchan.

Dr. Hapchan leaves the room.

Now Derek is back at home and he is on the phone talking to Jeff.

Derek says hi dad how are you doing?

Jeff says I am fine. How are you doing?

Derek says real good.

Jeff says did you find out when you will be having your surgery?

Derek says yes that's what I called to tell you. I'll be having my surgery in 3 days from now. That is the soonest the doctor could do it.

Jeff says what hospital is it going to be at?

Derek says at Care Medical Center at 8 am is when he scheduled to start the operation.

Jeff says ok I will tell your mother.

Derek says ok bye dad.

Jeff says bye son.

Then they both hang up their phone.

Now Derek picks his phone back up and dials Tommy's number. Tommy is at home and when his phone rings he picks it up.

Tommy says hello.

Derek says Tommy this is Derek.

Tommy says hi Derek.

Tommy says when are you going to have your operation?

Derek says that's what I called to tell you. The operation is in 3 days at Care Medical Center at 8 am.

Tommy says ok thanks for telling me. I will be there to support you.

Derek says thanks Tommy.

Tommy says you are welcome. I will also tell Gloria and Katrisha and the family to help you spread the word to your close friends.

Derek says thanks Tommy.

Tommy says you are welcome.

Derek says bye.

Tommy says bye.

Then they both hang up their phone.

Two Women Are Opposite Sex

Now Derek's phone rings and he picks it up.
Derek says hello.
Doug says hi Derek this is your brother Doug.
Derek says ok.
Doug says how are you doing?
Derek says ok.
Doug says I was just calling to see have you heard when you will be having you operation?
Derek says I just finished talking to Tommy and right before the phone rang I was just getting ready to call you and let you know when. The operation will be in 3 days from now at Care Medical Center at 8 am. I have already told dad and he said he would tell mother and spread the word for me.
Doug says ok I will be there to support you and help spread the word for you. I will see you in 3 days.
Derek says thank you Doug.
Doug says you are welcome my brother.
Derek says bye.
Doug says bye.
Then they both hang up their phone.

3 DAYS LATER

It is now 3 days later at 7:30 am and Derek is at Care Medical Center in his patient bedroom sitting up in his bed with the head of the bed slanted up and wearing his hospital gown and cap waiting for the hospital transporters to come and take him to surgery. The other bed in the room is empty. All his immediate family and close friend are in the room to comfort and support Derek. Jeff and Grace and Doug and Tina and Angela and Tommy and Gloria and Pam and Mike and Katrisha and Jake and Windle and Deana are all in Derek's hospital room.

Tommy says Derek you are doing a mighty good job at remaining strong through this.

Derek says I am just fine. I am getting more and more excited about this because I know when I am done with the operation my body will be changed into a human being that I've always wanted to be. A woman. So I am getting more and more excited. I feel like I am suffering in a man's body because this in not what I am happy being. Inside of me I have a woman's feelings so I am excited that I am about to change my body into a woman's body.

Jeff says Derek I was wondering after your surgery since you will be a woman are you going to keep your same name or are you going to change your name to a woman's name?

Derek says I have decided to change my name to a woman's name.

Grace says what will your woman's name be?

Derek says when my surgery is over my name will then be Clara Styles. At that time please start calling me Clara Styles.

Jeff says ok.

Grace says ok.

Now 2 hospital transporters come in the room to take Derek to surgery. One of the transporters lets Derek know what they are going to do.

Jan says are you Derek Styles?

Derek says yes I am.

Jan says we are transporters we are going to take you to surgery. Are you ready?

Derek says yes I am.

Grace says excuse me mam.

Jan says yes.

Grace says around how long does it take for a sex change surgery?

Jan says it usually takes around 6 hours.

Grace says ok I just wondered how long they will have my baby in there.

The transporters walk to the side of Derek's bed 1 on each side and unlock the bed brakes and roll Derek to the surgery room.

6 HOURS LATER

It is now 6 hours later and the surgery is over. Clara is still sleep under the anesthesia and the transporters are now bring her back into her hospital room. First they park the bed where it was then they lock the bed locks so the bed won't roll.

Jan says she'll probably sleep another 15 or 20 minutes longer because she is still under the anesthesia. But after then she should be waking up.

Jeff says ok thank you.

Jan says you are welcome.

The transporters leave the room.

Grace walks to the side of the bed where Clara's face is and looks at her face.

Grace says oh my baby looks absolutely gorgeous. If I didn't know any better I wouldn't think this gorgeous woman used to be my gorgeous son. And now she's my gorgeous daughter.

Jeff says honny let me take a look at her.

Grace steps back and Jeff walks up to look at Clara's face.

Jeff says you are right she is gorgeous. I don't know how that doctor did it but he gave us a gorgeous daughter.

Now every one else takes a turn and goes to look at Clara's face. When they finish looking at Clara's face then she wakes up and sees all her family and friends still there waiting for her to wake up. Jeff and Grace see Clara wake up and he is in front of her as they both walk over to her on the same side of her bed.

Together Jeff and Grace says welcome to your new life.

Clara says thank you mother and dad.

Jeff says my daughter I am so happy you made it through surgery.

Grace says my daughter I am happy for you too.

Clara says thank you both.

Jeff gives Clara a hug.

Then Jeff steps back and Grace gives Clara a hug.

Grace looks at every one in the room and says excuse me every one. I am happy and proud to announce my new daughter Clara Styles.

Then every one claps their hands.
Tina says may I give her a hug?
Grace says sure.
Grace backs up and Tina gives Clara a hug.
Tina says welcome to your new life.
Clara says thank you.
Doug gives Clara a hug.
Doug says welcome to your new life.
Clara says thank you.
Mike gives Clara a hug.
Mike says welcome to your new life.
Clara says thank you.
Tommy gives Clara a hug.
Tommy says welcome to your new life.
Clara says thank you.
Gloria gives Clara a hug.
Gloria says welcome to your new life.
Clara says thank you.
Pam gives Clara a hug.
Pam says welcome to your new life.
Clara says thank you.
Angela gives Clara a hug.
Angela says welcome to your new life.
Clara says thank you.
Katrisha gives Clara a hug.
Katrisha says welcome to your new life.
Clara says thank you.
Jake gives Clara a hug.
Jake says welcome to your new life.
Clara says thank you.
Wendle gives Clara a hug.
Wendle says welcome to your new life.
Clara says thank you.
Deana gives Clara a hug.
Deana says welcome to your new life.
Clara says thank you.

When they all finish hugging Clara she picks up the remote control and pushes the button to call her nurse Gabriel.

Gabriel says may I help you?

Clara says may I please have 2 orange juices?

Gabriel says yes I will get it.

Clara says thank you.

Gabriel says you are welcome.

Gabriel turns off the call light. Then she goes to the break room and gets 2 orange juices and takes them to Clara's room.

Gabriel walks into the room and says excuse me do you want to continue to be called Derek or a different name?

Clara says I have changed my name to Clara Styles. Please call me Clara Styles.

Gabriel says ok Clara Styles here's the 2 orange juices you requested for.

Clara says thank you.

Gabriel says you are welcome. Welcome to your new life.

Clara says thank you.

Gabriel goes back to the nurse's station and sits in her chair and dials Dr. Hapchan's office number. Dr. Hapchan is in his office and the phone rings and he picks it up.

Dr. Hapchan says this is Dr. Hapchan may I help you?

Gabriel says Dr. Hapchan this is Gabriel.

Dr. Hapchan says ok.

Gabriel says you wanted me to call you when Derek wakes up from the surgery. Well she just called and asked for some orange juice and I took it to her. So I know she is awake now.

Dr. Hapchan says thank you for calling me I will go down to her room and talk to her about the surgery.

Gabriel says ok bye.

Dr. Hapchan says bye.

Then they both hang up their phone.

Gabriel grabs Clara's patient chart and writes the name Clara above the name Derek.

Dr. Hapchan walks into Clara's room and says hello every one.

Every one says hello.

Dr. Hapchan says do you still want to be called Derek or what name?

Clara says I have changed my name to Clara Styles. Please call me Clara Styles.

Dr. Hapchan says ok Clara Styles. How are you feeling?

Clara says I am feeling fine.

Dr. Hapchan says that is great. I am glad your surgery went perfect. But even though your surgery went fine and you said you feel fine I still want to keep you in here at least 1 more day because I want to make sure you don't feel any pain from walking around and from urinating. If walking around and urinating does not cause you any pain then I will discharge you tomorrow ok.

Clara says ok it sounds good to me.

Dr. Hapchan says plus on your patient chart I will keep your old name their but right above it I will write your new name ok.

Clara says that's fine.

Now Dr. Hapchan leaves the room.

Doug says Clara my furnace in my house isn't working right and it's going to be a few days before I can get it fixed. So can I spend a few nights at your house until my furnace gets fixed?

Clara says yes.

Doug says where are your keys?

Clara points to her pants and says look in my pants pocket right there.

Doug walks over to Clara's pants and reaches into the pocket and pulls out the house keys.

Doug says since you are letting me sleep at your house then I'll pick you up when you get discharged.

Clara says ok.

THE NEXT DAY

It is now the next day at Care Medical Center and Clara is in her patient room by herself watching television and Dr. Hapchan walks into her room.

Dr. Hapchan says hi Clara.

Clara says hi Dr. Hapchan.

Dr. Hapchan says how do you feel?

Clara says I feel wonderful. Yesterday after you left I got out of bed and tested my body to make sure I did not feel any pain. I walked around this floor plus got on the elevator and went downstairs and walked around down there. Plus I drank lots of liquid to make myself urinate and when I did I felt no pain at all. Dr. Hapchan I don't know how you did it but the way my body feels you did an excellent job. Thank you for giving me the operation.

Dr. Hapchan says you are welcome Clara. Well from what you are telling me when you exercise and urinate you feel no pain. So I would say you are ready to go home now.

Clara says thank you dr.

Dr. Hapchan says if you have any problems in the future please feel free to contact me.

Clara says I will

Dr. Hapchan leaves the room.

Clara get on the phone and dials the number to her house. Doug is there and when the phone rings he picks it up.

Doug says hello.

Clara says Doug this Clara.

Doug says ok.

Clara says the doctor has discharged me and I am now ready for you to come and pick me up from the hospital. I'll be ready when you get here.

Doug says ok.

Clara says bye.

Doug says bye.

They both hang up their phone. Now Clara starts putting on her street clothes. At the same time at Clara's house Doug is getting in his car and driving to the hospital. When he gets to Clara's room Clara is dressed in her street clothes and Doug walks in and they both give each other a hug.

Doug says sister I am glad you got better. Let's go home.

Clara says that sounds good to me.

Clara finish grabbing all her belongings and her and Doug leave the hospital and get in Doug's car and drive to Clara's house.

When Clara and Doug get on the front porch Doug says Clara since this is your house I want you to go in the door 1st.

Clara says ok.

Clara grabs the door knob and opens the door all the way.

At the same time in a loud voice all the family and friends says SURPRISE. Welcome back home and welcome to your new life.

Clara puts a shocked look on her face and says oh this is a beautiful surprise thank you all very much.

Then she closes the front door and looks at how gorgeous they decorated the inside of the house for the surprise party. She even notices how gorgeously decorated the cake is and how pretty they decorated the food on the table in the living room.

Clara says I don't mean to interrupt but for 2 minutes let me 1st put my things away in my bedroom.

So Clara walks to her bedroom and puts away every thing from the hospital then returns to the surprise party.

Now it is 2 hours later and Jeff and Grace and Clara are sitting in the living room on the couch.

Clara says mother this is going to be so wonderful. I now get to wear fancy skirts and fancy tops and fancy heels.

Grace says oh you and I have to go shopping together. Tina is a woman but with her being a masculine gay woman she doesn't like to wear skirts and fancy tops and heels. She likes to wear men's clothes. Now that you're a woman I can go shopping with at least 1 of my daughters.

Clara says I am looking forward to it. Mother I'll be back I am going to speak to Katrisha.

Two Women Are Opposite Sex

Grace says ok.

Clara walks around and eventually finds Katrisha in the kitchen.

Clara says hey girlfriend it is good to see you.

Katrisha says it is good to see you too. It is wonderful to have you back home and even in your new life. Now I have another close girlfriend I can go shopping with.

Clara says yes. I am looking forward to it. It is going to be so nice when I talk about my women friends if I call them my girlfriend or say another woman is cute people won't judge me as gay or lesbian. Instead they will judge me as perfectly normal. Plus it seemed a little funny when I went to urinate I couldn't stand up to do it I now have to sit down because I don't have a penis any more. I now have a vagina. Plus if I decide to get married. I can now marry a straight manly man.

Katrisha says are you thinking about getting married?

Clara says right now I am thinking about it. My biggest problem is trying to find a man who will really love me just the same as I will love him. And be a good husband to me just as I will be a good wife to him.

Katrisha says it looks like that's just the way things are going to be for me and Jake. He really loves me and I really love him. And the different times we've dated and did entertaining things together he has been very nice to me. And I enjoy being with him. Another thing I like about him until we're married he's never tried anything sexual with me. Oh he would be romantic with me but he's never tried to physically or verbally get me to have sex with him. Plus he's never cheated on me. He may not be a church goer but he's still a good man to me.

Clara says just the kind of man Jake is to you that's the kind of man I want for my self.

Katrisha says do you want to get married?

Clara says yes I do.

Katrisha says since you want to get married and you like manly men. Try talking to Mike.

Clara says MIKE! Katrisha that man likes men. He doesn't like women intimately. Plus in the past I am the 1 who ended the relationship. So I know that will never happen.

Katrisha says before you had your sex change and had every body at your house to announce about your operation. I heard you say it was

223

a difficult thing for you to end the relationship because you both still loved each other. At the same time you chose to be a woman because you were tired of being discriminated against. You weren't tired of Mike. Plus when you 2 talk to each other and hug each other. I can hear the sound in your voice and see the look in your faces that you both still love each other. Plus it hasn't been a long time yet that you ended the relationship. It's only been a short time still. So I know that in your heart you both still have some feelings for each other. Just like when you 1st meet some one you are not immediately in love with that person. It takes time for your feelings to grow for that person. At the same time when 2 people end a relationship that existed for a long period of time they may not be together physically but in their hearts they are still together emotionally. Because that love is still there. And I can see it with you and Mike. That love is still there.

Now outside Tina and Angela are sitting and talking to Mike.

Tina says boy Mike all these people here and most of them have some one to share their life with. Jeff and Grace are married to each other. Tommy and Gloria are engaged. Doug and Pam are engaged. Katrisha and Jake are engaged. Wendle and Deana are engaged. Me and Angela are not engaged but we are still sharing our life together. Mike when Clara was Derek and he invited every one to his house to announce his operation did you say that you both still love each other?

Mike says yes I did.

Tina says Mike I know I like the same sex but I also know rather you're with the same sex or the opposite sex when 2 people decide to end a romantic relationship their feelings don't immediately disappear. I can tell by the way you 2 look at each other and the sound in your voices that you 2 still love each other.

Mike says so what are you trying to say?

Tina says ask Clara to marry you since that love is still there.

Mike says but the love I have is for the man she used to be not for the woman she is now.

Tina says it's still the same body you are in love with he just changed his sex.

Mike says if we got in a straight relationship. SHE won't be anything like HE was.

Tina says I am going to ask you a personal question. Have you ever had sex with a woman?

Mike says no I have not.

Tina says well I have had sex with a man and I am a gay woman. If I like the way a woman feels then I know you will especially since you have a penis. Since you 2 still have feelings for each other talk to her and try being with a woman. I know from experience there is nothing like sharing your life with some one you're in love with and that person is in love with you. Angela I want a piece of cake. I wonder has Clara cut her cake yet? Let's go and see.

Mike stays outside while Tina and Angela go inside. While Tina and Angela are cutting a piece of cake for themselves, Clara comes outside where Mike is.

Clara sits down and says Mike I want to talk to you.

Mike says ok.

Clara says in the past when I ended our relationship. I am very sorry if I hurt your feelings.

Mike says ok.

Clara says have you ever been married to a woman?

Mike says no I have not.

Clara says have you ever had a romantic girlfriend before?

Mike says no I haven't.

Clara says have you ever just thought about having a romantic girlfriend before?

Mike says no I haven't.

Clara says would you like to try a relationship with a woman?

Mike says that is hard to say because I have never thought about it before.

Clara says Mike when I was a man I liked manly men. Now that I'm a woman I still like manly men. When I was a man you and I was in love with each other and to be honest with you I am still in love with you. How would you feel about being in a relationship with me?

Mike says I am still in love with Derek.

Clara says I am still Derek's body I just changed my sex and name. So if you're still in love with Derek then in a way of speaking you're still in love with me. Are you or are you not?

Mike says I guess in a way I am still in love with the body. I really did not think about a woman before but since the guy I love is now a woman I am thinking about trying to be straight so I am willing to give the relationship a try to see will I like a woman and will it work out.

Clara says Mike are you serious? Because I am serious about getting back into a relationship with you.

Mike says I am serious.

Clara says so at this moment are we back into a relationship?

Mike says yes at this moment we are back into a relationship.

Clara says good lets go to the living room and get more of my cake and ice-cream.

Mike says that sounds great.

When Mike and Clara get to the living room Clara starts cutting cake for her self at the same time Mike gets every one's attention.

Mike says excuse me may I have every one's attention?

Every one looks at Mike.

Mike says Clara and I had a talk and we've decided to get back together and get engaged to get married.

Every one claps their hands and says yaaaaay.

Now all the couples Tommy and Gloria Doug and Pam and Clara and Mike and Angela and Tina and Katrisha and Jake and Deana and Wendle are all at the jewelry store looking at engagement rings and wedding rings. Wendle picks out the rings he likes then Deana picks out the rings she likes. Then Katrisha picks out the rings she likes then Jake picks out the rings he likes. Then Clara and Mike pick out their rings. Then Doug and Pam pick out their rings. Then Tommy and Gloria pick out their rings. Then they all pay for their rings.

Now every body is at the church for the wedding ceremony. Tommy and Gloria are marrying each other. At the same time Doug and Pam are marrying each other. At the same time Mike and Clara are marrying each other. At the same time Jake and Katrisha are marrying each other. At the same time Wendle and Deana are marrying each other. Pastor Luke is standing in front of the church behind the podium wearing his white robe. Tommy is in his white tuxedo standing in front of the church on the right side facing the audience. Doug is in his white tuxedo standing a few feet away from Tommy facing the audience. Jake is in his white tuxedo standing on the left side of the church facing the audience. Wendle is in his white tuxedo standing a few feet away from Jake facing the audience. Mike is in his white tuxedo standing between the middle aisle and Wendle so the brides can walk down the middle aisle and turn. He is facing the audience. Angela and Tina are in the audience along with all the parents and family members and close friends of all the brides and grooms. Every body is now ready and the music starts. All the brides are wearing white wedding dresses. One bride at a time comes into the congregation area and walks down the aisle up to their groom. First Gloria walks down the aisle and turns right and walks up to Tommy and stands next to him. Next Pam walks down the aisle and turns right and walks up to Doug and stands next to him. Now Mike steps over between the middle aisle and Pam. Next Katrisha walks down the aisle and turns left and walks up to Jake and stands next to him. Next Deana walks down the aisle and turns left and walks up to Wendle and stands next to him. Then Mike steps back into the middle aisle and Clara walks down the aisle up to Mike and stands next to him. Then the music stops and all the brides and grooms face each other. Then Pastor Luke walks up to the side of Mike and Clara standing a foot away and starts talking to all the grooms and brides at the same time.

Pastor Luke says dearly beloved we are gathered together here today in the presence of God and the presence of these witnesses to join these men and these women together in holy matrimony which is commended to be honorable among all men and therefore- is not by any-to be intered into unadvisedly or lightly-but reverently, discreetly, advisedly and solemnly. Into this holy estate these brides and grooms now come to be joined. If any person can show just cause why they may not be joined – let them speak now or forever hold their peace.

Nobody speaks up.

Now Pastor Luke walks up to Tommy and Gloria.

Pastor Luke says Tommy Cloud do you take Gloria Rich to be your wife to love and to comfort and to cherish and to honor in health and in sickness for better and for worse for richer and for poorer in joy and in sadness. For as long as you both shall live?

Tommy says I do.

Pastor Luke says Gloria Rich do you take Tommy Cloud to be your husband to love and to comfort and to cherish and to honor in health and in sickness for better and for worse for richer and for poorer in joy and in sadness for as long as you both shall live?

Gloria says I do.

Pastor Luke says may we exchange rings please?

Tommy puts a ring on Gloria's finger then Gloria puts a ring on Tommy's finger.

Now Pastor Luke walks over to Doug and Pam.

Pastor Luke says Doug Styles do you take Pam Smart to be your wife to love and to comfort and to cherish and to honor in health and in sickness for better and for worse for richer and for poorer in joy and in sadness for as long as you both shall live.

Doug says I do.

Pastor Luke says Pam Smart do you take Doug Styles to be your husband to love and to comfort and do cherish and to honor in health and in sickness for richer and for poorer for better and for worse in joy and in sadness for as long as you both shall live?

Pam says I do.

Pastor Luke says may we exchange rings please?

Doug puts a ring on Pam's finger then Pam puts a ring on Doug's finger.

Now Pastor Luke walks over to Mike and Clara.

Pastor Luke says Mike Cloud do you take Clara Styles to be your wife to love and to comfort and to cherish and to honor in health and in sickness for richer and for poorer for better and for worse in joy and in sadness for as long as you both shall live?

Mike says I do.

Pastor Luke says Clara Styles do you take Mike Cloud to be your husband to love and to comfort and to cherish and to honor in health and in sickness for richer and for poorer for better and for worse in joy and in sadness for as long as you both shall live?

Clara says I do.

Pastor Luke says may we exchange rings please?

Mike puts a ring on Clara's finger then Clara puts a ring on Mike's finger.

Now Pastor Luke walks over to Jake and Katrisha.

Pastor Luke says Jake Bake do you take katrisha Cloud to be your wife to love and to comfort and to cherish and to honor in health and in sickness for richer and for poorer for better and for worse in joy and in sadness for as long as you both shall live?

Jake says I do.

Katrisha Cloud do you take Jake Bake to be your husband to love and to comfort and to cherish and to honor in health and in sickness for richer and for poorer for better and for worse in joy and in sadness for as long as you both shall live?

Katrisha says I do.

Pastor Luke says may we exchange rings please?

Jake puts a ring on Katrisha's finger then Katrisha puts a ring on Jake's finger.

Now Pastor Luke walks over to Wendle and Deana.

Pastor Luke says Wendle Velet do you take Deana Humor to be your wife to love and to comfort and to cherish and go honor in health and in sickness for richer and for poorer for better and for worse in joy and in sadness for as long as you both shall live?

Wendle says I do.

Deana Humor do you take Wendle Velet to be your husband to love and to comfort and to cherish and to honor in health and in sickness for richer and for poorer for better and for worse in joy and in sadness for as long as you both shall live?

Deana says I do.

Pastor Luke says may we exchange rings please?

Wendle puts a ring on Deana's finger then Deana puts a ring on Wendle's finger.

Now Pastor Luke walks back to the middle of the aisle and stands a foot away from Mike and Clara.

Pastor Luke says now by the power invested in me by the state and by the power of Almighty God I now pronounce you all husbands and wives. You grooms may kiss your brides.

Now all grooms kiss their brides.

6 MONTHS LATER

It is now 6 months later in the evening time at Katrisha and Jake's house. Katrisha and Jake are sitting in there kitchen and they're almost finished eating dinner.

Katrisha says I am so glad I am off work all next week. With the weekend off and during the week and the weekend after that I will have a total of 9 days off.

Jake says that is good honny. I want you to enjoy yourself because you are my wife and I want you to be happy.

Katrisha says honey I know you and I are going on a few days vacation Monday morning. How would you feel about it if I invited Marsha to come with me tonight for just 1 night on a get away trip?

Jake says who's Marsha?

Katrisha says a lady I met at The Fun Place. She said her husband is gone a lot because he's a truck driver and plus their kids live out of town. So most of the time she's home by herself. She needs to make some friends.

Jake says where are you going?

Katrisha says for driving there's a camping ground an hour and a half away from here in between city limits. It's called Sun Camp. I want to invite her for just 1 night. We'll go tonight and come back tomorrow night so I will be back in time for our vacation Monday morning. She seems like a very friendly lady. Will it be ok with you if I take her there tonight?

Jake says that sounds ok with me honny.

Katrisha says ok I will call the camping ground and see do they have any tents to rent.

Katrisha gets up and dials the number to the camping place. After she sees they do have only 1 tent left to rent she pushes down the button to hang up the phone then she picks the phone back up and dials Marsha's number. Marsha is at home and when her phone rings she picks it up.

Marsha says hello.

Katrisha says Marsha this is Katrisha how are you doing?

Marsha says I am fine.

Katrisha says do you remember me?

Marsha says yes I met you at The Fun Place.

Katrisha says do you have any plans for tonight?

Marsha says no I am just sitting here watching television.

Katrisha says how would you like to come with me to a camping ground for just 1 night?

Marsha says that sounds like fun thanks for inviting me. I'm looking forward to it.

Katrisha says so am I.

Marsha says now are you coming by my house to pick me up? Or do I come to your house? And who's car are we riding in?

Katrisha says I'll come by your house and pick you up and we'll go in my car. I know exactly where it's at. Can you be ready in 2 hours?

Marsha says I sure can.

Katrisha says ok I will see you in 2 hours.

Marsha says ok.

Katrisha says bye.

Marsha says bye.

They both hang up their phone.

Katrisha says honny I called Sun Camp and they have only 1 more tent to rent and I reserved it for me and Marsha. I also called Marsha and she said she would love to come tonight. So I'm gonna go and pack my clothes.

Jake says ok honny.

Now Katrisha goes to the bedroom and pulls out a small suit case and starts packing her clothes. When she finish she looks for Jake and finds him in the living room watching television and walks over to him.

Katrisha says bye honny I will see you tomorrow.

Jake says ok.

Then they give each other a good bye kiss.

Then Katrisha walks out the door to the car and opens the back door on the driver's side and puts her bag on the seat and closes the door, then opens the driver's door and gets in and drives to Marsha's house. When Katrisha gets to Marsha's house then Marsha puts her bag on the back seat on the passenger's side then she closes the door and gets in the front passenger's seat.

Marsha says hi Katrisha.

Katrisha says hi Marsha.

Katrisha starts driving to Sun Camp.

Marsha says thank you for inviting me.

Katrisha says you are very welcome. This will be some socialization for you. I was hoping you would remember me from The Fun Place.

Marsha says yes I did. But I've noticed I don't see you all in there any more.

Katrisha says 2 of my close boy friends had a bad experience in there so we all haven't gone anymore because we're all close to one another.

Marsha says I can understand that. I wish we could make this trip last for a few days.

Katrisha says that would be nice but my husband and I are going on vacation for a few days starting Monday morning. That's why you and I are coming back tomorrow night. So I can get a little bit of rest before the vacation trip with my husband. I noticed you are wearing a skirt for camping. Camping is mostly an outdoor casual recreation thing. You didn't wear pants for that?

Marsha says I don't like wearing pants. For my opinion pants are strictly a man's garment to make him look masculine. I feel a woman should wear a skirt because It makes her look more feminine and lady like.

Katrisha says do you belong to some religion that teaches that?

Marsha says no I don't belong to any religion I just like to wear skirts because I feel it helps me to look feminine like a lady should look. And that's why I wore a casual looking skirt. Casual for the occasion and skirt since I'm a lady. For the same reason that's why I am wearing casual jewelry. Casual for the occasion and jewelry since I am a lady.

Katrisha says ok not for myself but for yourself you wear skirts only and jewelry because it makes you look more lady like.

Marsha says yes. I would not feel comfortable if I wore pants like you are doing. How much do I owe you for your gas?

Katrisha says nothing at all. I am paying cash for the whole

trip.
Marsha says thank you.
Katrisha says you are welcome.
Marsha says how far is the camping ground?
Katrisha says in between city limits it's an hour and a half.

A FEW HOURS LATER

Now it is night time and Katrisha and Marsha are walking into the same tent and their separate sleeping bags are lying side by side with the head of both sleeping bags next to each other. Katrisha and Marsha climb into their own sleeping bag at the same time and lay on their back.

Before they go to sleep Marsha says I am looking so much forward to tomorrow.

Katrisha says I hope you enjoy yourself.

It is now 1 hour later and Katrisha is just starting to doze off to sleep she closes her eyes and Marsha is still awake. Marsha looks over at Katrisha and Marsha moves her head over to Katrisha's head and Marsha holds her lips on Katrisha's cheeks for 3 seconds and Katrisha feels Marsha's lips on her cheeks and immediately opens her eyes and raises herself up and scoots over 1 foot away and with a shocked look on her face and a mad sound in her voice.

Katrisha says did you just kiss me?

Marsha says I love a woman on top of me.

Katrisha stands all the way up and in a mad voice she says OH NO NO WAY! Are you gay?

Marsha says yes.

In a mad voice Katrisha says I have gay boy friends and even gay girl friends but I myself am all the way straight. You may love a woman on top of you but I love my husband on top of me. When you try to touch me in a sexual way I don't deal with you anymore bye.

In a mad way Katrisha picks up her sleeping bag and walks out of the tent and goes inside the camping office and still a mad look on her face and mad sound in her voice yelling at the camping cashier.

Katrisha says I just had a bad experience in my tent and I want my money back.

Katrisha puts the tent key on the counter.

The cashier raises both hands at the same time and takes a deep breath and 2 times turns his head from left to right and says ok.

The camping cashier opens the cash drawer and gives Katrisha her money back.

Katrisha walks out of the camping office going toward her car. Marsha is standing outside by the office and sees Katrisha coming outside going toward her car.

Marsha says Katrisha where are you going?

Katrisha says do me a favor and find another way home.

Marsha says what do you mean?

Katrisha says I told you I am all the way straight. I don't like women in a sexual way.

Katrisha gets in her car by herself and drives all the way back home. When Katrisha gets back home Jake is in the bedroom he's got the ceiling light off but the lamp on the night stand is turned on and he's lying in bed on his back and he's reading a book and feeling sleepy so he lays the book on the night stand and turns off the lamp and pulls the covers up to his shoulders. Then immediately Katrisha opens the bedroom door and flips the switch to turn on the ceiling light and Jake immediately opens his eyes and raises his self up in bed with a mad look on his face and a mad voice.

Jake says OH MY GOODNESS YOU SCARED ME! Honny I am happy to have you home but I thought you and Marsha were gone on a camping trip.

Katrisha sits on the bed and says we did go but after we got in our tent then I had a horrible experience.

Jake says honny what happened?

Katrisha says night time came and we both laid in our sleeping bags and I was dozing off to sleep and I felt some lips on my cheeks so I immediately opened my eyes and jumped up and asked Marsha did she just kiss me? She told me yes. Then I said are you gay? She said yes she loves a woman on top of her.

Jake says WHAT!

Katrisha says I told Marsha oh no no way I am all the way straight myself. I have got gay boy friends and even gay girl friends but when you try to touch me in a sexual way then I don't deal with you any more. Plus I told her you may love a woman on top of you but I love my husband on top of me. BYE! Then I left her there by herself. Jake I couldn't believe what I was hearing and experiencing. I never even suspected that Marsha was gay. She wasn't wearing men's clothes. She was wearing a skirt and some pretty jewelry around her neck and even on her wrist. And she was very feminine like you would expect a lady to be. Plus she said she is married and got kids. So when she kissed me and said she likes a woman on top of her it really shocked me. I totally did not expect that.

Jake put his arms around Katrisha and says honny I am very sorry you experienced some thing like that.

Now at Wendle and Deana's house Wendle and Deana are sitting in the living room on the couch watching the baseball games on a video.

Wendle says honny how would you feel about it if I invite Victor over to watch the games with us and spend the night?

Deana says who is Victor?

Wendle says a guy I met at The Fun Place. He was sitting at the table with us. He told me his wife works a lot so most of the time he's home by his self. I want to give him some one to hang out with for some socialization. Would you mind if I invite him over for the game and to spend the night?

Deana says I don't care.

Wendle picks up the phone and dials Victor's number. Victor is home and when the phone rings he picks it up.

Victor says hello.

Wendle says hi Victor this is Wendle. Do you remember me?

Victor says yes I remember you from The Fun Place.

Wendle says how would you like to come over and watch the baseball game with me and my wife and spend the night?

Victor says that sounds good.
Wendle says can you be here in 1 hour?
Victor says yes.
Wendle says ok I will see you in 1 hour bye.
Victor says bye.
Then they both hang up their phone.

It is now 1 hour later and Victor is at Wendle's door and rings the bell. Victor still has his mustache and is wearing a pair of blue jeans and a casual pull over shirt and a pair of old tennis shoes. Wendle goes to the door and opens it.

Wendle says hi Victor come on in.
Victor walks in and says hi.
Wendle says let me take your bag.

Wendle puts the bag in the hall closet. Deana is sitting on the couch and Wendle looks at Victor and points to Deana.

Wendle says this is my wife Deana.
Victor says it is good to meet you.
Deana says it is good to meet you too.
The phone rings and Deana picks it up and says hello.
Deana waits 10 seconds and says this is Deana.
Then Deana waits 20 seconds and says ok I will come in.
Then Deana waits 5 seconds and says bye.
Then Deana hangs up the phone and says honny my boss just called me and asked if I could come to work today because they are short of help. And I said I would. So I will see you and Victor tonight ok.

Wendle says ok honny.
Now Deana leaves for work.

At the same time Wendle says Victor if you are hungry we have plenty of hot brats' worth on the stove and plenty of cold soda in the refrigerator.

Victor says sure I will take some.
Wendle says come to the kitchen with me.

In the kitchen Wendle gives Victor a can of soda and 2 brats' worth sandwiches on a plate and hands it to Victor. Then puts 2 brats' worth on a plate for him self.

Wendle says lets go sit on the couch so we can see the television.

4 HOURS LATER

It is now 4 hours later and Wendle and Victor are still sitting on the couch. Victor is sitting right next to Wendle and Wendle is feeling sleepy and Victor is watching him doze off to sleep. The second Wendle dozes off to sleep Victor puts his lips on Wendle's cheeks kissing him hard and loud and Wendle feels it and immediately jumps up and looks at Victor.
    Wendle says did you just kiss me?
    Victor says yes.
    Wendle puts a mad look on his face and in a mad voice says are you gay?
    Victor says yes. I love lying on top of a man.
    Wendle continues with his mad face and voice and says well you won't get on top of me. I love lying on top of my wife. I have gay girl friends and even gay boyfriends but I my self am straight all the way. When you get sexual with me I don't deal with you any more. Man if you don't get out of my house right now I will end up in prison because I will seriously hurt you.
    Victor says may I please have my bag?
    Wendle goes to the closet and grabs Victor's bag and hands it to him.
    In a firm voice Wendle says GET OUT!
    Victor leaves the house.

5 HOURS LATER

It is now 5 hours later at night and Deana comes home from work and sees Wendle sitting on the couch by himself watching the game.
    Deana says I thought Victor was going to watch the game with you and spend the night? Where is he at?
    Wendle says I made him go home.

Deana says well after you invited him here then you made him go home? That was mighty rude.

Wendle says honny he made a pass at me. He kissed me on my cheek and told me he likes to lay on top of a man.

Deana says WHAT!

Wendle says yes. That really shocked me too because I never seen any thing like that in him. He wasn't wearing women's clothes he was wearing men's clothes. Plus he wasn't feminine he was very masculine like you would expect a man to be. Then he also told me he has a wife and kids. Because of all those facts together I thought he was straight.

Deana says honny just because a man is wearing men's clothes it doesn't mean he is straight. He could be straight or gay or bi-sexual either way. If a man wears women clothes he could be straight or gay or bi-sexual either way. If a man is masculine he could be straight or gay or bi-sexual either way. If a man is feminine he could be straight or gay or bi-sexual either way. If a man is married to a woman he could be straight or gay or bi-sexual. If a man has got kids he could be straight or gay or bi-sexual. It is the same way with women. Just because a woman is wearing women's clothes It doesn't mean she is straight. She could be gay or bi-sexual either way. Just because a woman is wearing men's clothes it doesn't mean she is gay. She could be straight or bi-sexual either way. Just because a woman is feminine it doesn't mean she is straight she could be gay or bi- sexual either way. Just because a woman masculine it doesn't mean she is gay she could straight or bi-sexual either way. Just because a woman is married to a man it doesn't mean she is straight she could be gay or bi-sexual either way. Just because a woman has got kids it doesn't mean she is straight she could be gay or bi-sexual either way. When you sum up all these points now-a-days you can't only judge by outward appearance any more. You've got to see what's on the inside. Yes there is still a lot of straight people in this world and you and I are a part of the straight people. Plus just because some one has no kids and likes being single that doesn't make him or her gay either. But there is also a lot of gay people that you can not see by their outward appearance.

Now at Good Quality Pam Styles is now working in the men's department as a cashier and she has just finished ringing a male

Two Women Are Opposite Sex

customer's order she is putting his order in a plastic bag along with the receipt and gives the customer the bag.

Pam says have a good day.

There are no other customers in line.

Pam says Shirley I am going on break now.

Shirley says ok.

Pam walks to the men's department. In the men's department Pam walks up to the counter and sees Doug working with his last customer before break and is bagging a female customer's order. The lady customer has just bought 14 pairs of panties and 14 bras. When Doug has finished bagging the clothes he hands the bag to the lady.

Pam says Doug are you ready to go on break with me?

Doug says yes. Tina I am going on break now.

Tina says ok.

Doug and Pam are walking to the break room.

Doug says honny I need to go to the bathroom please wait for me in the break room.

Pam says ok.

Doug goes to the bathroom and Pam goes to the break room and sits down. When Doug comes to the break room he sits next to Pam.

Pam says how do you like working in the women's department?

Doug says it's nice I get to look at skirts and tops and dresses structured in a fancy way. But to me the work is no different than the men's department. Our new boss doesn't discriminate. Just like women work with men items so the men also work with women items.

It is now 2 hours later in the women's department and Tina has come to work the evening shift. Doug is finished with his last customer for the day.

Doug says Tina I will see you later I am off now.

Tina says ok.

Doug walks over to the men's department. When he gets up to the counter he sees Pam working with her last customer for the day. The male customer is buying 14 pairs of underwear and 14 shirts and 1 pack of Viagra. First Pam is putting the t-shirts in a plastic bag then 2nd she puts the underwear in the bag then the pack of Viagra then the receipt then closes the bag.

Pam says you have a nice day.

Pam looks at Shirley and says Shirley I am off now I will see you later.

Shirley says bye.

Pam says honny I am ready to leave now.

Doug says ok lets go.

Pam and Doug are in the car.

Doug says honny there are times when I feel my heart is beating faster than it should. This problem comes and goes occasionally. So if there is nothing you have to take care of then we'll 1st stop by the hospital and have a doctor check my heart.

Pam says no I don't have any thing I have to do besides cooking dinner. But we can eat out some where. Second of all honny you don't take chances with your health. Yes by all means let's go and get that checked out.

Doug says I am going to the same hospital that Clara was at Care Medical Center.

Pam says that's fine with me.

Now Doug and Pam are at the hospital sitting in the emergency room and waiting for the nurse to call Doug's name.

Pam says honny I will be right back I have to go urinate real bad.

They both can see the men's and women's bathroom from where they both are sitting. Both bathrooms are right next to each other. Doug and the other patients can see Pam knocking on the door to the women's bathroom.

Inside the bathroom the lady patient says some one is in here.

In a frustrated voice Pam says man I am about to urinate on myself.

Then Pam looks at the men's bathroom door.

Pam says as bad as I hate to do this.

She knocks on the men's bathroom door and gets no response because nobody is in there.

Doug sees it when Pam opens the bathroom door all the way and sees that it's empty and goes in. Now in the women's bathroom the patient lady comes out. Now 1st Pam finishes and comes out of the men's bathroom and goes back to sit next to Doug. Now 2nd Pam and Doug don't see it when a male patient goes to the men's bathroom.

Doug says honny I took an exlax and it's working on me. I'll be right back.

Pam sees Doug when he is standing in front of the men's bathroom and knocks on the door.

The male patient says someone is in here.

In a frustrated voice Dou says shshshshoot! I'm about to mess my pants.

Now Pam sees Doug knocking on the door to the women's bathroom. Nobody is in there so he doesn't hear any thing. Pam sees him open the door all the way and they see nobody is in there then she sees him go in there. Now Doug has finished in the bathroom and comes out and goes back to the waiting room and sits next to Pam.

Now the nurse Kimberly comes to the door with the clip board and speaks loud enough to be heard by every one in the waiting room.

The Kimberly says DOUG STYLES.

Doug says that's me.

Doug and Pam get up and walk toward the nurse.

Pam says I am his wife so I will come with him.

Kimberly says just follow me.

Doug and Pam says ok.

Kimberly walks them to the exam room and says you both wait in here until the doctor comes.

Kimberly pulls out a hospital gown for Doug to put on and hands it to him and says when I leave put this on and sit on the exam bed.

Doug says ok.

Kimberly walks out of the exam room and closes the door then Doug changes his clothes into the hospital gown. When he is done he sits on the exam bed. Then the lady doctor Cindy comes in with her chart.

Cindy says hello I am Dr. Cindy Pen. I will be your doctor. Now before I go any further let me say this. We've been having some patients to request for doctors of the same sex and some patients request for doctors of the opposite sex. Do you have any problem with a doctor of the opposite sex?

Doug says as long as my wife is in here with me it is fine with me.

Dr. Pen looks at Pam and says is it ok with you Mrs. Styles?

Pam says as long as I am in here it is fine with me.

Then Pam notices Cindy's face and says Dr. Pen years ago did you go to a high school called Wise High School?

Dr. Pen says yes I did.

Pam says I thought your face looked familiar. Do you remember me Pam. My maiden name is Smart. Pam Smart.

Dr. Pen took a 2nd look at Pam's face and says yes I remember you.

Pam says girlfriend come here and give me a hug and kiss.

They both hugged and kissed each other on the cheeks.

Pam says girlfriend you haven't changed a bit. You look just as cute now as you did in high school.

Dr. Pen says thank you. You look cute too.

Pam says and you became a doctor.

Dr. Pen says yes it's what I've always wanted to be.

Pam says girlfriend I am so proud of you.

Dr. Pen says thank you girlfriend.

Dr. Pen says Mr. Styles according to your chart occasionally you've been having problems with your heart beating faster than it should.

Doug says yes I have.

Dr. Pen hooks the earpiece of her stethoscope to her ears and puts the other end on Doug's chest to check his heart beat.

When she finishes she says I am hearing a normal heart beat. But before I prescribe any medicine I need to know when you cook do you eat a lot of fried foods?

Doug says yes.

Dr. Pen says do you use salt?

Doug says yes.

Dr. Pen says well when you fry stop using salt. We are going to see will that help your heart beat right again. Come back to me in 1 month and I want to see how you are feeling ok.

Doug says ok.

Dr. Pen says I'd rather tell a person how to protect their health rather than prescribe medicine.

Doug says it sounds good to me.

Dr. Pen says I will see you in 1 month from today ok.

Doug says ok. Oh by the way did you and Pam say you both went to the same high school?

Dr. Pen says yes.

Doug says would you ladies believe I graduated from there too.

Dr. Pen says that's amazing all 3 of us went to the same high school.

Pam says I had no ideal that 1 of the same guys I went to high school with I would be sharing the rest of my life with him.

Doug says Dr. Pen knowing that you wanted to be a doctor. When you were in high school and know that you had to put a lot of time into studying your books did you have any time to socialize with your friends?

Dr. Pen says well I had time to socialize with my friends but I made sure most of the time I hung around my girlfriends rather than my boyfriends because I wanted to make sure the boys did not try to get me into a romantic relationship until I finished all my schooling and got into my career and started buying a home. And so now that I am full time in my career and buying a home. I got blessed. A very nice male doctor approached me and asked me to marry him. And we have 2 kids a girl and a boy. So now I feel like I can't ask for any thing more. First of all and most important of all I have a wonderful god in my life. Our Heavenly Father, he's the most loving and powerful person throughout the ENTIRE universe. When showing love and power nobody can beat him or even match him. Second of all I have a career I love and I also have a wonder loving husband and 2 wonderful kids that we love. And also in between my god and my family and career I also have time for a social life. What about you did you have time for socializing with girlfriends and boyfriends?

Doug says I had time and since at that time I wasn't really thinking a lot about a career I hung around both my girlfriends and my boyfriends equally. Even now I hang around my girlfriends and my boyfriends equally. Dr. Pen I am curious did your husband go to Wise High School?

Dr. Pen says no he went to a different high school but had the same kind of dream to be a doctor.

Then Dr. Pen reaches into her pocket and pulls out a picture of her and her husband on their wedding day.

Dr. Pen says here is a picture of him on our wedding day. His name is Brad.

First Dr. Pen hands the picture to Doug. Doug looks at the picture for 5 seconds.

Doug says he's cute.

Dr. Pen says thank you.

Pam says Dr. Pen can I see the picture?

Dr. Pen says sure.

Doug hands the picture to Pam. Pam looks at the picture for 5 seconds.

Pam says Dr. Pen you looked cute in your wedding dress.

Dr. Pen says thank you.

Pam hands the picture back to Dr. Pen. Dr. Pen puts the picture back into her pocket.

Dr. Pen says Mr. Styles I will see you in 1 month from today.

Doug says ok.

Dr. Pen leaves the room. Doug now puts his street clothes back on.

Now Dr. Pen is sitting at the nurses station and flips through Doug's file to the page where Doug's home phone is and see the page and writes it down on a piece of note pad paper. When she is done she closes the file and puts it away.

It is now the next day at Doug and Pam's house. Pam is at home by herself and the phone rings and she picks it up.

Pam says hello.

Dr. Pen says hi this is Dr. Pen from Care Medical Center. May I please speak to Doug Styles or his wife?

Pam says Doug is at work this is his wife Pam Styles may I help you?

Dr. Pen says my husband and I are having a social gathering at our house for all our patients. And since me and you and Doug all went to the same high school together I want you and Doug to come to the party so you can meet my husband Brad. Don't bring any food my husband and I are doing a catering for all of his and my patients. It will be at 5pm this evening. Will you come?

Pam says sure I will tell Doug as soon as he gets home.

Dr. Pen says ok. I will see you tonight.

Pam says ok bye.

Dr. Pen says bye.

Then they both hang up the phone.

Now Pam drives to Good Quality, when she gets there she walks to the men's department where the pants are then she finds her size and puts the pants in the cart. Then Pam walks over to the men's shirts and looks for her size then puts the shirt in the cart. Then Pam walks over to the men socks and puts her size in her cart. Then Pam walks over to the men shoes and finds her size then puts them in the cart. Then she walks to the dressing room and takes her clothes out of the cart and goes into the dressing room and closes the door and lays her clothes down on the seat and takes her women clothes off and puts on the stores clothes. When she finish dressing she looks in the mirror to make sure the clothes look and feel right on her. After she sees that they look right then she takes off the stores clothes and puts her women clothes back on. Then she picks up the stores clothes and walks out of the dressing room and puts the clothes back in the cart and walks to the cashier. Tina is at the men's cashier by herself.

Tina says how are you doing Pam?

Pam says fine.

Tina says are you buying Doug some new clothes?

Pam says no these are for me. Since they are cheaper than some women's clothes I just want to see how they feel on me and if I like wearing men's clothes.

Tina starts ringing the price of the clothes and says oh I don't blame you. Honny you know me I don't wear nothing but men's clothes. I don't like wearing dresses or skirts. And not because I am a lesbian but I just think men's clothes are more comfortable. So that is why I wear them. Do you think it would bother Doug for you to wear men's clothes?

Pam says I don't think it would bother him. I have done a lot of other feminine things that women do and it did not bother him. So I don't see how this would bother him. Then Tina finishes the sale transaction.

Tina says you have a good day.

Pam says you too.

Pam goes back home. When she get home she goes to the bedroom changes into her men's clothes. After she finish changing then she walks to the living room then Doug walks in the door.

Doug says honny what did you cook for dinner?

Pam says I didn't cook because earlier Dr. Pen called.

In a scared voice Doug says oh my goodness is there something wrong with me?

Pam says oh no honny she called to invite all her patients to her and her husbands house for dinner. She said since you and I and her went to the same school she wants us to come and meet her husband. I thought It was very nice of them.

Doug says it was very nice of them to invite us. What food do we take?

Pam says Dr. Pen says her and her husband are doing a catering dinner. So we don't bring any food.

Doug says what time does it start?

Pam says at 5pm.

Doug says did you get some new clothes?

Pam says yes I just got these today from work.

Doug says it doesn't bother you to wear men's clothes?

Pam says since some are cheaper I wanted to see how they will feel on me and if I'll like it.

Doug says how do they feel on you?

Pam says well I just put them on and so far they feel comfortable. Honny I respect your feelings on this. Does it bother you for me to wear men's clothes?

Doug says my only concern is that you are not a lesbian rather open about it or in secret. I don't want a gay wife. I want strictly a wife who's all the way straight.

Pam says honny I promise you I am all the way straight. I would never deceive you in any way. And especially not with my sex life or even sexual preference. I love you way too much to do something like that.

Doug opens his arms and says come here.

Pam walks into his arms then they hug and kiss each other.

It is now 4:45pm and Pam looks at her watch.

Pam says honny we better get to the doctor's house.

Pam is still wearing men's clothes until she gets back home. When they get to the doctor's house they ring the doorbell. Cindy Pen and Brad Pen are both sitting in the dinning room eating when the door bell rings. Cindy and Brad walk to the door and greet Pam and Doug.

Cindy says hi come on in.

Doug and Pam step inside and see people in the living room and kitchen.

Cindy says I want you 2 to meet my husband.

Cindy points to Brad and says this is my husband Brad Pen. He's a doctor too. Honny this is Pam and Doug.

Cindy points to Doug and Pam and says honny this is Doug and Pam. Plus me and Pam and Doug all went to the same high school together.

Brad says that is neat.

Cindy says girlfriend give me a hug and kiss.

Doug is looking at Pam.

Pam walks into Cindy's arms and they hug each other and kiss on the cheeks.

Brad says Doug even though we didn't go to the same school together but still your face looks familiar. Were you raised up on Unity Street?

Doug says yes.

Brad says you and I were raised up on the same street we were close friends just like brothers. Good to see you again boyfriend.

Doug says good to see you again too.

Brad says come here and give me a hug and kiss.

Pam is looking at Doug.

Doug walks into Brad's arms and they hug and kiss each other on the cheeks.

Doug says when Cindy showed me your picture I thought your face looked familiar. Now that you said some thing I know for sure it was you.

Cindy says Doug and Pam welcome to our home.

Doug and Pam both say thank you.

Real happily Cindy says boy Pam other than the other day in the hospital exam room you and I haven't seen each other in years.

Pam says I know it's been too long.

Brad says Doug this is amazing we both grew up together and later you went to school with my wife. Welcome to my home.

Doug says thank you. This is very nice of you to invite us.

Brad says let us show you both where the food is.

Doug says ok I'm hungry.

Cindy and Brad take Doug and Pam to the dinning room where the food is.

Cindy says here's a wide variety.

Real happily Doug says boy all this food looks good.

Brad says help yourself and enjoy.

Pam says this is amazing. Someone I became close friends with became a doctor.

Now 1st Cindy and Brad grab their chair and sit back down and continue eating their food. Then 2nd Doug and Pam grab a plate and put food on it. When they fill up their plate they start looking around for empty chairs and notices they can't find any.

Pam says Cindy do you have any more empty chairs we can sit on while we eat our food?

Cindy says let me look in the storage room and the basement.

Cindy walks to the storage room and turns the light on and looks around and doesn't see any empty chairs then turns the light off. Next Cindy walks to the basement and turns the light on and looks around and still doesn't see any empty chairs and turns the light off. Then she goes back to the dinning room.

Cindy says Pam and Doug I am very sorry I looked all around the storage room and all around the basement and I didn't realize we had all the fold up chairs pulled out and being used by other guess.

Cindy and Brad sit down in their seat.

Cindy says Pam I have an ideal you can just sit on my lap.

Pam sits on Cindy's lap and they eat their food.

Brad says Doug you can sit on my lap.

Pam is watching Doug.

Doug sits on Brad's lap and they both eat their food.

Two Women Are Opposite Sex

Pam says how often do you both invite your patients over for a meal?

Brad says we like to do this around every 6 months around middle summer and again around late fall before winter comes in.

Cindy says what I like about it is it helps us to build a close relationship with our patients. Because to me it's a way of saying in my heart you are more than my patient. You are my friend. I'll be more than your doctor that you can trust. I'll also be your friend that you can trust. Because just think when you trust someone with your health and your life don't you want it to be someone you know well and have built a closeness with them?

Pam and Doug says sure.

Brad says that's why we do it. Plus just because we have good money coming in and have a gorgeous home it doesn't make us any better than someone with a lot less.

Cindy says that's another thing I like about it. It teaches us to be humble. Just because you have more materially than someone else it doesn't make you any better than that person. Because to God we all are still equal to one another.

Doug says how many rooms do you have?

Brad says we have 8 large bedrooms and 2 ½ large bathrooms and 1 large living room and 1 large sitting room and 1 large kitchen and 1 large dinning room and a 4 car garage. This house cost us $1,180,000.00. We're paying $3,277.09 per month to the bank.

It is now 4 hours later at the doctor's house and all the other guess have gone home.

Pam says well thanks again Cindy and Brad for inviting us we really enjoyed the food and association.

Doug says we did thank you both very much.

Brad and Cindy both say you both are very welcome.

Pam says I want to run an arron before Doug and I go home so we'll be leaving now.

Cindy says ok.

Cindy and Pam give each other a hug and say to each other I love you.

At the same time Pam sees Brad and Doug hug each other and say to each other I love you.

Now Doug and Pam leave the doctor's house.

While they are in the car Doug says honny did you say before we go home you want to run an arron?

Pam says yes I want to go to the retail store and get a few items.

Doug says are you talking about the store we work at?

Pam says yes.

Now Doug parks the car at Good Quality and Doug stays in the car and Pam walks to the men's department where the pajama pants are when she finds her size she puts it in the cart. Then she walks over to the pajama shirts and finds her size then she puts the shirt in the cart. Then she walks over to the pajama robe and when she finds her size then she puts it in the cart and walks to the cashier.

Tina says I see you are buying more clothes. Did Doug see you wearing the pants and shirt and shoes you bought?

Pam says yes he did.

Tina says did he complaint?

Pam says I don't mean any harm toward you but he said his only concern was that I am not a lesbian rather open about it or in secret about it. I understand his point since he's married to me.

Tina says I understand his point to since he's straight. With me being a lesbian and in a gay relationship I would not want Angela to be straight rather open about it or in secret.

Pam says I told Doug he has nothing to worry about I love him way too much to do him like that.

Tina says I feel the same way about Angela and I strongly believe Angela feels the same way about me.

Tina is now finished with the transaction and has put the clothes in a plastic bag and says Pam you have a good day.

Pam says you too bye.

Tina says bye.

Pam goes back to the car and gets in and Doug drives home.

When they get in the house they go to the bedroom and Pam takes out her new pajamas and lays them on the bed and puts her new robe

Two Women Are Opposite Sex

in the closet and changes into her pajamas. At the same time Doug takes pajamas out of his dresser drawer and changes into them.

When they both are finished changing Pam says honny do you like my new pajamas?

Doug looks at them and says honny they look nice.

Pam says since I have to work tomorrow I am getting in the bed now.

Doug says I am off tomorrow but since I ate I am on a full stomach so I am feeling sleepy now. So I am going to bed too.

Then they both lay in bed.

Pam says I don't like how they did our work schedule for this week. For today you worked and I was off. Now tomorrow I am working and you are off. I like it better when they schedule us to work the same day and be off the same day.

Doug says me too. That way we can spend more time together.

It is now the next day and Doug is at Good Quality looking at the women's skirts. When he finds a skirt his size he puts it in his cart. Then Doug walks over to the women tops and looks for his size when he finds it he puts it in his cart. Then he walks over to the pantyhose and looks for his size and puts them in his cart. Then he walks over to the women's heels and looks for his size then puts them in his cart. Then he walks to the cashier and Shirley is behind the counter and she is almost finished with her present customer. She is putting the lady customer dresses and pants in a plastic bag along with the receipt.

Shirley says you have a good day.

The lady customer leaves.

Shirley says Doug come on up.

Doug walks up to the counter.

Doug says hi Shirley.

Shirley says hi Doug.

Shirley starts the transaction and says looks like you picked out some nice clothes.

Doug says thanks.

When Shirley finishes the transaction she puts all the clothes in the plastic bag with the receipt and closes the bag.

Shirley says you have a nice day off Doug.

Doug says thanks I will.

LATER THAT EVENING

Later that evening Doug is at home in the bedroom and he has just finished putting on the women's clothes he bought earlier. The only thing he has left to put on is his shoes so now he sits on the bed and at the same time Pam walks into the bedroom and gives Doug a kiss on the lips.

Pam says hi honny.

Doug says hi honny.

Doug puts the shoes on and stands up and faces Pam.

Doug says how did your day go today?

Pam says it went ok. Did you get some new clothes?

Doug says yes I just got these today from work.

Pam says does it bother you to wear women clothes?

Doug says since some are cheaper I wanted to see how they would feel on me and if I would like wearing them.

Pam says do they feel comfortable on you?

Doug says VERY COMFORTABLE. Well you respected my feelings on this so I respect your feelings. Does it bother you for me to wear women's clothes?

Pam says Doug honny I am just like you. As long as you are not gay I am fine with it.

Doug says honny I am just like you I am strictly straight all the way. I would never deceive you in any way especially about my sex life or sexual preference. I love you way too much to do something like that.

Pam opens her arms and says come here.

Doug walks into Pam's arms and they hug and kiss each other.

Pam says we both are strictly straight all the way.

Doug says good that's right.

Pam says I need to go to the kitchen right quick.

Pam walks into the kitchen and looks in the refrigerator and speaks loud enough for Doug to hear her.

Pam says honny we need to get some groceries.

Doug walks into the kitchen and says when are we going to the grocery store?

Pam looks at Doug and sees he is still wearing the skirt and puts a hesitant look on her face.

Pam says now. Are you sure you want to go grocery shopping? I will go by myself.

Doug says honny I will go with you.

Pam says ok.

Pam walks to the bedroom and puts on men pants and a men's shirt and men's shoes.

Pam walks out of the bedroom and says are you ready now?

Doug says sure.

They both get in the car and drive to the grocery store. While at the store Pam is pushing the grocery cart. She tries to stay around 8 feet away from Doug. Pam notices how customers are staring at Doug wearing a skirt and she feels embarrassed. Doug picks up an item and looks up and sees Pam is about 8 feet away from him with the cart. Doug walks up to her.

Dou says honny here.

Then he puts the item in the cart then Pam puts and item in the cart and moves 8 feet away from Doug. Every time Doug picks up an item to put in the cart he looks up and Pam is 8 feet away from him. Doug has to keep calling her name and saying wait for him. He brings the item up to the cart and puts it in and Pam puts her item in and moves the cart 8 feet away from him. This keeps happening until the cart is filled to the rim. When the cart is filled up then Pam puts her last item in the cart and with an embarrassing look in her face.

Pam says Doug I am done lets go to the cashier and go home Doug says ok.

Now Doug and Pam are back home and they have just finished putting the groceries away.

Doug says honny I need to run an arron right quick there's something I forgot.

Pam says ok.

Doug gets in the car and drives to Good Quality. When he gets inside he walks to the women's department and flips through the pajama tops until he finds his size. When he finds it then he lays it in his cart and looks for the matching pajama pants. When he finds it then he lays it in his cart. Then he walks over to the robes and when he finds his size then he puts it in his cart and walks to the cashier.

When Doug gets back home he carries the plastic bag to the bedroom. When he gets there Pam is standing in front of the dresser looking into the mirror she has just finished putting on her men's pajamas. Doug takes off his skirt and top and heels and puts on his women's pajamas and they both climb in bed and hug each other.

Doug says honny I agree with you I don't like our schedule tomorrow either. I work and you are off.

Pam says I know.

It is now the next day and Pam is standing at Angela's front door and rings the doorbell. Angela comes and opens the door.

Angela says hi Pam come on in.

Pam says hi.

Pam comes in and stands at the door and says good to see you.

Angela says would you like something to eat or drink?

Pam says no thank you I just need to talk to you.

Angela says ok I have time to talk go ahead.

Pam says I have noticed Doug doing and saying things that I feel uncomfortable with. And so now I feel I want a divorce.

Angela says oh my goodness.

Pam says can you help me with a divorce in court?

Angela says to be honest with you as much as I love being a lawyer. I would not feel right helping you to divorce Doug.

Pam says I do not mean to be rude but why?

Angela says I have become close friends with both of you. I would not like to fight Doug to help you divorce him. At the same time I do not want to fight you to help Doug divorce you. If I go against either 1 of you then I am not being a friend. Even though I have known Doug longer but still since you 2 were engaged at Derek's house. I have known you every since and now I feel close to you both equally. So I am sorry but I can not help you with a divorce. You will have to find another lawyer.

Two Women Are Opposite Sex

Pam says I understand. I never thought about it like that so I do understand. I will go find another lawyer.

Angela says ok.

Pam says you have a good day.

Angela says you have a good day too.

Now Pam leaves and drives to the court house.

At the court house Pam is in the court clerk's office talking to Peter the court clerk.

Pam says I want to file for a divorce.

Peter says ok.

Peter walks to the file cabinet where the divorce forms are kept and opens the drawer and takes out the forms and walks back over to Pam and hands the forms to her.

Pam says how much does it cost to get a lawyer to help you with a divorce?

Peter says that depends on a number of things. For 1 thing it depends on how much the lawyer charges for their services. Plus you do not have to have a lawyer for a divorce. A lawyer can help you out a lot. But you do not have to have a lawyer.

Pam says ok I will save some money and not get a lawyer and just get a divorce.

Peter says we have a new judge now. At first it was Judge Sherri but she resigned. And I really missed her too because she was very fair. She treated every body the same regardless. At the same time I understand she was offered a higher paying judges job in a different state so her and her husband moved out of state. Our new judge now her name is Eloise.

Pam says I just hope she does every thing by law and is fair.

Peter says that we will find out.

Pam sits in a chair and starts filling out her forms. When she finish filling out the forms she takes them back to Peter.

Peter says thank you. I will give these to Judge Eloise.

Pam says thank you and leaves the office.

Later that evening at Doug and Pam's house they are in the living room watching television and Pam picks up the remote control and turns off the television.

Pam says honny I have some bad news for you.
Doug puts a curious look on his face.
Doug says what Is wrong?
Pam says I want a divorce.
In a mad voice Doug says WHAT! A divorce for what?
Pam says Doug you have been saying and doing some things I feel uncomfortable with.
Doug says what did I do?
Pam says Doug you totally embarrassed me the other day when we went grocery shopping and you wore a skirt.
Doug says honny I asked you did it bother you for me to wear women clothes and you said as long as I was not gay rather open or in secret about it then it did not bother you.
Pam says plus when you went to bed at night you wear women's pajamas. Doug please be honest with me. Are you having sex with men?
Doug puts a frustrated look on his face and says no way.
Pam says I am sorry Doug but I have a hard time believing that.
Doug says oh my god. I can not believe what I am hearing. If you do not believe me then why did you even ask me.
Pam says I wanted to see would you be honest with me. I have already filed for a divorce.
Doug puts a shocked look on his face and says YOU ALREADY DID WHAT!
Pam says I have already filed for a divorce.
Doug says Pam do you still love me?
Pam says I can not love a man in an intimate way when he is giving me the impression he is gay.
Doug says Pam do you still love me just says yes or no.
Pam says I am sorry Doug but no I do not.
In a frustrated voice Doug says I can not believe this is coming from my own wife. First you tell me you want a divorce then you say you think I am gay then you say you do not love me any more.
Pam says Doug I will be back. I want to treat my self to a movie.
Doug says would you like me to come with you?
Pam says I will go by my self.
Doug says ok.

Pam leaves the house. After Pam leaves then the phone rings and Doug walks to the phone and picks it up.

Doug says hello.

Jake says hi Doug this is Jake can Katrisha and I come over to socialize for a while?

Doug says sure come on over. You and Katrisha were on Vacation. How was it?

Jake says it was fun but we came back early because Katrisha was tired and I wanted her to get some rest before going back to work so we are back early.

Doug says I am glad you enjoyed your self. So come on over.

Jake says ok we will see you in a few minutes.

Doug says ok.

Jake says bye.

Doug says be.

Then they both hang up their phone. Then Doug walks a few steps away from the phone and the phone rings again and Doug walks back to the phone and picks it up.

Doug says hello.

Tommy says hi Doug this is Tommy.

Doug says ok.

Tommy says can me and Gloria come over for a while to socialize?

Doug says that is fine come on over.

Tommy says ok we will see you in a few minutes.

Doug says ok.

Tommy says bye.

Doug says bye.

Then they both hang up their phone. Then Doug walks a few steps away from the phone and the phone rings again and Doug walks back to the phone and picks it up.

Doug says hello.

Mike says hi Doug this is Mike will it be ok if Clara and I come over for a while and socialize?

Doug says come on over.

Mike says ok we are on our way.

Doug says ok.

Mike says bye.
Doug says bye.
Then they both hang up their phone. Doug walks a few steps away from the phone and the phone rings again and Doug walks back to the phone and picks it up.
Doug says hello.
Wendle says hi Doug this is Wendle.
Doug says ok.
Wendle says do you mind if Clara and I come over for a while to socialize?
Doug says that is fine come on over.
Wendle says ok we will see you in a few minutes bye.
Doug says bye.
Then they both hang up their phone. Doug walks a few steps away from the phone and the phone rings again and Doug walks back to the phone and picks it up.
Doug says hello.
Grace says hello son how are you doing?
Doug says I am ok. Thank God I am still living.
Grace says well I most definitely thank God too. You are my son and I love having you around. I want my kids to live forever. By the way me and your father want to know if we can come over for a while just to socialize?
Doug says sure I would love to have my parents here. Come on over.
Grace says thanks son we will see you in a few minutes bye.
Doug says bye.
Then they both hang up their phone. Doug takes a few steps away from the phone and the phone rings again and Doug walks back to the phone and picks it up.
Doug says hello.
Tina says hi brother this is Tina.
Doug says hi Tina.
Tina says do you feel like having any company?
Doug says yes come on over.
Tina says ok I will see you in a few minutes.

Doug says ok.

Tina says bye.

Doug says bye.

Then they both hang up their phone. Now Doug walks a few feet away from the phone and the phone rings again and Doug walks back to the phone and picks it up.

Doug says hello.

Angela says hi Doug this is Angela.

Doug says ok.

Angela says can I come over for a while to talk?

Doug says sure come on over.

Angela says ok I will be there in a few minutes.

Doug says ok bye.

Angela says bye.

Then they both hang up their phone.

It is now 15 minutes after Pam has left and every body that called has now showed up at the door. The door bell rings and Doug opens the door.

Doug says hi come on in all of you.

Every one comes in and sits down.

Grace it is good to see you son.

Doug says thank you. It is good to see you too mother.

Doug walks over to Grace and gives her a hug and she gives him a hug in return.

Grace says I love you son.

Doug says I love you too mother.

After hugging Grace Doug says would every one like a snack and some thing to drink?

Every one says sure.

Doug goes to the kitchen and grabs some snacks and soda for every one and takes them to the living room and sits every thing on the living room table.

Doug says now every one help your self.

Every one says thank you.

Doug says you all are welcome.

Grace says where is my daughter Pam Styles?

Doug says she went to the movies.

Grace says well I am happy to visit you but how come you did not go with her for entertainment with your wife?

Doug says I asked her did she want me to come with her and she said she will go by her self.

Grace says that sounds really strange your own wife goes to the movies by her self.

Jeff says why did she choose to go to the movies by her self?

Doug says I hate to tell you this but earlier today I just had the worst experience of my life with my own wife.

Tommy says either you found her cheating on you or she did not want to have sex.

Doug says Tommy neither was the case but you are pretty close.

Jeff says what happened?

Doug says I came home this evening and Pam told me she wants a divorce.

Grace puts a shocked look on her face and says WHAT!

Jeff says I can not believe what I just heard.

Doug says that is the same thing I told her.

Angela says you 2 just got married only around 6 months ago and already she wants a divorce?

Jeff says son what happened that made her want a divorce and then so soon.

Doug says she told me I have been saying and doing things that she did not feel comfortable with. The other day we went grocery shopping and she said I totally embarrassed her by me wearing a skirt. Plus when we go to bed I wore women's pajamas. She is now accusing me of being gay. I told her I am very straight. I would not cheat on her or be gay. She told me earlier that she already filed for a divorce. So now I am going to have to get a lawyer to help me in court. Angela would you be able to help me in court to stop the divorce? Because deep within I still love Pam. I do not want a divorce. I want to stop the divorce.

Angela says Doug as much as I would love to help you because I love being a lawyer but my only problem with it is I feel very close to you and Pam as well so I would not feel comfortable in court fighting against you or fighting against her. I would not be a friend to you nor to her if I did that. So as much as it hurts me to tell you. No I can not do it I am sorry. You will have to find another lawyer. Pam came to me earlier and asked me for the same thing and I gave her the same answer. Plus since you are trying to stop the divorce and save your marriage I will tell you this. You do not have to have a lawyer for a divorce case. A lawyer can help you out a lot but you do not need a lawyer.

Doug says thank you for telling me that. I understand why you do not want to do it. You do not want to fight against 2 people that you feel close to. I had not thought about it like that at first. At the same time since I do not need a lawyer for a divorce case then I will not pay some one else. I will just go to the judge and stop the divorce myself and save some money.

Angela says if you want to save some money it sounds like a good ideal to me.

Doug says I could not believe her earlier. It was like all of a sudden my wife just turned against me. And now I am battling to save my marriage. I love my wife but when some thing like this happens I understand why some single people who have never been married do not want to get married. I am sorry I know all of you came over to socialize and now I am telling you about all of my horrible experiences.

Jake says that is ok you need to talk to some one about your problems.

Wendle says at times every one needs some one to listen to their problems.

Tommy says you will be surprised at how much you can help a person emotionally by just listening to them.

Doug says Jake and Wendle and Mike and Tommy I am so happy that your wife is treating you all a lot better than my wife is treating me right now.

Clara says I love Mike way too much to miss treat him.

Gloria says Tommy means way too much to me to miss treat him.

Deana says I want my marriage to last a life time so I prefer to be good to Wendle.

Katrisha says I feel the same way about Jake so he is only getting good treatment from me.

It is now 2 hours later and every body is starting to feel tired.

Wendle says well Doug I am enjoying my self but I am on a full stomach and a full stomach makes you feeling sleepy and tired. So now I am going home to bed.

Every body else says me too.

Doug says well I enjoyed having every body here for a while.

Every body gets up and starts leaving. After every body is gone Doug goes to the bed room and keeps his day clothes on and sits on the chair. Then Pam comes home and goes to the bed room.

Doug says hi honny.

Pam says hi.

Pam reaches in to her dresser drawer and pulls out her men's pajamas and lays them on the bed. Doug is watching her take off her day clothes and put on her men's pajamas and lye in bed and pulls the cover over her. Then Doug takes off his day clothes and puts on his men pajamas and lye in bed next to her and pulls the cover over him. Then Pam takes the covers off her self and gets out of bed and goes to the linen closet and pulls out some blankets and pillows and walks to the living room and lies on the couch and pulls the blanket over her self. Then Doug gets up and walks to the living room and sees Pam lying on the couch with the blanket lying over her. Then Doug takes a deep breath and walks back to the bed room and gets back in bed and pulls the cover over him.

1 WEEK LATER

It is now 1 week later at the court house. Judge Eloise is walking out her office and goes to the court room. She opens the court room door.

Inside the court room Sam speaks loud enough so every one in the court room can hear. Sam says ALL RISE.

Every one stands up.

Judge Eloise walks to her seat and sits down.

Alex says YOU MAY BE SEATED.

Two Women Are Opposite Sex

Pam is standing on Judge Eloise left side as the plaintiff. And Doug is standing on Judge Eloise right side as the defendant.

Judge Eloise says ok we will get started. Sam will you swear them in?

Sam says ok.

Sam takes the bible up to Pam and holds it out to her and says will you please raise your right hand and place your left hand on the bible?

Pam does just so.

Sam says do you swear to tell the truth and the whole truth and nothing but the truth.

Pam says yes I do.

Then Sam walks over to Doug and holds the bible out to him.

Sam says will you please raise your right hand and put your left hand on the bible?

Doug does just so. Sam says do you swear to tell the truth and the whole truth and nothing but the truth?

Doug says I do.

Now Sam walks back to his standing spot.

Judge Eloise looks at Pam's divorce file.

Judge Eloise says according to your papers here Mrs. Styles you filed for a divorce because you are tired of your husband Doug Styles embarrassing you by saying and doing things not right for a man. Ok be specific with me. Exactly what kind of things was he saying and doing that is not right for a man to do?

Pam says well on the job he works in a retail store and he started off in the men's department then later took a position in the women's department actually working with women's dresses and even their panties and bras. I am actually seeing this with my own eyes. One day I asked him how does he like working in the women's department and he had the nerve to tell me he likes it. I thought he was going to tell me that he is going to tell his department boss he wants to go back to working in the men's department. But he did not.

Doug raises his hand.

Judge Eloise says Mr. Styles I am going to listen to you when Mrs. Styles is finished talking. So you do not need to raise your hand ok.

Doug says ok.

Doug puts his hand down.

Pam says I do not feel comfortable watching my husband work with women's clothes. Plus 1 day last week we were at the hospital sitting in the emergency room and he told me he had to go to the bathroom. When I looked around I actually seen him go into the women's bathroom. The only time a man should go into the women's bathroom is when he is on the job and there is nobody in there and he is employed as a house keeper. On his job Doug is not a house keeper and he most definitely was not on the job. I am starting to wonder about him. There is more things I need to tell you but so far do you see what I mean about Doug doing things not right for a man.?

Judge Eloise puts a firm look on her face and says stop right there before you go any further. You just asked me do I see what you mean about Doug. When you step into my courtroom you do not ask me questions about the case you are bringing to me. I will ask you questions about the case. I am the boss in my courtroom ok.

Pam says ok Your Honor.

Judge Eloise says now you said there are other things you want to tell me.

Pam says yes the other day we went to the grocery store and Doug totally embarrassed me he was wearing a skirt. I tried my hardest to stay away from him but he had to keep getting my attention to keep putting food items in the grocery cart. I could not wait to get out of the grocery store and back home because I was totally embarrassed. Plus while we were at the hospital in the exam room he gave me the impression that he is a secret gay man because while he was talking to the lady doctor he called his men friends his boyfriends. Plus the lady doctor showed us a picture of her and her husband on their wedding day and Doug actually told the lady doctor her husband is cute. Then a few days after that the doctors Cindy and Brad Pen invited us over to their house for a meal and to meet Brad. Brad told Doug to sit on his lap and I thought Doug was going to kindly refuse it but he did not. Doug actually sat on Brad's lap. Then later that day when we were leaving the doctor's house I seen it with my own eyes Doug and Brad actually hugged each other and kissed each other on the cheeks and said that they love each other. So when we got back home I asked Doug is he gay and he told me no. But after my ears hearing all these things and my eyes seeing all these things I believe he is lying to me. I am afraid I am married to a gay man. That is why I want a divorce Your Honor.

Judge Eloise says ok is there any thing else you would like to say?

Pam says that is all I can think of for now.

Judge Eloise says ok with the things you told me I understand what you mean. And since I am a straight woman and wife I agree with you. At the same time I have not heard from Doug yet. By law I am required to be fair by listening to both of you. Because there are 2 sides to ever story. Doug now I will listen to you. Go ahead and speak.

Doug says Your Honor 1st of all I want to fight the divorce because I still love my wife. Second of all Pam told you that on the job she does not feel comfort with me working with women's personal items but she did not tell you that on the job she works with men's personal items selling underwear and Viagra and condoms, there is no difference. When we went to the hospital in the emergency room I had to go to the bath room real bad and the men's bath room was being used and so I made sure no one was in the women's bath room and when I seen no one was in there then I went in there. Like I said I had to go real bad. But then later Pam went into the men's bathroom for the same reason. Pam told you that I embarrassed her in a grocery store by wearing a women's skirt and heels. She did not tell you that when the doctors invited us to their house that she was wearing men's clothes making her self look like a lesbian. She even wore men's clothes to the grocery store. She did not think I was supposed to feel embarrassed. Pam told you while we were at the hospital when Dr. Pen showed us a picture of her and her husband Brad I said he is cute. At the same time Pam said Cindy is cute. She told you that I calls my men friends my boyfriends. Well she also calls her women friends her girlfriends and I did not judge her as gay. But she is judging me as gay. Now later when the doctors invited us to their house the only reason why I sat on a man's lap is because the doctors did not realize that they ran out of fold up chairs for their guess. So the man doctor told me to sit on his lap and I did. But then Cindy told Pam to sit on Cindy's lap and Pam did it. And yes when we were leaving Brad and I hugged each other and kissed each other on the cheeks and even said we love each other meaning agape love. Not sexual love. Your Honor Pam was doing the same things with Cindy that I was doing with Brad. Then she tells me she wants a divorce. She is accusing me of being gay. I am not accusing her of being gay. Your Honor I still love Pam and I want to save my marriage.

The room stays silent for 4 seconds.

Judge Eloise says ok Doug is there any thing else you want to add to your testimony?

Doug says that is all I can think of for right now.

Judge Eloise says Mrs. Styles is there any thing else you want to add.

Pam says no.

Doug raises his hand.

Judge Eloise says yes.

Doug says Your Honor I am sorry to interrupt you but there is something I did forget to add.

Judge Eloise says ok go ahead.

Doug says Pam told you that I would wear women pajamas to bed but she did not tell you that she also would wear men pajamas to bed doing the same thing. That is all I needed to add Your Honor.

Judge Eloise says Mrs. Styles earlier I told you that I agree with you. And I do. Some cases that are brought to court are cases that a person did something illegal to another person. So the judge has to make a decision based on what the laws are concerning that case. There are other cases brought to court that do not concern the laws it is just a case where person A did something to person B and person B did not like it so person A took person B to court about it. Then the judge has to make a decision based on the Judges opinion. Now this case here is not a case where Doug did something illegal to you nor did he do anything illegal at all, he just did some things that society does not accept from men. There are no laws against what you are complaining about. He crossed dressed and went out in public and you crossed dressed and went out in Public. He put on women's pajamas and you put on men's pajamas. On the job he works with women's personal items and you work with men's personal items. Later he had to go to the bathroom real bad and the men's was being used so he went into the women's bathroom. You had to go to the bathroom real bad and the women's bathroom was being used so you went into the men's bathroom. He sat no a man's lap because there was no other chairs and you sat on a woman's lap because there was no other chairs. Mrs. Styles you were telling me what he did wrong but you were not telling me why he did it. You were making it sound like he just did not care or just acting gay. Or making it sound like it was something that it was not. At the same time you was not telling me that you were doing the exact same thing. You felt uncomfortable with him doing the exact same things you were doing.

Pam raises her hand.

Judge Eloise says you may speak.

Pam says Your Honor may I please ask you a question that is not about the case but about your self?

Judge Eloise says yes.

Pam says do you call your women friends your girlfriends?

Judge Eloise says no I do not. Because to me when a woman calls her women friends her girlfriends that sounds just as gay as when a man calls his men friends his boyfriend. To me there is no difference. I do not want my husband to call his men friends his boyfriends. At the same time I do not want my self calling my women friends my girlfriends. To me it sounds equally gay. So I call my women friends my friend. Not my girlfriend, but just my friend. Just like I do not want him wearing women clothes at the same time I do not want my self wearing men clothes. When a man cross dresses it makes him look gay. He is a man he should be wearing men's clothes. For my opinion it is the same way for a woman she is a woman she should be wearing women's clothes. For both sexes they should not cross dress because to me it looks equally gay. There is no difference. Mrs. Styles you are discriminating against your husband. You think it is fine when you do these things but you do not want your husband to do these things. I am going to ask you this. Has he ever hit you?

Pam says no he has not.

Judge Eloise says does he work to support you?

Pam says yes he does and we both work.

Judge Eloise says ok you have a man who does not hit you and he works to support you and you want to divorce him all because he was doing the same things with men that you were doing with women.

When you 2 got married you both said for better and for worse. You took each other for your good points and for each others faults. So Mrs. Styles since the man does not hit you and works to take care of you and you have been doing the same things he was doing you were wrong to accuse your husband of being gay and file for a divorce. So my decision is no. I am not giving you a divorce. Hold on to your good husband. Mr. Styles I grant to you your wife. You 2 are still married.

Doug says thank you Your Honor.

Judge Eloise says this case is dismissed.

Judge Eloise picks up her hammer and hits it on her block of wood and lays it down and walks back to her office. Sam and Alex escort Doug and Pam out of the courtroom.

It is now the next day at Doug and Pam's house and Doug is at work and Pam is at home and the phone rings and Pam picks it up.

Pam says hello.

Tommy says hi Pam this is Tommy is Doug home?

Pam says no he is at work but he will be home this evening.

Tommy says when he gets home I need to come by and ask him for a favor.

Pam says you can come by this evening he will be here.

Tommy says ok bye.

Pam says bye.

Then they both hang up their phone.

Pam pulls out a suitcase and starts packing her clothes. When she finish packing then she gets on the phone and calls a hotel in a different city.

Pam says I was wondering do you have a room for 1 person?

Pam waits 10 seconds then says how much is the room?

Pam says could you please hold it for Pam Velet?

Pam waits for 10 seconds and says ok thank you bye.

Pam hangs up the phone. Then she picks the phone back up and calls a cab to pick her up from her house. When she is finished talking to the cab company she hangs up the phone. Now the cab driver takes Pam to the bus station and she gets on the bus. When she get to her city destination she gets off the bus and get in a cab and tells the driver

Two Women Are Opposite Sex

what street to take her to. Whe she gets to the hotel Pam puts her bags in her hotel room.

Now back at Doug's house Doug comes home and looks at the clock. Doug goes to the kitchen and sees that Pam is not in there plus no dinner on the table. Then Doug walks to the bedroom and sees that pam is not in there. Then Doug walks to the bathroom and the door is wide open and he sees that Pam is not in there.

Doug says maybe she had to run an arron. I hope she is not getting more men pajamas. I will start cooking dinner for us.

Now back at Pam's hotel room. Pam calls a cab to pick her up from her hotel room. Then she hangs up the phone and walks outside and gets in the cab. Pam tells the cab driver what street to take her to. Now Pam gets inside the bar and sees 4 empty seats and sits down.

It is now 2 hours later at Doug's house and Doug is finished cooking and the phone rings and Doug picks it up.

Doug says hello.

Tommy says hi Doug this is Tommy.

Doug says oh hi Tommy.

Tommy says do you have a wrench I can borrow?

Doug says yes I do.

Tommy says can I come over now to borrow it?

Doug says yes you can.

Tommy says ok I will see you in a few minutes.

It is now 15 minutes later and Tommy is at Doug's door.

Tommy says hi Doug.

Doug says hi Tommy come on in.

Tommy says where is Pam?

Doug says I do not know she was gone when I got home. So I guess she is running an arron. Come with me and I will get the wrench.

After Doug gives Tommy the wrench then they sit in the livingroom and talk for 2 ½ hours. After 2 ½ hours Tommy looks at the clock.

Tommy says boy we have been sitting here talking for 2 ½ hours I am going to get home now.

Doug says ok I will see you later.

Tommy says ok bye.

Doug says bye.

Tommy leaves the house.

Now back at the bar a gorgeous man named Adam came into the bar and sees Pam and walks up to her and points to the seat next to her.

Adam says excuse me mam is any body sitting here?

Pam says no you can sit there I will not charge you.

Adam sits down and says my name is Adam what is your name?

Pam says my name is Pam.

Adam says mam I am not trying to flirt with you but I think you are a very attractive woman.

Pam says oh thank you. I think you are a very attractive man.

Adam says thank you. Are you married?

Pam says unfortunately yes I am but I am trying to get a divorce from my husband and find a new husband.

Adam says I am single and trying to find a wife. What is wrong with your husband?

Pam says I believe he is gay.

Adam says I am sorry to hear that. Has he had sex with another man?

Pam says no he has not done that.

Adam says so what makes you think he is gay?

Pam says he will say another man is cute and calls his men friends his boyfriends and he has gone into a women's bathroom plus he has wore women clothes plus he even hugs other men and even kisses them on their cheeks. After all of that would you say a man is gay?

Adam says yes I agree with you. Did you say you are looking for a new husband?

Pam says yes I did.

Adam says how would you feel about you and I dating each other?

Pam says how do you feel about calling your men friends your boyfriends.

Adam says I am highly against it. How do you feel about calling other women your girlfriend?

Pam says I am highly against it even for women.

THE END

STORY CHARACTERS

THE CLOUD FAMILY

Ben Cloud - the father
Mary Cloud - the mother
Katrisha Cloud - the straight daughter
Tommy Cloud - the straight son
Mike Cloud - the masculine gay son

THE STYLES FAMILY

Jeff Styles - the father
Grace Style - the mother
Derek Styles - the feminine gay son. After surgery Derek's name changes to Clara
Doug Styles - the masculine straight son
Tina Styles - the masculine gay daughter

THE VELET FAMILY

Rose Velet - the mother
Wendle Velet - the straight son

THE WING FAMILY

Dolly Wing - the mother
Angela Wing - the feminine gay daughter

THE SCHOOL STAFF

Wise High School - the high school
Mrs. Heather - the head principle
Mrs. Day - the senior principle
Mrs. Floral - the junior principle
Mrs. Reasha - the sophomore principle
Mr. Chime - the freshman principle
Mrs. Afflian - secretary of senior principle
Mrs. Bright - secretary of junior principle
Mrs. Sealer - secretary of sophomore principle
Mrs. Joy - secretary of freshman principle
Mrs. Smith - Tommy's teacher
Mrs. Gold - replaces Mrs. Smith
Mrs. Great - Tommy's 6th hour teacher
Dale Trade - 12th grade school trouble maker
KC Life - cosmetology man
Alisha Cream - cosmetology woman
Chase Ward - Tommy's classmate

THE BANK STAFF

Sonny Bank - name of bank that Ben works at
Joe Brag - bank teller manager
Amy
Bill Tote - male staff at bank
Mrs. Quote - 1st lady customer at bank
Kevin Firm - bank administrator
Mrs. Jet - 2nd lady customer at bank
Clay Dot - man customer at bank
Jennifer Teasle - lead teller at bank
Orletta - lady staff watching the women's bathroom for Ben he had to go badly
Buddy Long - bank district manager
Becky Short - district manager's secretary
Josh Skill - bank's owner
Kristine Plane - bank's assistant administrator

GOOD QUALITY RETAIL STORE STAFF

Good Quality - name of retail store
Denise Round - manager of women's department

Don Stream - manager of furniture department
Greg Crave - manager of men's department
Shirley Eater - Tina Style's straight female friend girlfriend at work
Larry Good - general manager
Katrisha Cloud - staff in women's department
Derek Styles - staff in furniture department
Doug Styles - staff in men's department
Tina Styles - staff in men's department
Arron Deli - male customer at Good Quality
Ron Fun - staff in furniture department
Scott Eter (husband) - male customer at Good Quality
Tonya Eter (wife) - female customer at Good Quality
Jarred - elderly customer on walker who Don is assisting
Russel Mone - customer talking to Doug about funeral
Joice Not - housekeeper lady cleaning flood in men's bathroom
Steve - security guard at Good Quality
Corey - Good Quality's district manager
Vern - Good Quality's owner
Maintenance guy - at Good Quality

COURT HOUSE STAFF

Sherri Fair - judge
Eloise Same - judge who works in Sherri's place
Peter Forth - courthouse clerk
Sam Gear - courthouse sheriff
Bob Suit - Vern's lawyer
Alex Push - courthouse sheriff

BAR STAFF

The Fun Place - neighborhood bar
Marsha - feminine gay lady at bar approached Katrisha
Victor - masculine gay man approached Wenlde
Ryan - bartender man at The Fun Place
Danny Wom - bar staff walking around the floor at the Fun Place
Brian Wrong - bar manager at the Fun Place

ADULT MOVIE COMPANY STAFF

Hot, Fabulous - adult movie company
Phillup Hold - owner of straight bar and adult movie company
Todd Mine - (husband) administrator of Hot, Fabulous
Mrs. Mine - wife of administrator
Troy Caught - manager of adult movie company
Jane - receptionist at Hot, Fabulous
Kenny Church - lawyer of Brian and Danny and Todd and Troy
Yavonne - Phillup's secretary
Hold Production - name of Phillup's corporate building

HOSPITAL STAFF

Care Medical Center - hospital where Derek gets his sex change
Dr. Hapchan - surgeon who gives Derek his sex change
Louis - hospital transporter
Jan - hospital transporter
Gabriel - Clara's nurse at nurses desk
Kimberly - the nurse who takes Doug to the exam room
Dr. Cindy Pen - the doctor who checks Doug's heart in the exam room
Dr. Brad Pen - Cindy's husband

CHURCH STAFF

Pastor Luke - the pastor that conducts the wedding ceremony

CAMPIING STAFF

Camping cashier - the cashier at Sun Camp camping grounds

GENERAL CHARACTERS

Jean - cashier at women's clothing store
Jerry - male staff at men's clothing store
Gloria Rich - Tommy's intimate girlfriend
Jake Bake - Katrisha's intimate boyfriend
Pam Smart - Doug Styles intimate girlfriend
Deana Humor - Wendle's Velet's intimate girlfriend

www.ingramcontent.com/pod-product-compliance
Lightning Source LLC
LaVergne TN
LVHW042244070526
838201LV00088B/13